HEAVEN'S *my* DESTINATION

BOOKS BY THORNTON WILDER

NOVELS

The Cabala

The Bridge of San Luis Rey

The Woman of Andros

Heaven's My Destination

The Ides of March

The Eighth Day

Theophilus North

COLLECTIONS OF SHORT PLAYS

The Angel That Troubled the Waters

The Long Christmas Dinner & Other Plays in One Act

The Collected Short Plays of Thornton Wilder Vol. 1

The Collected Short Plays of Thornton Wilder Vol. 2

PLAYS

Our Town

The Merchant of Yonkers

The Skin of Our Teeth

The Matchmaker

The Alcestaid

The Beaux' Stratagem (co-adapted by Ken Ludwig)

A Doll's House (translation)

LETTERS AND ESSAYS

American Characteristics

The Journals of Thornton Wilder, 1939–1961

The Selected Letters of Thornton Wilder

The Letters of Gertrude Stein and Thornton Wilder

A Tour of the Darkling Plain: The Finnegans Wake *Letters
of Thornton Wilder and Adaline Glasheen*

HEAVEN'S *my* DESTINATION

A Novel

THORNTON WILDER

HARPER**PERENNIAL** MODERN**CLASSICS**

NEW YORK • LONDON • TORONTO • SYDNEY • NEW DELHI • AUCKLAND

HARPER**PERENNIAL** ⬤ MODERN**CLASSICS**

A hardcover edition of this book was published in 1935 by Harper & Brothers, Publishers. It is reprinted here by arrangement with the Wilder Family LLC.

HEAVEN'S MY DESTINATION. Copyright © 1934 by the Wilder Family LLC. Foreword © 2003 by J. D. McClatchy. Afterword © 2003, 2020 by Tappan Wilder. All rights reserved. Printed in the United States of America. No part of this book may be used or reproduced in any manner whatsoever without written permission except in the case of brief quotations embodied in critical articles and reviews. For information, address HarperCollins Publishers, 195 Broadway, New York, NY 10007.

HarperCollins books may be purchased for educational, business, or sales promotional use. For information, please email the Special Markets Department at SPsales@harpercollins.com.

FIRST PERENNIAL EDITION PUBLISHED 2003.
FIRST HARPER PERENNIAL MODERN CLASSICS EDITION PUBLISHED 2020.

Designed by Renato Stanisic

The Library of Congress has catalogued the hardcover as follows:
Wilder, Thornton
    Heaven's my destination / Thornton Wilder.—1st Perennial ed.
        p. cm.
    ISBN 0-06-008889-3
    1. Traveling sales personnel—Fiction. 2. Textbooks—Publishing—Fiction. 3. Christian converts—Fiction. 4. Middle West—Fiction. 5. Depressions—Fiction. I. Title.

PS3545.I345H4 2003
813'.52—dc21

ISBN 978-0-06-299021-1 (pbk.)

20 21 22 23 24 LSC 10 9 8 7 6 5 4 3 2 1

George Brush is my name;
America's my nation;
Ludington's my dwelling-place
And Heaven's my destination.
> *(Doggerel verse which children of
> the Middle West were accustomed
> to write in their schoolbooks)*

Of all the forms of genius,
goodness has the longest awkward age.
—THE WOMAN OF ANDROS

CONTENTS

CONTENTS

FOREWORD

When Sigmund Freud first read *Heaven's My Destination,* he threw the book across the room. Wilder had visited Freud at his villa outside Vienna in the fall of 1935 and had given him a copy of the novel, which had been published earlier that year. Freud would have none of it. "I come from an unbroken line of infidel Jews," the doctor explained; as a boy he had been lectured at by his father that "there is no way that we could know there was a God; that it didn't do any good to trouble one's head about such; but to live and do one's duty among one's fellow men." But what had actually annoyed Freud about the book was, he said, the fun it made of religion. "Why should you treat of an American fanatic?" the old doctor asked. "That cannot be treated poetically."

Or so Wilder records the meeting in his journal. Of course, Freud wasn't the only reader to have been upset. Some thought it filled with an austere religious fervor, others thought it a broad satire of American Protestantism. Wilder himself, speaking with an interviewer many years later, recalled some of the public reaction to his hero, George Brush:

> George, the hero of a novel of mine which I wrote when I was nearly forty, is an earnest, humorless, moralizing, preachifying, interfering product of Bible-belt evangelism. I received many letters from writers of the George Brush mentality angrily denouncing me for making fun of sacred things, and a letter from the Mother Superior of a convent in Ohio saying that she regarded the book as an allegory of the stages in the spiritual life.

In fact, the book's first reviewers were puzzled because it could be read either way, because Wilder seemed such a dispassionate narrator, because the moral scales weren't tipped to one side or the other. Again, Wilder explained that *Heaven's My Destination*

> was written as objectively as it could be done and the result has been that people tell me that it has meant to them things as diverse as a Pilgrim's Progress of the religious life and an extreme sneering at sacred things, a portrait of a saint on the one hand and a ridiculous fool jeered at by the author on the other. For a while I felt that I had erred and that it was an artistic mistake to expose oneself to such misinterpretations. But more and more in harmony with the doctrine that the writer during the work should not hear in a second level of consciousness the possible comments of audiences, I feel that for good or for ill you should talk to yourself in your own private language and be willing to sink or swim on the hope that your pri-

vate language has nevertheless sufficient correspondence
with that of persons of some reading and some experience.

From the very beginning of his career, Wilder had been speaking his own "private language," however it may have been
schooled by the example of older stylistic masters. The baroque
suavities of *The Cabala,* the vividly poised moralizing of *The
Bridge of San Luis Rey,* the chaste decorum of *The Woman of
Andros,* had all earned for their author a reputation as a writer of
chiseled refinement. And because each novel was so different from
what had preceded it, the range of his imagination was also lav-
ishly praised. Early and easy success, however, invariably pushes
one's detractors front and center, and in 1930 Wilder was con-
fronted by an especially vicious attack on both his achievement and
his sensibility. Writing in *The New Republic,* critic Michael Gold
ignited a controversy that we must believe singed Wilder and
without a doubt inflamed the magazine's letters column for weeks
to come. Gold, whose ardent Communist views made Wilder the
convenient embodiment of "a small sophisticated class that has
recently risen in America—our genteel bourgeoisie," dismissed the
novels as "chambermaid literature" and accused Wilder's writing
of "the shallow clarity and tight little good taste that remind one of
nothing so much as the conversation and practice of a veteran
cocotte." It was a vulgar, snide, tendentious piece, and it went on to
hammer at Wilder's lack of "nativism." Why had he taken refuge
in a "rootless cosmopolitanism"? Italy, Peru, Greece—remote cul-
tures and effete characters—glossy high finish and etiolated aristo-
cratic emotions. Why, in other words, wasn't Wilder a Tolstoy, or
at least a Sinclair Lewis? Instead, his serenity is that of a corpse:
"Prick it, and it will bleed violet ink and *apéritif.*" Why won't
Wilder plunge into the burly realities of American life, the world
of stockbroker suicides and labor racketeers, steel mills and back

streets, prairies and mesas? "Let Mr. Wilder write a book about modern America," Gold concluded. "We predict it will reveal all his fundamental silliness and superficiality."

Despite the fact his defenders rushed into print, Wilder—who never publically commented on Gold's attack—was said privately to be hurt. Though I doubt Gold's article was a direct cause, it may have started a train of thought, one that gathered considerable baggage in the years directly following, when Wilder had moved on to a lively part-time teaching base at the University of Chicago and was also crisscrossing the country on the lecture circuit. He hadn't written about America before because, as he once explained, "I didn't know enough about it." He had plucked his characters from books. Now he learned firsthand the scenery and sounds of America and was ready to take advantage of them. In any case, his very next novel was distinctly "American." It set itself down in the Mississippi Valley and points west during the Depression, offered an array of social types, analyzed their living conditions and legal system, and probed both the country's beliefs and its true religion, business. It was enough to warm any Marxist's heart. In a letter to John Dos Passos, Edmund Wilson wrote: "Thornton Wilder has taken up the challenge flung down by Mike Gold and written the best book of his life. I wish you would overcome your prejudice against him and read it."

It would be inaccurate to claim that Wilder had deliberately remade himself as a novelist—had, as it were, gone native. (Though *Our Town* arrives just three years later.) The settings and characters of *Heaven's My Destination* bear subtle affinities with Wilder's fiction, both earlier and later. And its hero, George Brush, shares the ardent loneliness of all of Wilder's protagonists. But it is fair to say that Wilder did turn from the exquisite cadences and lambent, layered textures of his first three novels. His style here is drier, flatter, jumpier. It's the effort to create an "American speech" for his book, to give its narrative the clipped, moral tone of its cast and culture. It's what might be called a Grant Wood style. Of course Wilder was not writing a satire, though he's content to skewer pretensions and injustices. Instead, he'd set out to write a comedy, and he needed a light touch to capture the incongruities of American life, at once innocent and egotistical. It is a comedy in the highest sense, and moves easily from hayseed farce to superstitious magic (Father Pasziewski's spoon) to moral argument (the concluding courtroom scene is the book's masterstroke).

It's said there are only two stories, two basic situations which all novels weave variations on. In one, our hero leaves home and is beset by adventures. In the other, a stranger comes to town and occasions adventures. *Heaven's My Destination* combines the two patterns. Its premise is an old joke—did you hear the one about the traveling salesman and the farmer's daughter?—and its plot has put readers in mind of the perilous progress of Bunyan's Christian pilgrim or of the chivalric quest of Cervantes' Don Quixote. It's clear from his own testimony that, indeed, Wilder had such figures in the back of his mind as he worked. Candide or Tom Jones, Pip or Stephen Dedalus—literature abounds in innocents and their "education." The hero of Wilder's novel, George Brush, seems a familiar enough figure. (His name too is familiar, and calls up the once ubiquitous door-to-door Fuller Brush man, as well as a more recent teetotaling, fundamentalist president.) In the movies he might have been played by Tom Hanks or James Stewart—or even, as Wilder apparently hoped, Gary Cooper. But, though we know he was born in Michigan and graduated from Shiloh Baptist College in South Dakota, he still seems a mysterious presence, and that's because Wilder intended to portray a saint—the sort of person who is always more than a little unworldly. He appears and disappears faster than mortals ought. "I'm the happiest man I've ever met," he boasts while assuming the sorrows of others. Even saints have to live in the world, however, and the novel's epigraph, taken from *The Woman of Andros,* tells us about the narrative shape of this book: "Of all forms of genius, goodness has the longest awkward age." As he *brushes* up against the world, with its whorehouses and seedy hotels, its newspapermen and thieves, he does not *learn* the ways of the world, the world learns his ways. Still, battered and defeated, as unloved and lonely at the end of the novel as he was at its start, exactly a year earlier, he changes less in his own eyes than in ours. We witness his awkward age with an amazement that tempers to pity. "I may be cuckoo," he says at the end, in a way that any reader may both admire and deplore, "perhaps I am: but I'd rather be crazy all alone than be sensible like you fellows are sensible. I'm glad I'm nuts. I don't want to be different. Tell the fellows I'll never change——." The only thing to do with Gandhi—George's own particular patron saint—is to follow him or shoot him. All saints are first fallen men, and the women men fall for have a lot to answer for. George was converted by a drug-addled sixteen-year-old tent evangelist named Marian Truby, and his one roll in the hay loft with Roberta Weyerhauser drove him to seek and marry her—with disastrous results. He is drawn to these women, and to older matronly women as well, like Queenie and Mrs. Crofut, because he longs for love. His head is filled with ideas, his heart is empty. He wants "an American home," a Norman Rockwell family image, but saints aren't allowed wives and kids. Instead, as George says, and it is a mean substitute, "I have the truth."

Heaven's My Destination was written in the midst of the Great Depression, a time when all Americans were called on to redefine themselves. The national upheaval was a time of private soul-searching as well as of government programs. It was Wilder's genius to have made George's idealism seem like a solution that solves nothing. So cannily has Wilder drawn his portrait that his picaresque hero, in adventure after adventure, erodes the very sympathy he builds in us. George is annoying in part because we live—now as then—in a culture of Meddlers and Experts, a culture of tireless self-improvement, in which, from television spot or bumper sticker, we are constantly urged to get right with God, lose fifty pounds, quit smoking, discover the ultimate stain remover, and accept Jesus as our personal savior. No one wants to be goaded into goodness or exasperated to salvation. Above all, we loathe logic, and George Brush is not a romantic but a logician. Creatures of satisfying habits, we resent change, resent thinking about our comforts; we prefer the bromides and slogans, the sheer unselfconsciousness of animal life. "You'll learn in time," George is told. "I guess you'll find your place in time, see? Only don't come around us any more. We got our own ideas and our own lives all arranged, see? and we don't like to be interrupted."

But George is also annoying because he is a saint. "Isn't the principle of a thing more important than the people that live under the principle?" he asks, and wonders why his marriage collapses. "It's not important if Roberta and I are different, as she calls it. It's not important if we don't get on like some couples do. We're married, and it's for the good of society and morals that we stay together until we die." This is his devastating innocence. It causes him to despair, and only a miracle can save him. The brilliance of Wilder's technique in this novel is to reenact in the reader the same drama that the characters who encounter George face. We are asked to think, to see the light—and then watch the realistic shadows fall.

Wilder's brother Amos, in his 1980 book *Thornton Wilder and His Public,* tried to trace the lineage of George Brush, and he put it most accurately when he noted that Brush's ancestor is less a specific literary character than a mythological type: "the American Adam." This is a figure central both to our literature and to our imaginings of ourselves. Thoreau and Whitman, Hemingway and Fitzgerald—our writers have tried continually to embody this innocent, vital ideal. Wilder was fond of Thoreau, whose own annoyingly soulful self-righteousness could have been a model for Brush's. But in fact, it was Emerson (who couldn't see the poison snake in the grass, in Wilder's skeptical reckoning) who, in his clarion 1837 oration "The American Scholar," most notably defined the American Adam, whom he calls "the scholar":

> The office of the scholar is to cheer, to raise, and to guide men by showing them facts amidst appearances. . . . He must accept . . . the state of virtual hostility in which he seems to stand to society, and especially to educated society. For all this loss and scorn, what offset? He is to find consolation in exercising the highest function of human nature. He is one, who raises himself from private considerations, and breathes and lives on public and illustrious thought. . . . Whatsoever oracles the human heart, in all emergencies, in all solemn hours, has uttered as its commentary on the world of actions—these he shall receive and impart. And whatsoever new verdict Reason from her inviolable seat pronounces on the passing men and events of to-day,—this he shall hear and promulgate.

This moves to the heart of what has been called the American Religion as both our greatest prophet, Emerson, and our subtlest analyst, William James, have seen it. George Brush is less a Baptist than a believer in this hybrid religion that doesn't much resemble historical Christianity. The Christian asks, "Who will save me?" The American asks, "What will make me free?" And because the American strives for individuality and the pragmatism of feelings and experiences (rather than desires and memories), he lives as a solitary, his inner loneliness at home in an outer loneliness of wilderness or urban enormity. Salvation for the American comes not through the congregation or community but is a singular confrontation, an exclusive reliance on the empowered self. The American is known not by his pious submission but by his radical innocence. Here again is Emerson, with his scholar:

> In silence, in steadiness, in severe abstraction, let him hold by himself; add observation to observation, patient of neglect, patient of reproach; and bide his own time— happy enough, if he can satisfy himself alone, that this day he has seen something truly. Success treads on every right step. For the instinct is sure, that prompts him to tell his brother what he thinks. He then learns, that in going down into the secrets of his own mind, he has descended into the secrets of all minds.

In 1930, two years before he started working on *Heaven's My Destination,* Wilder wrote to a friend about his earlier three novels, and saw in them a common theme. "It seems to me that my books are about: What is the worst thing that the world can do to you, and what are the last resources one has to oppose to it?" The best of those novels, *The Bridge of San Luis Rey,* asked whether "the intuitions that lie behind love are enough to justify the desperation of living." There is, finally, a shimmering ambivalence in Wilder's answer. In *Heaven's My Destination* he asks if the honest man's pursuit of truth is enough to sustain him in a deceitful world. I'm not entirely convinced Wilder could answer his own question, and neither was he. The ending of the novel seems rushed, substituting a crisis for a conclusion. Wilder admitted as much, both in his journal and in letters to friends. "Sure, I made a lot of mistakes," he wrote to one. "As you say, at the close especially." Twenty years later, he blamed it on a sense of "procrastination, the inability to call my wits together for a deep concentration" that forced him to rush toward the last page.

He was being too harsh on himself. It may be that, though the plot conforms to its circular mythic pattern, Wilder had so identified with Brush that he couldn't in the end see the emotional ramification of his protagonist's decisions. Asked by an interviewer if, as a young man, he resembled George Brush, Wilder answered:

> Very much so. I came from a very strict Calvinistic father, was brought up partly among the missionaries of China, and went to that splendid college at Oberlin at a time when the classrooms and student life carried a good deal of the pious didacticism which would now be called narrow Protestantism. And that book is, as it were, an effort to come to terms with those influences. The comic spirit is given to us in order that we may analyze, weigh, and clarify things in us which nettle us, or which we are outgrowing, or trying to escape. That is a very autobiographical book.

All of Wilder's novels, of course, are at some level "autobiographical." In this one, surely, there was a side to his own personality that Wilder projected onto Brush. He was not unaware of the overanimated intellectuality of his own social manner or of a certain emotional naïveté. In 1933, he wrote mockingly to a friend, "What a good parson I would have been. How diligent, and how I would have loved it. How anxiously I would have watched them gather; and how concerned I'd have been, visiting them in their homes. It would have played squarely into all my faults." And behind his own manner were large shadows—above all, his father's. Amos Parker Wilder was the embodiment of the zealous, interfering, righteous, moralizing Calvinist ethic. A letter to his children would say, for instance, that "the kingdom of Heaven is to be brought to earth, the bad fiends yielding—then it fills a youth with ardent aspirations to be in the midst of the fight—to give his fellow man the best that is in him. He knows that when he is right he is on sure ground—that the right must conquer." Wilder, instinctively drawn to his mother's softer, more cultivated and literary character, nonetheless inherited some of his father's driven energies. The difference between them is that the son had a sense of irony. Late in his life, Wilder wrote to his oldest friend, Robert Maynard Hutchins, of his father's "all too freighted unshakeable obtuseness."

The inward gaze alerts us to nuances of characterization, but to dwell exclusively on George Brush would be to miss most of the comic brio of this novel's storytelling as well as its astute realism. If John Steinbeck's mighty *Grapes of Wrath* is the tragic novel of the Great Depression, then *Heaven's My Destination* is its comic masterpiece. This was the era of "failing banks, falling businessmen," and the touching scene of Brush's Camp Morgan encounter with Dick Roberts, the suicidal real estate man, has an eerie edge. This was the era of an imploding economy and desperate measures, and Brush's lectures to the bank president or the stickup man about his ingenious moral ideas have a still astonishing (because still right, still untried) poignancy to them. This was the era of crushing poverty and odd bedfellows, and Wilder's description of Queenie Craven's derelict boarding-house in Kansas City is wonderfully evocative:

a high, narrow, blackened edifice, standing amid the similarly blackened hulks of former mansions ... its broken windows patched with newspaper, its yard full of weeds and overturned bath-tubs, against the last invasion of negro gamblers, cats and the night quartering of tramps. Queenie's back windows overlooked a cliff strewn with bottles and automobile tires descending to a waste of railroad tracks and the sluggish soot-covered river.

This was the era too of Gandhi's call to passive resistance, and his presence in the novel—along with Tolstoy's—is an unlikely counter.

But there is a side of George Brush's crusade that has all the activism of the best of the New Deal. He wouldn't think of cheating on his expense account, thinks everyone should be burdened equally by the Depression, has advanced views on child rearing and capital punishment, and in Louisiana once rode in a Jim Crow railroad car because he believes in the equality of the races.

But today we read *Heaven's My Destination* less for its anatomy of an era than for its brilliant storytelling. There are countless cameo roles to appreciate—blowsy Margie McCoy, the gaggle of giggling prostitutes at the cinema, or little Rhoda May with the placard (I AM A LIAR) around her neck—each composed of small details with large implications. The opening scenario is ingenious. The narrative pace is exhilarating. And the big set pieces are ideally situated. The Molière in Wilder has a fine nose for hypocrisy and cant. The Marxist in Wilder (Groucho, not Karl) has a sure sense of comic timing, as when his friends get our hero drunk. Throughout the novel advanced ideas are dealt with nostalgically, and that's because, as Wilder wrote in a letter, the novel is about "all of us when young; you're not supposed to notice the humor—you're supposed to look through it at a fella who not only had the impulse to think out an ethic and plan a life—but actually *does* it." So what are we laughing at? The fella who *does* it? Or ourselves when young and filled with ambitions? The best comedies bring us smack against a contrary world and implicate both their cast of smart fools and our own tangled hearts. *Heaven's My Destination*, Wilder's funniest novel, is a comedy of American manners, a pageant of absurdities and miracles, logic and belly laughs, a truly sophisticated, at times even unsettling, corn-belt classic.

—J. D. McClatchy
Stonington, Connecticut

HEAVEN'S *my* DESTINATION

1

George Brush tries to save some souls in Texas and Oklahoma. Dore-
mus Blodgett and Margie McCoy. Thoughts on arriving at the age of
twenty-three. Brush draws his savings from the bank. His criminal
record: Incarceration No. 2.

One morning in the late summer of 1930 the proprietor and several guests at the Union Hotel at Crestcrego, Texas, were annoyed
to discover Biblical texts freshly written across the blotter on the
public writing-desk. Two days later the guests at McCarty's Inn,
Usquepaw, in the same state, were similarly irritated, and the
manager of the Gem Theater nearby was surprised to discover that
a poster at his door had been defaced and trampled upon. The
same evening a young man passing the First Baptist Church, and
seeing that the Annual Bible Question Bee was in progress, paid

his fifteen cents and, taking his place against the wall, won the first prize, his particular triumph being the genealogical tables of King David. The next night, several passengers on the Pullman car "Quarritch," leaving Fort Worth, were startled to discover a young man in pajamas kneeling and saying his prayers before his berth. His concentration was not shaken when he was struck sharply on the shoulder by flying copies of the *Western Magazine* and *Screen Features*. The next morning a young lady who had retired to the platform of the car to enjoy a meditative cigarette after breakfast, returned to her seat to discover that a business card had been inserted into the corner of the window pane. It read:

George Marvin Brush, Representing the Caulkins Educational Press. New York, Boston, and Chicago. Publishers of Caulkins' Arithmetics and Algebras, and other superior textbooks for school and college. Across the top of the card the following words had been neatly added in pencil: *Women who smoke are unfit to be mothers.* The young lady reddened slightly, tore the card into flakes and pretended to go to sleep. After a few moments she sat up and, assuming an expression of weary scorn, looked about the car. None of the passengers seemed capable of such a message, least of all a tall, solidly built young man whose eyes, nevertheless, were gravely resting on her.

This young man, feeling that he had made his point, picked up his briefcase and went forward to the smoking-car. There almost every seat was filled. The day was already hot and the smokers, having discarded coat and collar, lay sprawled about in the blue haze. Several card games were in progress, and in one corner an excitable young man was singing an interminable ballad, alternately snapping his fingers and stamping his heel to mark the beat. An admiring group was gathered about him, supplying the refrain. Congeniality already reigned in the car and remarks were being shouted from one end of it to the other. Brush looked about him appraisingly, and chose a seat beside a tall leather-faced man in shirt sleeves.

"Sit down, buddy," said the man. "You're rocking the car. Sit down and lend me a match."

"My name is George Brush," said the younger man, seizing the other's hand and looking him squarely and a little glassily in the eye. "I'm glad to meet you. I travel in school books. I was born in Michigan and I'm on my way to Wellington, Oklahoma."

"That's fine," said the other. "That's fine, only relax, sonny, relax. Nobody's arrested you."

Brush flushed slightly and said, with a touch of heaviness, "In beginning a conversation I like to get all the facts on the table."

"What did I tell you, buddy?" said the other, turning a cold and curious eye on him. "Relax. Light up."

"I don't smoke," said Brush.

The conversation did the rounds of the weather, the crops, politics, and the business situation. At last Brush said:

"Brother, can I talk to you about the most important thing in life?"

The man slowly stretched out his full lazy length on the reversed seat before him and drew his hand astutely down his long yellow face. "If it's insurance, I got too much," he said. "If it's oil wells, I don't touch 'em, and if it's religion, I'm saved."

Brush had an answer even for this. He had taken a course in college entitled "How to approach strangers on the subject of Salvation"—and two and a half credits—generally followed the next semester by "Arguments in Sacred Debate"—one and a half credits. This course had listed the openings in such an encounter as this and the probable responses. One of the responses was this, that the stranger declared himself already saved. This statement might be either (1) true, or (2) untrue. In either case the evangelist's next move was to say, with Brush:

"That's fine. There is no greater pleasure than to talk over the big things with a believer."

"I'm saved," continued the other, "from making a goddam

fool of myself in public places. I'm saved, you little peahen, from putting my head into other people's business. So shut your damn face and get out of here, or I'll rip your tongue out of your throat."

This attitude had also been foreseen by the strategists. "You're angry, brother," said Brush, "because you're aware of an unful-filled life."

"Now listen," said the other, solemnly. "Now listen to what I'm saying to you. I warn you. One more peep of that stuff and I'll do something you'll be sorry for. Now wait a minute! Don't say I didn't warn you: one more peep—"

"I won't trouble you, brother," said Brush. "But if I stop, don't think it's because I'm afraid of anything you'd do."

"What did I tell you," said the man, quietly. He leaned over, and picking up the briefcase that was lying between Brush's feet, he threw it out of the window. "Go and get it, fella, and after this learn to pick your man."

Brush rose. He was smiling stiffly. "Brother," he said, "it's lucky for you I'm a pacifist. I could knock you against the roof of this car. I could swing you around here by one leg. Brother, I'm the strongest man that was ever tested in our gym back at college. But I won't touch you. You're rotted out with liquor and cigarettes."

"Haw-haw-haw!" replied the man.

"It's lucky for you I'm a pacifist," repeated Brush, mechani-cally, staring at the man's eyes, the yellow strings of his throat, and the blue stain his collar button had left.

By now the whole car was interested. The leather-faced man threw his arm over the back of the seat and included his neighbors in his pleasure. "He's nuts," he said.

Voices in the car began to rise in a threatening tide: "Get the hell out of here." . . . "Put him out."

Brush shouted into the man's face: "You're full of poisons—Anybody can see that. You're dying. Why don't you think about it?"

"Haw-haw-haw!" said the man.

The noise in the car rose to a roar. Brush went down the aisle and entered the toilet. He was trembling. He put his hand on the wall and laid his forehead against it. He thought he was going to throw up. He muttered over and over again, "He's rotten with liquor and cigarettes." He gargled a mouthful of cold water. When his breathing had become regular again, he returned to the car "Quarritch." He walked with lowered eyes and, sitting down, he held his head in his hands and stared at the floor. "I shouldn't hate anybody," he said.

The train reached Wellington an hour later. Brush went to the hotel, engaged an automobile, and retrieved the briefcase. He spent the day calling on the department heads in the high school. On coming out of the dining-room after dinner he went to the writing-desk, printed a Bible text neatly on the blotter, and went early to bed.

The next morning brought his twenty-third birthday. He rose early and started to leave the hotel for a walk before breakfast. In one hand he held a rough draft of his resolutions for the year, along with a list of his virtues and faults. As he passed through the lobby he noticed that a fresh blotter had been placed on the writing-desk. He went up to it, took out his fountain pen, and stood a moment irresolute. Then without sitting down he printed across the top the words, "Thou, Lord, seest me."

A negro who was crouched on the floor, polishing spitoons, raised his eyes slowly and said, with guarded animosity: "You'd better not write on that blotter. Mr. Gibbs is awful mad about that. He's had to change it once already and he's awful mad."

"Does it do any harm to anybody?" asked Brush, calmly, returning the pen to his pocket.

"The folks don't like it. Mr. Blodgett, who's stayin' here, 's all roused up."

"Well, tell Mr. Blodgett to speak to me about it. I'd like to meet him," replied Brush, crossing to the water-cooler and starting to draw himself a drink of water. At that moment the manager of the hotel came down the stairs, followed by a man and a woman. The man was short and fat; he had a round red face and a pair of mobile black bushy eyebrows. He crossed the room to the writing-desk and picked out a piece of stationery.

"Look't this!" he cried, suddenly, pointing at the blotter. "Look't this! Now that's the second time. God! it gives me a pain."

"You can't stop'm, Mr. Blodgett," said the manager, sadly. "Why, last year, there was a fellow—"

"Well, I'd like to meet one. I'd like to tell'm what I think."

The manager whispered a few words to Blodgett and indicated Brush with his thumb.

Blodgett whistled. "You don't say!" he said.

The woman interposed loudly: "Now Reme, you're always picking up some crazy galoot or other. You'll get into trouble one of these days. Come in to breakfast and let'm be."

"Well, sister, you gotta have some fun when you're on the road, don't you?" said Blodgett. "This is a chance. Watch me now."

As Brush started to go to the street Blodgett put out his hand. "Say, buddy," he said, quietly, one eyebrow subtly raised, "where are you holding meetings?"

"I'm not holding any meetings," replied Brush, seizing his hand and looking dynamically into his eyes. "I think your name is Blodgett. Mine is George Brush. George Marvin Brush. I travel in textbooks. Glad to know you, Mr. Blodgett."

"Yes, sir, every time," said Blodgett. "Doremus Blodgett, Ever-last Hosiery. So you travel, do you?"

"Yes."

"Well then, what's the idea of writing all over these blotters? You're young and healthy. See what I mean?"

"I'm glad to talk about it," said Brush.

"That's the way. Now look here, Brush. I'm glad to see you're a reasonable fella. We were afraid you were going to be one of these faynatics. See what I mean? Brush, I want you to meet the finest little girl in the world, my cousin, Mrs. Margie McCoy."

"Glad to know you," said Brush.

Mrs. McCoy had a large puffy face heavily covered with powder. It was surmounted by a fine head of orange, brown, and black hair. She did not acknowledge the introduction.

"Fella to fella," continued Blodgett, "What's the idea of writing over all these blotters, eh? I don't say it isn't all right for preachers. They get paid for it."

"Mr. Blodgett, I've found a good thing and I want to tell everybody about it."

"Let'm be, Reme. Let'm be," said Mrs. McCoy, beckoning her cousin toward the dining-room door with jerks of her head and the movements of her sullen eyes.

"Well, I don't like it," continued her cousin, suddenly belligerent.

"If you don't like it," continued Brush, "that's because you're aware of an unfulfilled life."

Blodgett began to shout. "That's the trouble with you stinking reformers, you think everybody——"

Here Margie McCoy flung herself between them: "Have some breakfast first, for Gawd's sake! Now stop it! Stop it, I say! You're always trying to get into a fight. Besides, the doctor told you you gotta keep calm."

"I don't fight, Mrs. McCoy," said Brush. "Let him say what he wants to say."

Blodgett began again in a calmer tone. "I don't say it isn't all right for preachers, but what gripes me is when some . . . Goddam it! everything has its place."

"Aw, come on and get some cawfee," said Mrs. McCoy, adding, under her breath: "He's just a nut. Let'm be."

"Say, why aren't you a preacher, anyway? Why aren't you in a church, where you belong?"

"There's a reason for that," replied Brush, staring fixedly at the wall behind Blodgett.

"Couldn't you get enough money?"

"No, that wasn't the trouble. . . . I had a very personal reason."

"Stop right there!" cried Blodgett. "I don't want to hear anything that's not my business. All I say is that it looks to me like you had a still more personal reason for going in."

Brush stared at him somberly. "I'm not afraid to tell," he said. "I did something . . . I did something that a minister can't do."

"Oh, I see!" said Blodgett, out of his depths. "Well . . . of course, that makes a difference."

"What did he *say?*" asked Mrs. McCoy.

"He said . . . he did something that a minister can't do." Then turning to Brush, Blodgett took on a conspiratorial air; lowering his voice, he inquired, "What was it?"

"I wouldn't like to tell that with a lady here," said Brush.

Blodgett raised his eyebrows and whistled compassionately: "Ain't that terrible! There's a woman in it, eh?"

"Yes."

"Tchk-tchk-tchk! You know you ought to marry the poor girl."

Brush looked at him sharply. "Of course I want to marry her. Only I can't find her."

"I gotta get out of here," cried Margie McCoy, abruptly. "I'm going cuckoo. Let'm be, Reme. He's crazy. He's nuts," and she hurried into the dining-room.

Blodgett's manner took on the hushed and prudent manner he would have assumed had Brush informed him that he was talking to Napoleon. "Say, ain't that terrible! How did it happen?"

"I'd rather not talk about it," said Brush.

Blodgett asked some questions about the road and about business conditions in Texas. Then he said: "How about coming up to the room tonight, eh?—little talk?"

"I'd like to, but I'm leaving this morning for Oklahoma City."

"What? We'll be there tomorrow. Where do you put up, boy?"

It seemed that they both planned to stay at the McGraw House and a meeting was planned for the following evening. "Good! About eight, see? Come up to the room and have a little drink."

"I don't drink, but I'd like a little talk."

"Oh, you don't drink?"

"No."

"Sure, I realize it's against the law," said Blodgett, generously.

"It undermines the nervous system and impairs the efficiency," added Brush.

"Damn it, you're right. You're right. I'm going to stop it one of these days. You never said a truer word. But you won't mind if the little lady and I have something while you're there?"

"No."

Mrs. McCoy appeared at the door. "Reme, you come here," she cried. "Come here. He might shoot or something."

"Marge, what do you mean, shoot. He's all right. He's a fine fella." He slapped Brush on the back, then lowering his voice, added, confidentially: "No ill-feelings, see? The little girl's always that way when you first know her."

Blodgett winked intimately and followed his cousin in to breakfast.

Brush left the hotel and walked down the street in the shade of the cottonwood trees. He listened enviously to the domestic sounds that came from the houses to his right and his left. Housewives were shaking rugs out of windows or shifting saucepans upon a stove. Children were heard calling in shrill voices, every sentence beginning and ending with a querulous "Ma." A few men had taken advantage of the early coolness and were cutting the lawn; others were flinging open the doors of their garages and casting a first reassuring glance at their car. At the edge of town Brush left the road and followed a path through some deep grass; passing some rubbish-heaps and a deserted sawmill he came upon a clear stream that, flowing rapidly, seemed to carry a load of tangled weeds towards a pond. He lay down beside the pond, face downward, and gazed at the scene. Two water snakes glided by, weaving in and out of each other's shadow. In the middle of the pond a turtle, with two small turtles on her back, climbed out upon a rotting plank. More turtles followed and, settling themselves squarely, drew their heads partly into their shells and closed their eyes. The very bird calls announced a hot day.

Brush had come out to think. This was his twenty-third birthday, and birthdays were solemn occasions for him. Two years before he had risen up from a swinging hammock on his father's porch, had crossed the town of Ludington, Michigan, and proposed marriage to a widow ten years older than himself. He had been refused, but he never forgot the exhilaration of having done it, nor the look in her eyes as she stood drying her hands on her apron, while her children crawled about on the floor, untying his shoestrings. One year before he had spent the evening in the Public Library at Abilene, Texas, reading the life of Napoleon in the Encyclopædia Britannica. When he finished he had taken a pencil from his pocket and written in the margin, "I am a great man, too, but for good," and had signed his initials. The perspiration had stood out on his forehead.

And now before the pool near Wellington, Oklahoma, he prepared to examine himself on his twenty-third birthday. Tremendous were the good resolutions adopted that morning. It was to be a great year. He never forgot the solemnity of that hour, even though, at the end of it, still on an empty stomach, he fell asleep.

As a result of one of the decisions made by the pool near Wellington, Brush found himself towards noon on the same day in Armina, forty miles away, whither he had come to draw his savings from a bank in that town. The bank consisted of one big room, high and well lighted, with a pen in the middle, walled in with a show of marble and of bright steel gratings. Beside the door the president sat in his smaller pen, filled with despair. Short of a miracle his bank had little over a week to live. Banks had been failing all through these states for months, and now even this bank, which had seemed to him to be eternal, would be obliged to close its doors.

Brush glanced at the president, but, resisting the temptation to go and talk to him, went to a desk and, drawing out his bankbook, made out a slip. He presented himself at the cashier's window.

"I'm closing up my account," he said. "I'll draw out everything except the interest."

"I beg your pardon?"

"I'll take out the money," he repeated, raising his voice as though the cashier were deaf, "but I'll leave the interest here."

The cashier blinked a moment, then began fumbling among his coins. At last he said, in a low voice, "I don't think we'll be able to keep your account open for so small a sum."

"You don't understand. I'm not leaving the interest here as an account. I don't want it. Just return it back into the bank. I don't believe in interest."

The cashier began casting distraught glances to right and left. He paid out both sum and interest across the grating, mumbling: "I . . . the bank . . . you must find some other way of disposing of the money."

Brush took the five hundred dollars and pushed the rest back. He raised his voice sharply and could be heard all over the room saying, "I don't believe in interest."

The cashier hurried to the president and whispered in his ear. The president stood up in alarm, as though he had been told that a thief was entering the vaults. He went to the door of the bank and stopped Brush as he was about to leave.

"Mr. Brush?"

"Yes."

"Might I speak to you for a moment, Mr. Brush? In here."

"Certainly," said Brush, and followed him through a low gate into the presidential pen. Mr. Southwick had a great unhappy sheep's head rendered ridiculous by a constant fluttering adjustment of various spectacles and pince-nez and black satin ribbons. His professional dignity reposed upon an enormous stomach supported in blue serge and bound with a gold chain. They sat down on either side of this monument and gazed at one another in considerable excitement.

"Mm . . . mm . . . ! You feel you must draw out your savings, Mr. Brush?" said the president, softly, as though he were inquiring into an intimate hygienic matter.

"Yes, Mr. Southwick," replied Brush, reading the name from a framed sign on the desk.

". . . And you're leaving your interest in the bank?"

"Yes."

"What would you like us to do with it?"

"I have no right to say. The money isn't mine. I didn't earn it."

"But your money, Mr. Brush—I beg your pardon—your money earned it."

"I don't believe that money has the right to earn money."

Mr. Southwick swallowed. Then in the manner he had once used while explaining to his daughter that the earth was round, he said: "But the money you deposited here, that money has been earning money for us. The interest represents those profits, which we share with you."

"I don't believe in profits like that."

Mr. Southwick edged his chair forward and asked another question: "Mm . . . mm . . . ! May I ask why you have thought it best to withdraw your money at this time?"

"Why, I'm glad to tell you, Mr. Southwick. You see, I've been thinking about money and banks a lot lately. I haven't quite thought the whole matter through yet—I'll be able to do that when my vacation comes in November—but at least I see that for myself I don't believe in saving money any more. Up till now I used to believe that you were allowed to save *some* money—like five hundred dollars, for instance, for your old age, you know, or for the chance your appendix burst, or for the chance you might get married suddenly—for what people call a rainy day; but now I see that's all wrong. I've taken a vow, Mr. Southwick; I've taken the vow of voluntary poverty."

"Of what?" asked Mr. Southwick, his eyes starting out of his head.

"Of voluntary poverty, like Gandhi. I've always followed it somewhat. The point is to never have any money saved up anywhere. Do you see?"

Mr. Southwick mopped his forehead.

"When my pay check comes every month," continued Brush, earnestly, "I immediately give away all money that's left over from the month before, but I always knew that at bottom that wasn't honest. Honest, with myself, I mean, because all this time I had five hundred dollars hidden away in this bank here. But from now on, Mr. Southwick, I won't need any banks. You see, the fact that I had this money here was a sign that I lived in fear."

"Fear!" cried Mr. Southwick. He rapped the bell on his desk so hard that it crashed to the floor.

"Yes," said Brush, his voice rising as the truth became clearer to him. "No one who has money saved up in a bank can really be happy. All the money locked up here is being saved because people are afraid of a rainy day. They're afraid, as they say, that worst may come to worst. Mr. Southwick, may I ask if you're a religious man?"

Mr. Southwick was deacon in the First Presbyterian Church and had passed a red velvet collection bag for twenty years, but at this question he jumped as though he had been struck sharply in the ribs. A clerk approached him. "Go out at the corner and get Mr. Gogarty at once," he commanded, hoarsely. "Get him at once!"

"Then you know what I'm talking about," continued Brush. His voice could now be heard throughout the hall. Clerks and depositors had stopped what they were doing and were listening in consternation. "There is no worst coming to worst for a good man. There's nothing to be afraid of. To save up money is a sign that you're afraid, and one fear makes another fear, and that fear makes another fear. No one who has money in banks can really be happy. It's a wonder your depositors can really sleep nights, Mr. Southwick. There they lie, wondering what'll happen to them when they get old and when they get sick and when banks have troubles—"

"Stop it! Stop what you're saying!" cried Mr. Southwick, very red in the face. A policeman entered the bank. "Mr. Gogarty, arrest this man. He's come here to make trouble. Get him out of here at once."

Brush faced the policeman. "Arrest me," he said. "Here I am. What have I done? I haven't done anything. I'll tell the judge. I'll tell everybody what I've been saying."

"Come on along. You come on quiet."

"You don't have to push me," said Brush. I'm glad to come."

He was taken to the jail.

"My name is George Marvin Brush," he said, seizing the warden's hand.

"Take your dirty hand away," said the warden. "Jerry, get the fellow's prints."

Brush was led into another room to record his fingerprints and to be photographed.

"My name's George M. Brush," he said, seizing the photographer's hand.

"How are yuh?" said the other. "Glad to see yuh. My name's Bohardus."

"I didn't catch it," said Brush, politely.

"Bohardus—Jerry Bohardus."

Jerry Bohardus was a retired policeman with a kindly disposition and a dreamy, fumbling manner. A shock of long gray hair fell into his eyes. "Kindly step up in front of this glass table for me," he said. "It's fine weather we're having."

"Oh, fine," said Brush. "It's fine, outside."

"Now put your hand down lightly on this pad, Mr. Brown. That's the ticket. That's right. That's fine." He lowered his voice and added, confidentially: "Don't feel badly about this business, Mr. Brown. It's just a form we gotto go through, see? It don't mean anything. They send these here prints to Washington, where there are eighty-five thousand others; some of them belong to sheriffs and mayors, too, yes, sir. I wouldn't be surprised if there were a few senators. Now the other hand, my boy. That's the ticket. So you never had this done before?"

"No," said Brush. "The other town I was arrested in didn't seem to care about it."

"Probably they didn't have the ay-paray-tus," replied Bohardus, complacently knocking the glass table with his knuckles. "We give two thousand dollars for all this, and it's a dandy."

Brush earnestly examined the result. "That thumb's not very clear, Mr. Bohardus," he said. "I think I'd better do it over again."

"No, that's clear enough. You've got a fine thumb. See them spirals?"

"Yes."

"They're just about the finest spirals I ever saw. Some say they stand for character."

"Do they?"

"That's what they say. Now we'll take your picture. Will you kindly put your head in this frame? . . . That's the ticket. It's funny about fingerprints," continued Bohardus, placing a board of numerals against Brush's chest. "Even if there were a trillion con-trillion of them no two'd be alike."

"Isn't that wonderful!" replied Brush, his voice lowered in

awe. Bohardus retired under a dark cloth. "Do you want me to smile now?" called Brush.

"No," answered Bohardus, emerging and adjusting his lenses. "We don't generally ask for a smile in this work."

"I suppose you've seen lots of criminals in your day, Mr. Bohardus?"

"I? I certainly have. I've bertillioned people that have killed their folks and that have poisoned their wives and that have spat on the flag. You wouldn't believe what I've seen. . . . Now we'll get your side face, Mr. Brown. . . . That's the ticket." He came forward and turned Brush's head. He took the occasion to ask, delicately, "May I inquire what they think you did, Mr. Brown?"

"I didn't do anything. I just told a bank president that banks were immoral places and they arrested me."

"You don't say. . . . Chin up, Mr. Brown."

"My name isn't Brown. It's Brush—George Brush."

"Oh, I see. Well, what's a name, anyway? . . . There, now I guess we got some good pictures."

"Do you sell copies of these, Mr. Bohardus?"

"We're not allowed to, I reckon. Leastways, there never was no great demand."

"I was thinking I could buy some extra. I haven't been taken for more than two years. I know my mother'd like some."

Bohardus stared at him narrowly. "I don't think it shows a good spirit to make fun of this work, Mr. Brown, and I can tell you I don't like it. In fifteen years here nobody's made fun of it, not even murderers haven't."

"Believe me, Mr. Bohardus," said Brush, turning red, "I wasn't making fun of anything. I knew you made good photos, and that's all I thought about."

Bohardus maintained an angry silence, and when Brush was led away refused to return his greeting. The chief of police, Mr. Southwick, and other dignitaries were in earnest conference when

Brush was led into the warden's office. At once he approached Mr. Southwick.

"I still don't see what was wrong in the things I said. Mr. Southwick, I can't apologize for a mistake I don't understand. I can see that you might feel hurt because I haven't a very high opinion of the banking business, but that's not a thing you can put me in prison for, and it's not a thing I can change my mind about, either. Anyway, all I ask is a fair trial and I think I can clear myself in half an hour. And I hope there are as many people in the courtroom as possible, because in these depression times a lot of people ought to know what Gandhi thinks of money."

The chief of police came toward him threateningly. "Now stop this foolishness!" he said. "Stop it right now. What's the matter with you, anyway?" He turned back to his men. "Jerry thinks this guy's screwy. Perhaps we ought to take him up to Monktown for some tests. . . . How about it, young fella? What's the matter with you, anyway? Are you nuts?"

"No, I'm not," cried Brush, violently, "and I'm getting tired of this. You can see perfectly well I'm not crazy. Give me any old test you like—memory, dates, history, Bible. I'm an American citizen, and I'm of sound mind, and the next person that calls me crazy will have to answer for it, even if I am a pacifist. I told Mr. Southwick that his bank and every other bank is a shaky building of fear and cowardice. . . ."

"All right, dry up, pipe down," said the chief. "Now looka here, Brush, if you aren't out of this town in an hour you get the strait-jacket and a six-months' sanity test upstate. Do you hear?"

"I'd like to take it," said Brush, "but I can't spare six months."

"Gogarty," said the chief, "see him to the depot."

Gogarty was a tall man with a great bony jaw and pale blue eyes.

"Boy, are you coming along quiet?" asked Gogarty.

"Of course I'll be quiet," said Brush.

After they had gone a number of blocks in silence Gogarty stopped, turned, and putting one forefinger on Brush's lapel, asked in a confidential tone:

"Say, boy, where did you get that idea about the Armina Savings Bank bein' shaky? Who told yuh?"

"I didn't mean that bank only. I meant all banks."

This answer did not satisfy Gogarty. Lost in thought, he continued to peer over his spectacles into Brush's face. Then he turned and stared up the street.

"Looks to me like there's a lot of people at the door of that bank now," he said. Suddenly he was roused to action. "Boy, you stick by me," he said. He dashed into the house before which they were standing. A woman was washing the dishes. "Mrs. Cowles," said Gogarty, severely, "as constable in this town I am obliged to use your telephone."

"Why, certainly, Mr. Gogarty," said Mrs. Cowles, nervously.

"And I'll have to ask you, ma'am, to go out on the front porch while I'm talking here."

Mrs. Cowles obeyed. When Gogarty had received a reply he said: "Mary, put on your hat. Do what I tell you. Go down and draw out all the savings, down to the last cent. And run. Only got half an hour. And don't tell nobody what you're doing."

He left the house with Brush and allowed Mrs. Cowles to return to her work. He again peered up the street, and deciding that his duty lay there, trusted Brush to reach the railway station by himself.

Mr. Southwick went home and lay down in a darkened room. From time to time he moaned, whereupon his wife, moving about on tiptoe, would rise and change the damp cloths on his forehead, whispering: "Sh, Timothy dear! There's nothing to worry about. You just take a nap. Sh!"

2

Oklahoma City. Chiefly conversation. The adventure in the barn. Margie McCoy gives some advice.

Brush arrived at the McGraw House in Oklahoma City on the same evening. The following morning he set about putting in a hard day's work. He called on all manner of school superintendents, principals, and heads of departments. He drove out to a reformatory and was persuaded to address the assembled student body.

At eight o'clock in the evening he knocked at Blodgett's door. For a moment there was the sound of voices in loud altercation, then Blodgett came out into the hall and closed the door behind him.

"Say, Brush," he said, "about tonight. I just want to ask you to be a little careful. You know. My cousin's kind of nervous. Just keep off subjects that might upset her. You get the idea."

"All right. I'll try and remember."

"Yeah. She's had a lot of fuss lately. She only got a divorce last month, and you know how it is."

"She's a . . . divorced woman?" asked Brush, softly.

"Yeah, yeah. So you see!" and Blodgett winked with fraternal complicity. Then he opened the door and announced, with nervous cordiality: "Well, Marge, look who's here."

Margie McCoy was sitting on the bed, her feet on a newspaper, her back against the iron bedstead. Her face was still sullen. She held a tall glass in one hand, and a cigarette in the other. She acknowledged Brush's greeting by only the slightest movement of her eyes, after which she continued gazing implacably at the wall before her.

The conversation proceeded with the greatest difficulty. Brush went carefully, not sure which subjects were likely to unnerve a woman who had recently passed through the harrowing experience of obtaining a divorce. After forty minutes of this discomfort he rose to go.

"Well, thank you very much for letting me come around," he said, backing to the door. "I'd better be going. I still have some reports to draw up, and . . ."

To the surprise of both the men, Mrs. McCoy spoke: "What's the hurry? What's the hurry?" she asked, irritably. "Sit down. Don't you smoke, either? No wonder you feel like a fool, just sitting and talking. Remus, give'm some ginger ale, anyway. That way he can at least hold something in his hand, my-God!"

A second attack was made on conversation. Brush let fall the news that he had been arrested and taken to jail since last he saw them. He was encouraged to tell the story and was soon recounting his conversation with Mr. Southwick. He explained the theory of voluntary poverty. Now Mrs. McCoy's eyes were resting on him in astonishment. At the end of his exposition the same question rose simultaneously to the lips of both the listeners.

"What would you do if you lost your job?" they asked.

"Well, I don't know exactly. I never really thought about it. I guess I'd find something. Leastways, it doesn't seem very likely. I keep getting raises all the time. They even make me nervous."

"The raises make you nervous?" asked Mrs. McCoy.

"Yes."

"What would you do if you got sick?" she asked.

"What are you going to do when you get old?" asked Blodgett.

"I already explained that to you," he said.

Mrs. McCoy solemnly put her feet on the floor and, placing her hands on her hips, she leaned forward: "Listen, baby," she said. "Let me look at you. Are you trying to kid me?"

"Why, no, Mrs. McCoy. I'm serious."

She just as solemnly returned to her position on the bed. "Well, something's the matter," she muttered, looking distrustfully into her glass.

"Buddy," said Blodgett, "why did you say that it made you nervous to get raises?"

"Because hardly anybody else's getting raises these days. I think everybody ought to be hit by the depression equally. You see?"

Mrs. McCoy said dryly: "Sure I see. Your ideas aren't the same as other people's, are they?"

"No," said Brush, "I should think not. I didn't put myself through college for four years and go through a different religious conversion in order to have ideas like other people's."

"I see. Now answer me another: When you get married what are you going to use for money?"

"I beg your pardon?"

"How do you know your wife'll be willing to throw away all your money every month, and how do you know she'll be willing to look forward with a big thrill to the poorhouse, like you do?"

"Oh, she will," said Brush.

"You're engaged, are you?" asked Blodgett.

"I'm . . . I'm practically engaged. Well, I don't know whether I'm engaged or not."

"Is she a . . . she's a nice girl, eh?"

"I don't know that, either—not for sure." Brush glanced at Blodgett. "I'd better not talk about it," he said. "It's all a part of that big mistake I made. You said you didn't want me to mention things like that tonight."

"I can stand anything now," said Mrs. McCoy. "After the big poverty idea I can stand anything. The other morning was different. I couldn't stand it on an empty stummick, that's all. Come on and tell us what happened."

Again Brush looked at Blodgett.

"Sure," said Blodgett, "Go ahead."

"I know it's a pretty intimate thing to tell people . . . people that I've only known a short time. But you'll see how badly I need advice on it. Before I begin I think I ought to explain to you how I feel about women."

"Just a minute, buddy," said Blodgett, trimming a cigar. "You're sure you can stand it, sister?"

"What did I tell you? I can stand anything."

Brush looked up in surprise. "There's nothing hard to stand about this. I just wanted you to know that until this thing happened I was looking everywhere for a wife. Really, everywhere. It was almost the only thing I thought about. You see, I'm twenty-three years old; in fact, that was my birthday when you met me yesterday."

"Well, well!" said Blodgett. "Many happy returns of the day."

"Thank you a lot . . . and I should have settled down long ago . . ."

"I see."

". . . and founded an American home."

"What?"

Brush leaned forward earnestly. "You know what I think is

the greatest thing in the world? It's when a man, I mean an American, sits down to Sunday dinner with his wife and six children around him. Do you know what I mean?"

"Six, eh?"

"Yes, and the more the better. Well, that's the thing I want most of all, so everywhere I go I keep looking for a wife. And every now and then I used to think I'd found her. For instance, I was singing in church one day—I guess I never told you I had a very good tenor voice—"

"No."

"Well, I have; so when I come to a town where I have to stay over Sunday I go to the minister of a church and offer to sing at the service. It makes the service more inspiring. And one day I was singing and I saw a girl in the congregation that looked perfect to me. I was singing 'The Lost Chord,' and when I came to the loud part you can imagine how I put everything into it. After service everybody came up and asked me to go home to dinner with them. That's what always happens. And the father of this girl came up and asked me to go home with them. All during dinner I sat by her and I thought she was the finest girl I'd ever seen in my life, even though she didn't say hardly a word. But all the time I was afraid something would spoil it. I brought the conversation around to evolution and I found she was all right there; they didn't believe any of that about monkeys. Well, you can guess what happened."

"No," said Blodgett, "I don't know as I can."

"We were sitting around after dinner and she asked her brother for a cigarette."

"You don't say!"

"Her mother was pretty disappointed in her and said so, but she wasn't as disappointed as I was. I guess she wanted to show off, with a singer in the house, that she wasn't just a village girl. That was in Sulphur Falls, Arkansas. Now I can never hear about Sulphur Falls without a funny feeling in my stomach."

"That's quite a story," said Blodgett. "Eh, Margie?"

"Did she ever know what she lost?" asked Mrs. McCoy.

Brush smiled. "It wasn't only me she lost, Mrs. McCoy," he said.

Blodgett broke in hurriedly. "Do they ever refuse to let you sing?"

"Sometimes they give me a test, but after a few notes they know it's all right."

"You ought to be able to pick up some handy money, that way."

"No, I don't believe in taking money for it. Once in Plata, Missouri, a man came up and offered me two hundred dollars to sing at the Elks' convention in St. Louis, but I couldn't. I would have done it for them free of charge, only my route didn't go anywhere near St. Louis at that time. That's another of my theories. A voice like mine is just a gift, that's all. It's not to anybody's credit to have a fine voice. It's just a thing of nature, like any other. Niagara Falls and the caves of Kentucky and John McCormack are just gifts to the public. It's like strength. I happen to have that, too. I'll help you move your trunk or your piano all day, but I wouldn't take money for it. Do you see?"

"Yes," said Mrs. McCoy, "I see something. Only, when are you going to get back to the other story?"

"It's a hard story to tell. It was in the vacation before my senior year at college——"

"What college was that?" asked Blodgett.

"Shiloh Baptist College, in South Dakota, a very good college. Summers I used to cover Missouri, Illinois, and some parts of Ohio, selling the Children's Encyclopedia. I walked and hitchhiked from one place to another. And one day I got lost. I must have been about twenty miles from Kansas City, sort of southwest. It got dark and began to rain. So I stopped at a farmhouse to ask if I could sleep in the barn. The farmer and his wife took me into their kitchen and gave me some coffee and bread and butter. They said they were Methodists and I could see there were three or four beautiful daughters moving around; but I couldn't see them very well because they stayed out of reach of the lamplight. But I noticed them and they all seemed to be quiet, beautiful girls. I said to myself that I'd make a good note of the house in the morning and come back again some day. Then I thanked them and said good night and went to the barn and went to sleep." Here Brush took out his handkerchief and wiped his forehead. "From now on it's kind of delicate," he said, "and I don't want to hurt your feelings, but I guess you've both been married."

"Yes," said Blodgett, "we know the worst."

"I woke up in the pitch dark and heard a girl's voice laughing, and then later it was half laughing and half crying. She asked me if I wanted something to eat. Well, I can always eat something—"

"Have an apple?" asked Mrs. McCoy.

"No, thank you, not now . . . We had a long talk. She said she wasn't happy on the farm. I asked her what her name was and she said 'Roberta.' Anyway, it sounded like Roberta. And that's important, because maybe it was Bertha. And one day in the newspaper I saw that there was a girl's name called Hertha. It might have been any one of those names."

"What does it matter what her name was?" cried Mrs. McCoy.

"You'll see. Anyway, she cried and I tried to comfort her. So I decided she was the person I was going to marry."

There was a pause; the others looked at him inquiringly.

He repeated with emphasis, "So I decided she was the person I was going to marry."

Blodgett leaned forward and asked in a low, shocked voice, "You mean you ruined the girl?"

Brush turned pale and nodded.

"Give him a drink!" cried Mrs. McCoy, abruptly, "Give him a drink, for Gawd's sake!"

"I don't drink," said Brush.

"Remus, you give'm a drink," she cried, still more violently.

"He's gotta take it. I can't stand seeing him act like a big baby. Now you drink that down and stop being a fool."

Brush accepted the glass and made a pretense of sipping at it. To his surprise, a weak sweetish taste lingered on his lips.

"Hurry up," said Mrs. McCoy. "How does it end?"

"That's about all," he continued. "I tried to tell this girl I'd be back the next day to marry her, but she ran back into the house. So I went down the road in the rain and walked all night. I walked for hours, planning what I'd say to her father and everything. But, you know, I've never been able to find that house again. I've been up and down every road that side of Kansas City a dozen times. I asked everybody about a farmhouse with daughters that were Methodists. I talked to all the R.F.D. postmen, but it was no good. Now you know why I can't think of being a minister."

There was a pause.

"And you love the girl, huh?" asked Blodgett.

Brush was displeased with the question. "It's not important if I love her or not," he said. "All I know is that I'm her husband until she or I dies. When you've known anybody as well as that, it means that you can never know anybody else as well as that until one of the two of you dies."

Mrs. McCoy leaned out of the bed and peered at the glass in his hand vindictively. "You're not drinking that drink!" she cried. "Drink it up. Don't you fool with it. Drink it up."

"I don't drink, Mrs. McCoy."

"I don't care whether you do or don't. I tell you to."

Blodgett himself was alarmed at her intensity. He raised one eyebrow expressively as a signal to Brush who took another swallow. Mrs. McCoy watched him belligerently. Then again she lowered her feet solemnly to the floor. She said, slowly, "Do you want advice?"

"Yes, I do."

"Naw, naw. I'm *asking* you, do you want some advice?"

"Yes."

"From who? From me?"

"Yes."

"Then listen! Now listen! Since you've tried as hard as you can; since you can't find the girl; since the girl let herself in for it, anyway—see?—since all these things are so, *forget it*. You're clear. You're free. Begin again. Begin all over."

"I can't do that. Don't you see I'm married already?"

"What are you talking about? You're not *married*. You have no license. You're not married."

"Mrs. McCoy, if you say I'm not married you're just quibbling with words, because I certainly am."

Mrs. McCoy stared at him wrathfully, then, shaking her head, returned to her former position.

Brush continued with lowered eyes: "Anyway, it's perfectly clear to me. And maybe it means that I can't settle down and found an American home. Sometimes I think I may get so discouraged that I may fall sick—or worse. Because that's all sickness is— discouragement. That's one of my theories, too. I have a theory that all sickness comes from having lost hope about something. If they find out they're not as good as they thought they were—in business or in anything else—or if they've done wrong and can't undo it, then they gradually fall sick. They really want to die. They haven't any real interest left in wanting to see the sun come up on the next day. They *think* they want to live, but secretly they don't. Anyway, I'm going to think it through next November when I get my vaca- tion. In the meantime I'm a good example of it. Look at me; I'm so worried about this that I got influenza last Spring. I've never been sick in my life. And another thing—if you'll excuse my mentioning it—I never used to have to take laxatives; but now I have to take laxatives all the time. I know what causes it, too. It means that I don't want to live unless I can settle down and have an American—"

At this point Margie McCoy became distraught. "Can't you stop him? Name-a-God, is this going on forever! Seems like we been here hours talking about this one thing. Change the subject. I'm going nuts. And you there, take another drink. No-o-o, none of those bird-sips."

Brush took another swallow and then rose. "I guess I'd better be going," he said. "I have to leave on a two o'clock train for Camp Morgan. Thank you for letting me come to see you."

He stood lamely in the middle of the room, waiting to see whether Mrs. McCoy intended shaking hands with him. She rose and strolled towards the door, swinging her hips as she went. She leaned against the wall by the door. The two men looked at her in some trepidation.

"Now, listen! Listen to me!" she said, emphatically. "You make me sick. Where do they get yuh, your the'ries and your ideas? Nowhere! Live, kid,—live! What'd become of all of us sons-a-bitches, if we stopped to argue out every step we took? Stick down to earth."

Brush looked at her with furrowed brow and said in a low voice, "It seems to me I live."

To the astonishment of both men, she placed her hand on his shoulder. "I mean, look around you. We'll be dead soon. Thinking doesn't change anything. It only makes you twice as blue."

"It doesn't make me blue," he said.

Mrs. McCoy turned back angrily into the room and lit another cigarette. "Oh, go to hell!" she said.

Blodgett followed Brush into the hall.

"I wish she'd at least shaken hands with me," said Brush.

"Don't get her wrong," said Blodgett, confusedly, "That's the way she is when you first know her. She'll be all right when you know her better."

Brush returned slowly to his room. Before beginning to pack, he stood at the window and looked out into the rain. "I talk too much," he said to himself in a whisper. "I must watch that. I talk too damn much."

3

Good times at Camp Morgan. Dick Roberts' nightmares. Dinner with Mississippi Corey.

George Brush's trip to Camp Morgan was in obedience to a telegram he had received on his arrival in Oklahoma City. The telegram came from his superior in the publishing-house and read: JUDGE LAKE MORGAN CAMP SETTLE GUTENBERG ALDUS CAXTON GIVE HIM THE WORKS SKIES THE LIMIT EINSTEIN. This message was not so difficult of interpretation as it appears to be. Howells, the sender, was a debonaire soul who signed his official communications with any signature that occurred to him as being improbable. "Judge Lake Morgan Camp" meant that Representative Corey, judge by inheritance from his father, was spending the week-end at the Lake Morgan Chautauqua and Recreation camp,

Morganville, Oklahoma. Judge Corey was the most influential member of the educational committee at the legislature; the choice of the textbooks for the public-school system lay largely in his hands. "Settle Gutenberg Aldus Caxton" meant that Brush was to persuade him to recommend certain textbooks published by his house. The names of the great printers served as code convention for Caulkins' *First Year Algebra,* Mademoiselle Desfontaines' *Les Premiers Pas,* and Professor Grubb's *A Soldier with Caesar.* "Give him the works skies the limit" referred to an elaborate joke between Howells and Brush, a joke that reposed on the pretense that representatives could be bribed. It implied that Brush was empowered to offer Judge Corey an honorary directorship in the League for the Improvement of Secondary Education. This post carried with it a retaining fee of seven hundred dollars a year. The joke had long since lost its freshness for Brush, but Howells returned to it month after month. Howells even insisted that a rival publishing-house practiced such a device in all seriousness, offering certain legislators a seat on the advisory counsel of an Education for Better Citizenship Union, carrying a retaining fee of a thousand dollars a year. Brush knew that Caulkins and Company would be incapable of such strategy, and, besides, he was unable to see how one opened the conversation that would lead to such an offer. At all events, he was able to place textbooks before millions of school children without such aids, and he was highly regarded by his firm in spite of his eccentricities.

In fact, his eccentricities gave the publishing-house no little pleasure. Brush's expense-account statements were unlike any others ever received in the office. He recorded every nickel and expended a large amount of ingenuity in saving the firm's money. He never doubted that the great Mr. Caulkins examined his reports in person, and he was right. Mr. Caulkins not only read them; he took them home to his wife, and carried them about with him in his pocket to show his friends at the club. There was only one point on which Brush and Howells came to strife. Brush not only refused to accept appointments with school officials on Sunday; however pressed his time, he refused to travel by train or bus on Sunday in order to reach an appointment on Monday morning. At a pinch he would consent to walk and hitch-hike. To ride a train on Sunday broke the Sabbath and prevented the trainmen from going to church and from passing the day in meditation. Howells pointed out to him that trains ran on Sunday anyway, "to carry sons and daughters to the bedside of their parents who had suddenly been taken ill." Brush replied that most parents would be willing to wait another day.

Brush left Oklahoma City at two and, employing a complicated chain of trains, buses, trolleys and taxicabs, crossed the greater part of the state and arrived at Morganville the next afternoon. During the journey he approached no one on the subject of salvation, but he reasoned with a Greek proprietor of a lunch-wagon on the matter of profanity, urged a farmer's boy to work his way through college, persuaded a garage proprietor to adopt a famished cat, and "thought through" the matter of capital punishment and the life sentence.

At Morganville he climbed into a bus hung with Chinese lanterns and banners that read: "Good times at Camp Morgan." He faced an advertisement on the back of the seat before him that read: "Girls, extend your acquaintance. Our Name-Badge Dances introduce everyone." The bus, advancing wildly through a pine wood, first passed a company of women in bloomers who were being instructed in nature lore, then a shoal of men in underwear who staggered by, their eyes starting out of their heads, their heels rapped by the cane of a sneering athletic coach. The road skirted a lake that was dotted with canoes and rowboats. In the middle of the lake a great balloon, advertising an automobile gasoline, was moored to a projecting rock. Brush dismounted at the administration shed and bought a registration card accompanied by a handful of tickets—bed assignment, meal coupons, and admission to a performance of "The Rivals" by the Normal School Forest of Arden Players.

His cot was one of six in a tent named "Felix." It belonged to the Oranges. His tentmates greeted him cheerfully, for the next morning the Oranges were to have a tug of war with the Blues, and Brush looked as though he could pull six men off their feet. He took a walk around the grounds, without enthusiasm. Seeing there was to be a camp-fire sing and marshmallow roast, he sought out the entertainment director, offered his services as soloist, and was accepted. Then he called upon the manager of the dining-hall, and had a place reserved for him at Judge Corey's table.

Returning to his tent, he began to unpack. He arranged his tooth-brush and shaving outfit on the shelf above his bed. On the cot next to his a man of forty lay, recovering from his exertions on the reducing squad. He opened an eye from time to time to observe Brush as he went about his work. Presently he raised himself up and, putting his feet on the floor, sat forlornly on the edge of his bed, his head in his hands.

Brush glanced at him sharply. "Don't you feel right?" he asked. "Did you overdo it?"

"Oh, I feel all right," said the man. A silence fell on his dejection. Brush glanced at him again and found the man looking at him with an absurd woe in his eyes. To recover himself the man said: "I don't know why I came to this place. I wish I were back in the office."

"It's Friday already," said Brush. "You wouldn't be doing anything in the office over the week-end, would you?"

"No, nor any other time. But I got the habit; I just go and sit there. I'm in real estate, and let me tell you we get heart failure every time the phone rings. I go and sit there and fool around the desk. I don't know."

"Sundays?"

"Yes, I manage to be there Sundays, too. There isn't anything else to do."

There was another pause. Brush began putting on a clean shirt for dinner.

"My wife dragged me here. She said it was good for the kids to get these lectures and shows. Yeah, she said it was good for the kids to take in these shows and concerts. Say, fella, my name's Dick Roberts of Meyrick."

"Glad to meet you. My name's George Brush. I travel in school books. My home's in Ludington, Michigan."

"Michigan, eh? Is there anything doing in your line?"

"Yes . . . yes," said Brush, tying his tie and frowningly studying Roberts' face in the mirror. "We keep selling pretty well."

Roberts struggled with himself and finally said, with effort: "Brush . . . mm. I may have to ask you to do a little favor for me."

"Sure. What can I do?"

"It may not be necessary, see, but just on the chance it is. I see as you've got the next cot to mine. My wife tells me I talk in my sleep. Just wake me up if I do."

"You mean that you snore?"

"No, I don't snore. She says that sometimes I sort of shout. Not very often, but sometimes. If I do it these nights, just hit me, see? Then I'll get up and go and sleep by the lake where I won't trouble anybody."

"Sure I'll do that."

"I just mentioned it. I don't sleep very well, anyway," continued Roberts, staring at the ground. "I guess I haven't slep' for weeks, not what you'd call slep'. That's why I went on that damned running squad. I wanted to get tired out."

The tent "Felix" stood beside the road that led through the camp-ground to the water's edge. Brush became aware of a woman standing in the road and calling: "Oh, Dick! Dick Roberts!"

"There's your wife calling you now," he said.

Roberts went out to her. Brush could hear her saying: "Lillian wants you to come in swimming and hold her up. Perhaps you're too tired now, though. I think there's just time before dinner and it might do you good."

"Yes, I'll be right along."

"Are you going to be comfortable, Dick?" she asked, peering anxiously towards the tent.

"Yes, it's fine. Everything's fine," he said, adding, "Wait a minute."

Roberts came back into the tent. "I'd like you to shake hands with my wife, if you're not busy," he said.

"I'd like to," replied Brush.

Mrs. Roberts was a short, slight woman with a manner that was at once vivacious and shy. After the introduction the three started walking slowly down the hill. Mrs. Roberts' eyes returned frequently with concern to her husband's face; his rested on the ground or affected to be interested in some object across the lake.

"We're so glad we came," said Mrs. Roberts. "The children are just as happy as they can be. You'd think they'd been here all summer, and of course they simply love it. I suppose you've come for a good rest and change."

"No," said Brush. "I don't like this kind of place. I've come on business to contact a man."

"Oh!" said Mrs. Roberts, glancing quickly at his face. "Well, I hope I see you again, Mr. Brush. Now I expect you'll be wanting to talk to some of these pretty girls around here."

"I'll get my suit on," said Roberts, and left them.

Brush did not move away. He continued walking gravely by Mrs. Roberts. She again glanced nervously at his face, and, stopping, said with great effort:

"Mr. Brush, since you're in my husband's tent, I think I ought to tell you something."

"I know. He told me."

"About his nightmares, you mean?"

"Yes."

"Perhaps it won't happen. But it would be very good of you to wake him up at once. I'm afraid he worries about that business too much. He just sits all day and all evening in that office, and I think he broods, that's a fact. That's why I came here to Camp Morgan—though it's quite expensive—to give him a change. Oh, I don't know what to do and I'm just sick about it!"

Here Mrs. Roberts began groping feverishly in her handbag for a handkerchief. Brush glanced down at her hands out of the corner of his eyes, standing ready to offer her his own, then continued solemnly looking at the lake.

"And what's more," added Mrs. Roberts, ". . . six weeks ago he had a kind of awful experience and he's never been the same since. And very likely he broods about that, too."

"Was he in an automobile accident?"

"No; it wasn't that. I'd like to tell you about it, if you're not . . . if you're not going any place. You see, Mr. Roberts and I were at one of those foolish amusement parks and we were riding on a roller-coaster, and a man in the same car as we were fell out and was killed. While he was dying, though, he wanted to dictate a letter to his family in Fort Wayne, Indiana, and Mr. Roberts, being an Elk, too, volunteered to take it. It was a simply awful accident. This man—though I hate to say it—was a perfect fool, Mr. Brush. He was one of that show-off kind and I guess he was trying to catch the attention of some girls in the same car. Mr. Roberts and I just hated him and there wasn't anybody that thought his jokes were funny. But the more people were disgusted with him the more he cut up. And the second trip, going around a curve, he stood right up in the car and pretended to dive. And sure enough, naturally, he fell. He fell hitting all those girders and things. Then while he was on the ground, waiting for the ambulance, he kept calling: 'Is anybody here an Elk? Is anybody here an Elk?' Seems he wanted to talk to an Elk, so Mr. Roberts volunteered. It made a terrible impression on him."

"I'll be glad to watch out for him tonight, Mrs. Roberts," said Brush. "I didn't think he looked very happy."

She turned and said, quickly, with nervous emphasis: "You know, that's a fact—he's *not* happy. I suppose I really oughtn't to tell you anything about this . . . you being so young and everything . . . but, Mr. Brush, I think he was going to commit suicide last week."

"Do you?"

"I don't know. I don't know. And I've never mentioned it to a soul. But one night I got up. I saw a light in the bathroom, and he was standing there just thinking . . . and with such a look on his face, Mr. Brush, such a sad look. And now when he calls out in his sleep I think it's about *that*. There's no business at his office any more, not to speak of, and he worries about me and the children." Here she suddenly lowered her head and whispered, passionately: "I don't mind if we're going to be poor. I don't care if we're as poor as dirt. I don't care if the town pays for us, only I don't want him to be so miserable."

"You ought to tell him that," said Brush.

"I can't. Somehow I can't. He's real proud. He thinks so much of having a nice home in a good neighborhood. He's real proud. Sometimes it seems like he thinks the depression's his own fault. You know, he'd kill himself for the insurance. I know he would. And I'm just sick about it."

"Apart from the nightmares, does he sleep very well?"

"I . . . I don't know. I listen to his breathing and sometimes I think he just imitates sleeping, so as not to worry me."

At this minute a boy of nine, dripping wet, came running up the slope, calling: "Mamma, I gotta turtle. I gotta turtle, mamma. Look't." But as his eyes caught sight of the tears on his mother's face the words stuck in his throat. He glanced from his mother to Brush, then back again, then continued in a low voice; "Look, mamma, I gotta turtle. See."

"George, this is Mr. Brush. He rooms in the same tent with your father and you. Can you say how-do-you-do?"

A queenly woman with a badge on her chest approached them. "Don't forget the costume ball tomorrow night," she said. "You can make a costume by adding some amusing detail. If you can't think of anything, come to the desk and we will be happy to give you some suggestions. Ah, the darling little turtle. Aren't you *happy* you found it? Mr. Macklin is the nature man and he will *explain* it to you."

She went on her way. Brush said, "I think I can do something."

"And don't tell. You won't tell, will you?"

"No-no, not if I can help it."

Brush turned back towards the main hall. On the veranda a large red-faced man was making himself loudly agreeable to some embarrassed children.

"How do you do, Judge Corey?" said Brush.

"Stop right there!" cried the judge. "I know your name as well as I know my own. Don't tell me!"

"My name's George Brush. I've come to see you about putting some of Caulkins' textbooks on the recommended lists for your schools."

"Good. Fine. Always glad to do the people's business. We'll have a little talk about that after dinner."

Brush began talking at once about the excellence of his books, but the judge's mind began to wander.

"They sound fine, buddy. They certainly do. I don't want to miss any of that. Be sure you write me a letter about it."

"I've written you three letters, Judge."

"Good. My secretary's saving them for me. What states do you cover, buddy? Been down to Texas lately? How's Bill Winderstedt? D'you know Bill? Say, Brush, I want you to meet my wife and daughter." He peered about him. "Don't know where they've gone. My daughter Mississippi don't know many people here yet. Say, I got an idea. What table you sittin' at, young fella? Don't say a thing! I'll tell 'em to sit you at our table. They're throwing a novelty dinner tonight. You'll like it. They do things well at this camp. Yes, sir, they see everybody has a good time. Table M. Remember that—Table M."

"Thanks, Judge. I'd like to."

The judge drew nearer and assumed a confidential expression. "I got another idea. A coupla us fellas are going over to Morganville to the Depot Hotel about ten for a little game of poker. All right?"

"I don't play, Judge."

"Oh, you don't play?"

"No."

"Tell the truth, I get tired of it myself. It's harmless, y'know, but it takes up too much of a fella's time. See what I mean? There's my wife and girl now." The judge turned his back on his approaching family, as though he feared that they might read his lips, and whispered: "Say, sonny, if you're staying around the lot here you might keep an eye on my little girl. She don't know many people here. A little canoe ride y'know . . . no rough stuff . . . just a half-hour canoe ride, something like that."

Mrs. Corey was a tall, stiff woman with a frightened expression on her face; her daughter greatly resembled her. The mother wore a pince-nez hung upon a long gold chain; Mississippi wore thick blurred spectacles.

"Girls," said the judge, "I want you to meet Jim Bush, one of the finest fellas you could hope to see. Jim, this is my wife. She's put up with me for thirty years and she's a prince. And *this* is Mississippi, the sweetest and snappiest little home-girl in Oklahoma, if I do say it."

"I didn't catch the name," said Mississippi, politely.

"Jim Bush! Jim Bush!" roared her father.

"Isn't that funny! I know so many boys named Jim!"

"Well, this Jim is sitting at our table," continued the judge, with a wink, "and I don't want to see any monkey business going on, like there was last week."

"Why, Leonidas!" cried Mrs. Corey, fingering the gold chain. "I don't know what Mr. Bush'll think."

"Well, if he thinks what I think, he'll think plenty," cried the judge.

"Papa, listen!" exclaimed Mississippi, coquettishly, flinging her elbow against her ears and burying her hands in the small of her back. "Listen, I know what let's do. Let's not eat here. Let's row across the lake, papa, and eat at that place above the water with the lanterns. Papa, do that for 'Sippy."

"Girlie, I'd do it if I could. I'd do it in a minute, but I can't. Y'see, Jim, I'm stockholder in this camp, and I've got to make an important announcement at dinner tonight."

"Tell him, papa; it's your idea. Listen, Mr. Bush."

"Yes, sir, about how everybody who mentions the depression must pay a fine of fifteen cents. D'you like it?"

"Yes," said Brush.

"But you young people run across the lake and try it. You try it and tell me how it is."

"Now don't stay too late, Mississippi. You know how I worry," said her mother.

"I can't go tonight, Mrs. Corey," said Brush. "I've been asked to sing at the camp fire at eight o'clock." Back of his words lay his astonishment that anyone could propose paying for a meal in one place when the meal had already been paid for at another.

"Why, it's only six o'clock! Seems like you could be over and back in that time," said Mrs. Corey, and in a sudden burst of noise the Coreys settled the matter.

The judge then pretended to have misgivings. "I don't know if we can trust our girlie to a big six-footer like Jim here," he said, striking Brush sharply on the back.

Brush went down to the waterfront and prepared the canoe, and ten minutes later the couple were sitting down at the Venice Inn, prepared to consume the seventy-five cent chicken dinner. Mississippi talked without pause, and as she talked she continually fingered, for coquetry, the hair at the back of her head and the folds of her dress over her lean clavicles. She declared an increasing admiration for Brush. "Now when can you come to Okey City, 'cause I want to give a big, big party for you. My father loves for me to give parties and I know our crowd would be crazy about you. Really, our crowd has the *best* time. We're not foolish, you know what I mean; we're just friends together. When can you come, Mr. Bush?"

"I don't go to parties very much," said Brush, slowly, "but I'll call you up some day and I'd like to have a talk."

Mississippi swallowed and said, with affected casualness: "Of course, I don't know whether you're married or not, Mr. Bush, but I don't think it matters much when one's just friends. Do you?"

Brush kept his eyes on the plate. "I'm practically engaged," he said. "I'm about married."

This announcement led Mississippi to share with him her ideas on love and marriage. Brush became fascinated by the spectacle of so many disadvantages heaped upon one person. From sheer distress his mind began to wander and he only caught fragments of her remarks. "You know," she said, "I don't care how poor a man is, honest I don't, but he must have high ideals. My girl friends say I'm foolish; but I'm funny that way. I couldn't bring myself to marry a man that didn't have good ideals." When, however, Mississippi began boasting about her adventures with gin, and when she began smoking a cigarette, Brush could contain himself no longer. Suddenly his lips spoke without his knowing it.

"You shouldn't talk baby talk," he said.

Both were shocked. "Why, James Bush," said Mississippi, "I didn't think you were rude. I don't talk baby talk. A person can't help how she talks."

"I . . . I beg your pardon. I didn't know what I was saying," said Brush, rising and turning very red. "I never did a thing like that before, Miss Corey. I apologize."

"But I don't . . . do I? Do I talk baby talk? If there's anything about me you don't like, I want you to tell me so, honest. I'm not conceited. I like people to tell me my faults. Honest, Mr. Bush, I'm not sore."

"My name's Brush, George Brush. Your father got it all wrong. George Brush."

"Really, I want to be told my faults. I don't think I'm perfect; honest, I don't."

Brush sat down again. He leaned forward, his elbows on his knees, and stared into her distorting spectacles. "Miss Corey, I've made a great study of girls. Everywhere I go I study them and watch them. I think they're about the most wonderful thing in the world. And I've been studying you, too. May I ask you to take off your glasses a minute?"

Mississippi turned pale. With a trembling hand she removed her spectacles. A frightened, pinched face looked uncertainly into his.

"Thank you," he said, gravely. He rose and took a few steps about the table. "You can put them on again."

There was a silence. Then he returned to his former position before her, and lowering his head, began with great earnestness: "Now, out of all my study I've drawn up a few rules for girls. Can I tell them to you? You might get to be a really nice girl if you worked on these rules." Her hand fluttered to her mouth, a gesture which he took for consent. "In the first place, always be simple in everything you do. Never laugh loud, for instance, and never make unnecessary movements with your hands and eyes. A lot of girls never get married because they have no friend to tell them that. In the second place, of course, never drink liquor or smoke. When girls do that, it's hard to recognize them for girls. And third and most important . . ."

At this point Mississippi Corey had hysterics. Brush was never to forget those ten minutes. There was weeping and laughing and gasping for breath; there was choking over a glass of water; there was lying down on a hammock and falling off a hammock. When at last the girl's sobs were under control, she was leaning on the parapet above the water, clutching Brush's hand and exclaiming: "Aren't I *terrible* to act like that in public! I think I'm terrible! But, honest, I'm not mad. I like to be told my faults. Goodness! I don't know what you'll think of me!"

Brush carried her down the steps to the dock and placed her in the canoe. For a time they paddled about the middle of the lake in silence. Mississippi washed her face. She seemed to regard herself as permanently dependent upon Brush's guidance. When he finally deposited her upon the shore, the campers were already beginning to seat themselves under the trees about the fire, and were singing of their own accord. "Working on the Railroad" was trying to drown out an upstart "Indian Love Call." Some boys were trying to amuse the company by throwing lighted flashlights from hand to hand. Brush excused himself and withdrew to clear his throat and gargle. He had asked to be first on the program, because he liked leaving an audience in the midst of its applause, in order to take a walk and savor the strange excitement that never failed to invade him after he had sung in public. When the program began he announced his selection: " 'Oh, for the wings of a dove,' by Felix Mendelssohn-Bartholdy, 1809–1847."

This pedantry and the title of the song threatened to endanger its reception, but soon all was going well. Brush then sang " 'The Lost Chord,' by Sir Arthur Sullivan, 1842–1900." He then bowed twice and disappeared among the trees. The audience settled down to prolonged applause and, when their singer failed to reappear, began to clap rhythmically in triple beats crying "We—want—*more!* We—want—*more.'*" The entertainment director anxiously darted amont the tents and trees, hunting for his singer, but Brush hid himself behind the canoe-shed until he heard the announcement that the Reverend Mr. Kedworth would give a little philosophy talk on "Smiles," and then moved on. The squares and lanes of the camp were empty in the moonlight. He stopped before the shelf of books in the social-room, but there was no Encyclopædia Britannica, and he moved on. He looked in the window of the house marked "First Aid"; a doctor in a white coat was reading by a lamp. He was tempted to enter and engage him in a professional conversation, but, feeling an unaccustomed lassitude, he turned away and went on up the hill. There he came upon the brightly lighted windows of the kitchen. An army of young men and women were still washing the dishes of the week-end crowd. These were college students working their way through the summer. This was a thing he knew all about. Filled with happy excitement, he entered and offered his services. He was given a dishcloth and assigned to wiping glasses at the side of a gray-eyed girl, who immediately made a great impression on him.

4

Further good times at Camp Morgan. Important conversation with a girl named Jessie Mayhew. Dick Roberts' nightmares concluded. George Brush refuses some money.

A tournament was taking place in the kitchen. The students were being made to sing the songs of the various colleges from which they came. The girls at the silverware-sink sang the song of Texas Wesleyan. Then a man and a girl at the cups and saucers table sang "Wisconsin, thy halls are ever fair." Then the gray-eyed girl who was working beside Brush was called upon for the song of McKenna College in Ohio. She made a speech first, saying that she had no ear and no voice, but that she would do what she could so as not to be an exception. She turned out to be a monotone, but her manner and her sportsmanship were so pleasing that she received an ovation. Then came a man from Georgia Tech, and a girl from Missoula. Then a Swedish cook, who had never been to college, but who had cooked for the students at Upsala, sang one of their songs. Then a demand arose for a song from the superintendent. No one had liked her very much, but from this evening, when she had turned very red and did what she could with the Goucher College song, opinion turned in her favor. Then the newcomer, George Brush, was called upon. He sang his Alma Mater so beautifully that all the workers held their breaths; he, however, went on the while swiftly and silently polishing glasses. The workers crowded about him, dishcloths in hands, asking him how long he was staying in the camp. Presently the superintendent called for silence by beating on a dishpan. "It's nine o'clock," she said. "At this rate we'll never get done. Hurry, everybody; let's finish up as soon as possible." Whereupon there followed a last ten minutes of concentrated work.

Brush whispered to the gray-eyed girl, "Can I call on you now?"

"What did you say?"

"Can I pay a call on you as soon as we're through?"

"Why . . ." she began, hesitatingly, . . . "why, yes."

"I'd like very much to talk to you."

They worked on in silence. At the signal for release there was a wild rush for the door on the part of those who wished to claim the canoes reserved for the workers. The superintendent crossed the room and, holding herself very straight, said to Brush: "I have a place vacant, if you'd like to stay and work in the dining-room."

"Thank you. I must leave tomorrow noon," he said, his eyes anxiously fixed on the back of the gray-eyed girl, who was going out of the door.

When he caught up with the girl he said, "Would you like to sit on the bench at the end of the pier?"

She did not answer. He saw that she had changed her mind

and was hunting for the words with which to excuse herself. He said, abruptly and with unexpected intensity: "I know you must be pretty tired after all this extra work at the week-end, but I wish you'd make an exception for me. I'd rather call on you tomorrow, only I must leave before noon, and I guess we both have a good deal to do in the morning. So as a great favor would you let me call on you now?"

She looked at him. "We can sit in the clubroom," she said, briefly, and led the way to the farmhouse that had been set aside as a dormitory for the waitresses. The house, as they approached it, was in a state of bedlam. Girls' voices could be heard calling from room to room. "Louise, lend me your sandals." "You won't need a sweater; you'll die in it." Several young men were waiting at the steps. A girl appeared at a window on the second floor and called out, "Where's Jessie?"

"Here I am," said the gray-eyed girl, quietly.

"Jessie, honey, can I borrow your bandana?"

"Yes. Only, do be quiet when you come in, Hilda."

The parties went off in a shower of excited conversation, and the house promptly fell into a profound silence. Jessie led Brush into the clubroom on the first floor. It was fitted out with the castoff furniture of the social rooms farther down the slope: a card-table one of whose legs was mended with adhesive tape, a dilapidated leather center, some kitchen chairs. It was in great confusion. Jessie began mechanically putting it in order, gathering up the pillows, motion-pictures magazines, ukuleles and tennis rackets. She sat down on the couch and began untying the ribbon that bound her hair.

"What's your name?" she asked.

"George Marvin Brush. I was born in Michigan. I'm a traveling salesman in school books. I came to this camp to see a man on business. This evening I asked if I could help in the kitchen, because I like to be where students are and where people are working. I've had to do that kind of work almost all my life."

Jessie leaned far back on the couch, slipped the ribbon off her hair, and shook her head from side to side. She listened to Brush with abstracted self-possession. "You have a fine voice," she said. "Everybody hoped you were going to stay on and work here."

"I wish I could."

"Won't you sit down?"

"Thank you."

Jessie rested her head on her elbows and looked at the ceiling. The pause that fell was so alarming to Brush that he broke it by moving his chair forward a few inches and beginning with gravity: "I live traveling around on trains all the time and I meet a lot of people, but almost everybody I meet depresses me really terribly. Why, just this afternoon and evening in this camp I've met the most depressing people and it was beginning to have a bad effect on me. And then I saw you and I knew at once that you were a very fine person, and I can't tell you what a difference it made. So this talk we're having is very important to me; and as we haven't much time, you being so tired and everything, I want you to forgive me if I seem to be pretty personal on so short an acquaintance. I want you to know who I am and what I'm like so that I can write letters to you."

Slowly and a little guardedly Jessie began to sit up straight. She now fixed her eyes on his, full of surprise, but without fear or repugnance.

"There's no one in the whole world that I get any pleasure writing letters to," he continued. "So when I meet a person as fine as you, I don't want to lose the chance to know you better. And so that we can get to be . . . almost friends, I want to tell you who I am and what I'm interested in. Is that all right?"

Jessie blushed slightly. "Yes," she said.

"Well, as I said, my name is George Marvin Brush. I'm twenty-three years old. I graduated two years ago from the Shiloh Baptist College in Walling, South Dakota. I'm a Baptist and I'm pretty religious. I grew up on a farm in Michigan . . . Can I ask you to tell me a few things like that about yourself?"

The girl drew in her chin abruptly, as though she were about to make a rude answer. She thought better of it, however, and said, with only a touch of curtness: "My name is Jessie Mayhew. I'm twenty-two years old. I'm a senior at McKenna College in Ohio. When I graduate I'm going to be a teacher. I'm Methodist."

The gray eyes looked coolly into the blue.

"Can I ask you . . . have you a father and mother?"

"No," said Jessie. After a pause she added, with assumed casualness: "I was brought up in an orphanage and then I was adopted by some people who died. I've supported myself since second year high school."

"I guess we're pretty much alike in some ways," said Brush. The ticking of the alarm clock on the mantel filled the room. "There isn't much more to tell about me. I grew up on the farm. I've got a father and mother and two brothers, both older. One of my brothers went away to be a sailor; the other's still on the farm. I go back to see them Christmas, but . . . you know, I feel like an orphan, too, almost. I love'm, of course, but always there is a kind of wall between them and me. You see, they didn't want me to go to college." He scanned her face to see the effect of this severe indictment. "So I worked my way through, just as you've been doing. You'd know that I'm not bragging when I tell you that I got the highest grades of anybody, and I was captain of track. I'd have been captain of football and baseball, too, only, working all the time, I didn't have time for practice and I had to drop them. I know without your telling me that you get high grades."

"Yes," said Jessie, reddening again, "I got all A's."

Brush smiled. He smiled very seldom. "Before I ask you to let me write you letters," he continued, "it's only fair I tell you my faults. I think you ought to know that there are some things about me that are hard to like. What I mean is that people are always getting mad at me and . . . even disgusted. But before I tell you my faults, I want you to know that since my conversion I haven't done anything bad *intentionally.* Naturally I haven't told a lie, except one, when I told a man that I'd once been to New York City. The next day I went back to the town where he was and told him I hadn't. And my other faults, like saying things in a temper and being tight with money, I've always apologized for those pretty soon after."

"Why do people get disgusted with you?" asked Jessie.

"Because my ideas aren't the same as other people's. For instance, I was put in jail the other day because they didn't like my ideas about money." Whereupon he told the whole story of his arrest in Armina, adding to it accounts of his theories of voluntary poverty, pacifism, the punishment of criminals, and the story of his previous incarceration. "But even when I don't get taken to jail," he concluded, "I've always been called crazy. Do you see what I mean."

"Yes."

"Does that make you think I'm an . . . an inconvenient sort of person to know?"

"No."

"I don't mind my friends telling me once in a while that I'm crazy—as a joke, you know—but do you think . . . have you begun to feel like calling me crazy in earnest?"

"No," said Jessie. "I don't care anything what other people think. I like people to be different."

"Then I want to tell you about the three big secret disappointments in my life. They're getting to be less and less all the time, and when I can tell them to a person like you I see that they have no reason to be important at all. The first one is . . . is that at college the fellows never elected me to one of the three literary societies. I was the top student in the whole college and I was the captain of my teams, but they never elected me to Philomathian or Eunostia or to the Colville Society. I used to feel pretty badly about that; I used to wonder why they couldn't stand me. And the second disappointment, Jessie, was something that one of my teachers said to me. He was my prof. in Religion A 6, and I admired him more than any other that was there. I used to take questions to him at his house and I thought he liked it. He used to get mad at me often, but just joking mad. You know how it'd be. But one time he got really mad. He said: 'You've got a closed mind, Brush, an obstinate, closed mind. It's not worth wasting time on you,' he said. 'I wash my hands of you,' he said; *'you'll never get anywhere!'* Imagine someone saying that! 'Now go away,' he said. 'Get away from me. Don't trouble me any more.' You know that was awful to me. Sometimes it comes back to me still, like it was the moment he said it, and the sweat—I mean the perspiration—comes out on my forehead. I don't want to live if I've got a closed mind and can't get anywhere—anywhere in *thinking,* I mean. But I don't believe what he said any more. I keep getting new good ideas all the time. I learn things as I go, at least that's the way it seems to me. As to the third disappointment, I don't want to tell you that just yet, but I'll tell you some day. But, Jessie, I don't want to give you the impression that I'm miserable or anything; because, really, at bottom, I'm the happiest man I've ever met. Sometimes it looks like everyone's unhappy except me. Just today in this camp I met such a mess of unhappy people that it began to get me; and then I saw you and I felt better right away." There was a pause, at the end of which he added, lamely; "So . . . I guess . . . that's how it stands."

Jessie said, without sharpness and with the beginning of a smile, "You do talk a lot."

"I know," he agreed, eagerly, "but I had to talk fast for lots of reasons." He gazed enthusiastically at her face a moment, then rose and said: "Will you let me give you a present to remember me by? This wrist watch is brand new and it's the best one I've ever had."

Jessie moved off the couch quickly. "No, no," she said, "I never like to have presents from people. I never like to. It doesn't mean I don't like people . . . but I don't like to take presents from them. Thank you just the same, though. Now, Mr. Brush, we're not old friends, and I don't like you to pretend we are. I'm interested in what you're saying about yourself," she added, seeing how crestfallen Brush had become. "I didn't say what I said in order to send you away, because I like what you've been saying."

"Will you tell me a few things about how you grew up?" asked Brush, sadly returning the watch to his own wrist.

Jessie remained standing. She began to walk back and forth, as though to mark the casualness of what she chose to say. "Well, as I told you, I'm an orphan. I was found in a field. First I lived in an orphanage. That was near Cleveland, Ohio. Some people think I look Slovak. I don't know and I don't think it matters. When I was ten I was adopted by an old German shoemaker and his wife. They both died and ever since second year at high school I've supported myself by working in a hotel. I'm majoring in Biology and some day I'll either teach Biology or maybe I'll try to be a doctor."

"You don't believe," began Brush, fearfully—"you don't believe in all that about evolution, do you?"

"Why, yes, of course I do."

Brush almost whispered: "You don't think the Bible'd tell a lie, do you? Do you mean you can't see there's a difference as big as the whole world between a human being with a soul and a monkey jumping around in a tree?"

There was an awful silence. Then Brush put another fateful question: "You don't believe in women smoking cigarettes, do you?"

Jessie stopped and looked at him. "Do you think such things are important?"

"Yes, I do—terribly important."

"Well, I don't. I hardly smoke any, myself, but I like to see women doing things that show they can be taken just as seriously as men are." Her eyes remained on him. She saw how crushed he was. "I'm surprised that you're the kind of person that still thinks such things are important. I was just beginning to think you were the only young man I ever met who wasn't silly."

Brush continued to look at the floor. He said: "My vacation comes in November. Can I come to McKenna College and see you then?"

Jessie began walking up and down again. "You can do what you like, I guess," she said. "It wouldn't do any good, though. There wouldn't be anything to talk about, if you have ideas like that. Besides . . . I live by myself. For these years, anyway, I'm *enough,* just myself. Besides, I haven't really got time for any new friends. Ever since sophomore year I've been head waiter in the dining-hall, and the rest of the time I study."

"But can I come?"

"Yes, you can come, like anybody else."

"I mean . . . would you go for a walk with me? Or have dinner or something?"

"Yes."

"Well, good-by," said Brush, putting out his hand.

"Good-by. I don't know why you're acting so serious. I've only known you an hour and a half. You look as though you'd lost your last friend."

"All I want to do now is think, so I'll say good-by."

"Good-by."

He went out into the hall, full of thought. Then he turned with sudden energy and said through the door: "Will you promise to think about it, at least? I don't see how a fine girl like you can believe that the Bible tells lies and that we come from monkeys, and that it's all right for girls to smoke cigarettes. What becomes of the world if we let all those ideas into it? What good is living in the world if we become like the foolish city people that believe things like that? Why . . . why you'd just be an ordinary person if you had ideas like that!"

"I'll think about it," said Jessie, wearily and a little bitterly, as she went back to the task of straightening the room. When that was done she went up to her room and sat down. She laid her arms firmly along the arms of the chair and stared at the wall in front of her. From time to time she muttered, "He's crazy." Then realizing that there was no sleep for her, she changed her shoes and walked around the lake.

Brush returned to the tent "Felix" and went to bed. He had hardly fallen asleep, however, when he became aware of a great tumult. He awoke with a start. Dick Roberts was thrashing about on his cot. In a choked voice that increased every moment in volume he was crying out: "I can't . . . I can't . . ." In the vague light that entered the tent from the moonlight outside, Brush could see the other occupants who had raised themselves on their elbows and were angrily turned towards Roberts' cot. "What the hell's going on here?" they were saying. "Who's throwing a fit, for God's sake?" Dick Roberts' son was wailing, "Papa, papa . . ."

Brush jumped out of bed and, seizing Roberts' hand, began to pump it up and down. "Hey, Roberts! Hey, Dick Roberts!" he called, adding to the others: "It's nothing, fellas. Just a nightmare. It's all right. . . . Hey, Roberts, y'all right?"

Roberts sat up and wiped his forehead. Then somberly and in silence he leaned over and began putting on his shoes. Brush hastily put on his shoes and trousers.

"Golly! what a row!" grumbled one of their tentmates.

"Sorry," said Roberts, and picking up his bathrobe started to leave the tent.

"Papa, where y' goin'?" asked his son, in terror.

"'Sh! Go to sleep, George."

"Papa! I wanta come."

"No, no. You go back to sleep."

Brush picked up a blanket and followed Roberts out of the tent. He caught up with him in the dusty road that led through the camp. Roberts was standing with lowered eyes in the moonlight; he was perfectly still and seemed to be thinking of something remote and profound. Brush stood and waited.

"You go on back," said Roberts, in a whisper, still without raising his eyes. "I'll find somewhere to sleep down by the shore here."

"Don't you think you'd better get your pants on? We'll go for a walk."

"I wouldn't go back to that tent for a million dollars."

"It doesn't hurt what those fellas say. What does it matter what people say?"

"I want to be alone," said Roberts, turning abruptly. He continued down the hill. Arriving at the water's edge, he took a paddle off the rack and pushed a canoe into the water. Brush did the same. Roberts whispered, savagely: "Beat it! Get out of here! I want to be alone, I said!"

"I must go wherever you go," said Brush.

Roberts started to direct his canoe toward the center of the lake. He beat the water first on one side, then on the other. The canoe wheeled in circles. Roberts became distraught with rage and began shoveling the lake furiously. Brush's canoe glided out like a seal. He pointed it in another direction, tactfully as though he had come out for a meditative hour in the moonlight. Roberts lost his paddle. Brush drew near. "I'll get it for you," he said.

"No! No! Get out!" cried Roberts in hoarse whispers. "What the hell is this, anyway? I'm not crazy yet. I don't need a guard to follow me around. I'm not crazy."

"Mr. Roberts, I'll be quiet. I won't trouble you. I just want to make sure you're all right."

Roberts stared at him a moment, then began plowing the lake again. His canoe turned over and in a moment he was noisily swimming towards shore.

"This is getting complicated," muttered Brush, shepherding canoe, paddle and swimmer. When he reached land, Roberts was trying to dry his pajamas by shaking himself and by wringing out the folds. Brush replaced the canoes and the paddles. "Wait a minute," he said. "I'll get you a towel." The bathhouse was locked, but Brush vaulted the board fence. He found some sour and blackened towels on the floor and threw them over the partition. When he vaulted back he found an old and nervous night watchman waiting for him with a flashlight.

"That's all right, boys," mumbled the watchman. "Have your fun, only don't make any noise."

"Borrow his flashlight," said Brush, "and go back to the tent and get your clothes on."

Roberts seized the flashlight, but before he started off he breathed, hoarsely, at Brush: "Go away! Get out! I want to be alone, I tell you!"

"I can't. I promised I'd follow you everywhere."

The night watchman shuffled along behind them: "Have all the good times you want, boys, only quiet," he said.

When Roberts emerged from the tent he was dressed. He held his automobile key in one hand and, running and stumbling, he started for the large field where scores of automobiles were drawn up in ranks. Brush ran along beside him. "If you don't take me along," he said, breathlessly, "I'll have to get some other people to help me."

Roberts was trembling so he could scarcely fit the key into the lock. Brush jumped upon the running-board, pleading with him.

The motor started and Roberts savagely turned the handle that closed the window where Brush's hand was resting. Brush ran to the First Aid house and burst in upon the doctor. "Doc," he cried, "lend me your car, quick! There's a man here who I think may be trying to commit suicide."

"What? Wait a minute. I must get someone to take my place."

"I can't wait. I may lose him. Give me your car key."

They hurried out together. "What's the matter with him?" asked the doctor.

"He's . . . well, he's just not happy," explained Brush.

Roberts had taken some time in extricating his car from the ranks, and Brush started out eagerly after the dim red tail-light speeding through the lanes of the forest. Morgan's Wood was a vast checkerboard of roads. Rustic benches and tables had been set at intervals among the scrawny trees, and occasionally cement fireplaces had been built. Towers of scaffolding, roughened with carved initials of thousands of visitors, rose above the tree-tops, furnishing lookouts for sight-seers and fire wardens. Occasionally a boarded-up refreshment stand stood beside the road, like a vast piano-box in the moonlight. As Brush overtook Roberts, the latter gave him a glance and stepped on the accelerator. They drove abreast for a time, shouting at one another, their cars lurching from side to side. They suddenly emerged into the main street of Morganville. Roberts was in need of gas and drove up to the still-lighted garage. Brush, avoiding Roberts' sudden turn, swerved to one side and struck a hitching-post in front of the Depot Hotel. There was a terrific din of shaken metal and shattered glass, and in the silence that followed it one wheel slowly and drunkenly crossed the street, looked about for a bed, and lay down.

Some white-clad figures appeared on the second-story porch of the hotel. Judge Corey's voice called out, "Who's dying down there, folks?"

"Judge, this is George Brush. Can I see you a minute?"

"Are you all right, boy?"

"Yes."

"Side door's open, Jim. Come up and have a drink."

"I don't drink."

"Come up, anyway, Jim. It's a great big free country."

Brush dashed up the stairs and burst into the room. "Judge," he said, breathlessly. "I want you to lend me your car . . ."

"Jim boy, you just had one."

"I know, but we gotta save a man from killing himself."

"Where is he?" asked the Judge, looking alertly into the hall. "Say, buddy, we can't have any of that around Camp Morgan. What's the matter with him, anyway?"

"I don't know, Judge. He's just not . . . happy."

"*Not happy?* Is he nuts?"

"No . . . it's . . . it's business, partly. It's the depression."

"Jim," said the Judge, angrily, "now don't you go mentioning the depression. That's what causes all this. Don't you say that word again. Where is the fella?"

"He's getting gas at the station next door."

"All right." The Judge turned and clapped his hands. "Folks, we're going for a ride in the woods. Say, Bush, Bough, Beach—By the way, what's your name, Jim?"

"Brush, George Brush."

"Brush, I want you meet these princes. This is Helma Solario, the best little trouper you could hope to know. Jeannie Socket, Bill Watkins, Mike Kusack. Girls, fellas, shake hands with Bush, friend of my daughter. By the way, Jim, you made a big impression.

"We must hurry, Judge. Really."

"My husband runs that garage," said Helma Solario, a plump black-eyed little woman, in an advanced stage of negligé and intoxication. "Mike, run down and tell him not to give the guy any gas." She went out on the porch and gave further instructions from there. "Bring the dope in here. We'll give him something to live for. Does he play poker? Ask him?"

"Come on, girls, we'd better go after him ourselves," cried the judge.

Brush descended the stairs, four at a time, and caught sight of Roberts driving off. The poker party followed in high spirits. They all climbed into the judge's car. Helma Solario sat on Brush's lap.

"This baby's alive, anyway," said Helma, tickling his ear. "Where do you come from, sweetness?"

"Michigan," replied Brush, peering anxiously into the forest at the right and the left of the road.

"All right, Michigan, when you find this guy tell him life's a big thrill. See? Tell him to stick around; we're going to have some more world wars. He'll love it. Tell him from me the depression's only begun. Next year's going to make this year look sky-high."

"You pay a fine for that," said the judge.

"Has he a family and kids?"

"Yes," said Brush.

"Sure he oughta wait around awhile until his kids grow up and call him an old boob. Why, he doesn't know the half of it yet. Old age is great, too, tell him."

"Now that's enough, Helma," said the judge.

"All right, tell him about the family life and old age of Judge Leonidas Corey. No one can ever say you aren't happy, can they, Leon? Just one damned million after another."

Brush saw Roberts' car drawn up in the undergrowth. "Stop the car, Judge. I've found him. Listen. I can do this alone from now on. Thanks a lot for bringing me here. I won't need you now."

"I want to talk to the fellow," said the judge.

"That'd be the last straw," said Helma. "God! Leave it to Michigan here. Good-by, baby. Tell him life's a big thrill."

The party drove off, leaving Brush still carrying his blanket, to peer about the woods for his friend. The car was empty. The surroundings lay in deep shadow. Brush listened carefully and heard nothing. Finally raising his eyes, he saw Roberts standing on the highest platform of one of the watchtowers. He went over to the foot of the tower and stood looking up.

"Damn it," said Roberts, "there you are again! Go away! Go on home!"

Brush did not answer. He waited for half an hour. Finally Roberts laboriously and awkwardly climbed down the ladder.

"It's getting chilly," muttered Brush. "You might want this blanket."

Roberts stared at him a moment, then started towards his car.

"I'm not going to let you get in the car," said Brush. "I'm stronger than you are."

Roberts began walking through the bushes, with Brush six feet behind him. This journey went on for over an hour. At times they found themselves at the lake's edge. Once they suddenly entered Morganville, where Roberts sat down for ten minutes on someone's front steps while Brush stood out in the middle of the street, tactfully gazing into the distance. Then plunging back into the forest again, they roamed through the clearings. Coming upon one of the picnic havens, Brush cleared his throat and said:

"Why don't you lie down here and get some sleep?"

"I tell you I never do sleep. How do I know I'll ever be able to sleep again?"

"It's two o'clock. I think you'll be able to sleep. I'll build a fire."

Roberts turned and again began stumbling through the trees. Brush caught up with him and seized his arm firmly. "You're not going any farther," he said, in a loud voice. "And you're not going to think any more about these things. I know what you're thinking all the time, and you've got to stop it. The world isn't as bad as you think it is . . . even if it looks bad. Now you lie down on that bench or table, wherever you like. I'm going to make a fire and sit here till morning. If you can't sleep, never mind; just look up through the trees. I shouldn't have let you tramp around with your head full of thoughts like that."

He laid the blanket on one of the benches. Roberts stretched himself on it and turned his contorted face away. After collecting several piles of dry sticks, Brush laid a fire according to the rules that had once gained him a badge in Ludington, Michigan. He sat down and looked into it. He asked, in a low voice: "Can I sing? Do you mind if I sing?" There was no answer. He began to sing softly. He tried "Far above Cayuga's Waters" and "The wings of a dove." He sang "Lie down, little croppies, lie down," and "Cowboy, go back to the hills." From there he went on to almost everything he knew. Finally he must have nodded, for he awoke with a start to find that day was breaking. The birds were beginning to make interrogative noises in the trees. He saw with surprise that an apparently cloudless sky could suddenly reveal itself as covered with soft pink clouds. As Roberts was snoring, Brush nodded off again. When he awoke, Roberts was looking at him. Without saying a word, Roberts picked up the blanket and started off. He was pale and embarrassed. They returned to the camp in silence and went to bed in the tent "Felix."

Brush was a little late for breakfast at table M. He found Judge Corey alone.

"Jim, how did it go?" asked the judge.

"He'll be all right today, Judge."

"You're a prince, Jim. We couldn't have a thing like that happen at Camp Morgan. The doctor came and told me about it. Don't you worry about the car."

Jessie Mayhew stood by Brush. "How do you like your eggs?" she asked.

"Jessie," said the judge, "you give the fella the best of everything the camp's got. Nothing's too good for Jim. . . . My wife and daughter tell me you have a fine voice, too. Jim, young fella, lean your ear over here. I want to ask you something: When are you leaving camp?"

"Sometime this morning."

The judge paused, then began in a cordial and confidential tone: "Jim, young fella, you made a big hit with my daughter, a big hit. I know that little girl and it's not every man that interests her, no, sir. Now listen. I want to give you a little tip. Just between you and I, see? . . . just man to man. That girl ought to have a nice home of her own. See what I mean? You might say she ain't really happy up at our house. Jim, thirty-five thousand dollars goes with that girl. Yes, sir, if she can find a good home, thirty-five thousand dollars goes with her. Depression year, too. Think it over. Yes, and what's more, I'm in a position to settle a young man in some good job around the Capitol, too. Well, that's just between you and I . . . How does it appeal to you, eh?"

Brush turned scarlet. Jessie Mayhew had been placing his cereal and coffee before him. He glanced at her face. "I . . . I hope she finds a good home, Judge," he said.

"Yeah, yeah. Well, think it over, boy, and in the meantime I'll see your school books get a high place. Yes, sir."

5

Kansas City. Queenie's boarding-house. First word of Father Pasziewski. George Brush drunk and disorderly.

Brush no longer regarded the farmhouse in Michigan as his home; he had no home, and for that reason when his itinerary brought him to a town or city where he had already made friends, he looked forward to the visit with a more than usual expectancy. Kansas City contained one of these substitute homes. Queenie's—Miss Craven's—boarding-house was a high, narrow, blackened edifice, standing amid the similarly blackened hulks of former mansions near where Eighth Street crosses Pennsylvania and Jefferson Avenues. Here a colony of rooming-houses barely maintains its existence, though near the center of the city, holding out, its broken windows patched with newspaper, its yards full of weeds and overturned bath-tubs, against the last invasion of negro gamblers, cats, and the night quartering of tramps. Queenie's back windows overlooked a cliff strewn with bottles and automobile tires descending to a waste of railroad tracks and the sluggish soot-covered river.

Brush ran up the steps and rang the bell. Queenie came to the door with a mop in her hand.

"Hello, Queenie!"

"Why, Mr. Brush! I'm glad to see you."

"Are any of the fellows home, Queenie?"

"Seems like I heard'm all go out. You can go up and see. Will you be staying here tonight?"

"Yes, Queenie, I'll be here three nights."

"Well, I'll come right up and make your bed. Looks even worse'n usual up there, Mr. Brush, but you know how it is. They say they'll kill me if I clean up any, beyond just making the beds. I wish you'd persuade'm to let me come up and clean around."

"I'll try. Is there any news?"

"Let me think. Mr. Morris got his pay cut over to the hospital; yes, and Mr. Callahan got reduced, too."

Brush descended a few steps: "Has Herb been drinking bad, Queenie?"

"Well, you know I never know what goes on, but I think he's been drinking some. I don't know how it happened, Mr. Brush, but the whole banister come off the staircase the other day. And Mrs. Kubinsky—lives next door—said she saw somebody hanging by their finger nails to the gutter on the roof one night, only he was pulled back at the last minute. 'T's a wonder they're still alive after five years, Mr. Brush, if you ask me, because they're at death's door once a week; that's no zaggeration."

"I know," said Brush, with concern. They looked at one another. Brush added: "We've just got to work on them slowly, Queenie. Never say die. How's Father Pasziewski, Queenie?"

"He's pretty good. He's back on the job again. He takes the seven and nine."

"The kidney trouble just blew over?"

"They think now it was gall stones. Mrs. Kramer gave him some water from the River Jordan and he put it in his tea every day and it melted'm down. I was over to the St. Veronica Guild, serving, and Mrs. Delehanty said that with him, if it wasn't one thing it'd be another, she said. He's not long for this world, she says."

Brush climbed the stairs to the top floor, which his four friends had rented from Queenie in perpetuity. Most of the doors had long been smashed, and after lying about as boards had finally disappeared in smaller and smaller fragments. Several partitions between the rooms contained holes, opened up in some historic rough-house, and now offering the testimony of their splintering edges and crumbling plaster. A smell floated about, made up of foul clothes, antiseptic soap, gin, and lemon-peel. Brush sat down on one of the beds and looked sadly about him. Here lived Herb and Morrie, two newspaper men; Bat, a mechanic in sound pictures; and Louie, a hospital chemist who in hard times had been obliged to descend to the duties of an orderly.

Brush's friendship with these tenants reposed upon a complicated treaty. On his part, Brush promised not to harangue them, unless invited, on religion, temperance, chastity, and tobacco; and they in turn promised to remain within reasonable limits of decency in conversation and in the invention of practical jokes. The cement of this precarious friendship lay in the fact that Brush carried a wonderful second tenor and that the practice of singing in parts constituted their chief pleasure. Brush could do things in the refrain of "Wasting in despair" that threw his companions into an ecstasy that was almost anguish. On the first note at the close of the refrain "If she be not fair to me-ee," he would rise an octave in soft portamento and, holding the note, pass from a whispered falsetto to a golden fortissimo, then, as the three other singers, pale and shaken, moved on to the second note, he would stride majestically down the chord into the bass register. He could phrase "Far above Cayuga's Waters" so that it seemed to allude to some infinitely sad leave-taking, years ago, probably in the depths of a forest, with discouraged horns blowing in the distance. It required all this proficiency, however, to hold the group together. The treaty was drawn up abruptly on the night of Brush's first visit to the boarding-house. He had knelt down beside his bed to say his prayers.

"Either you drop that or you keep out of here forever," they said.

"Well, if I don't do it," he replied, darkly, "remember it's not because I'm a moral coward."

"Oh, get out of here!" cried Louie. "Get out and stay out! Go to hell!"

But the thought of "All through the night" intoned *mezzo-voce* returned to them; they swallowed their anger and the treaty was drawn up.

Brush now sat on the bed and sadly reviewed the problem presented by the room before him. Queenie entered with the linen.

"If I clean up now, will you protect me against them, Mr. Brush?" she asked, doubtfully.

"Can you do it tomorrow, Queenie? I don't feel awfully well. I'm going to take a nap."

"You don't *feel* well? Where do you feel bad?"

"It's not anything special. I'm just sick of hotels and trains. I'm sick of lots of things."

Queenie respected dejection. She moved quickly about the bed-making. At last she said: "I've got a coffee-pot on the stove, Mr. Brush. It might peck you up a bit."

"No, thanks," he answered, gazing at the ceiling. He was suddenly surprised to hear himself saying, "Did you ever wish you were dead, Queenie?"

Queenie was immediately aroused. "Now don't you say that!

Why, I'm ashamed to hear you say things like that, Mr. Brush. I once said something like that in confession in Spokane, Washington, and Father Lyons almost bit my head off. It's not like you, either."

Brush smiled, abashed. "I was only joking, Queenie. It just jumped out."

"A healthy young man like you, with a fine tenor voice."

Queenie stood by with further reassurances until she noticed that Brush had fallen asleep. She took a step forward, looked at him narrowly a moment, and tiptoed downstairs. As she entered the front hall the door was noisily flung open and Louie rushed in.

"Hello, Queenie!" he cried. "Hitch up your pants, Queenie; the depression's over. They've found a plan to make the ocean fresh water. You'll love it."

"Now don't you go making any noise. Mr. Brush is up in your room, asleep. He's kinda sick, he says."

"What? Jesus sick? Well, well! Say no more. I know how to cure him."

Louie dashed upstairs and had a look at the patient. Brush woke up.

"How the hell did you catch it?" asked Louie, drawing up a chair before him.

"Catch what?"

"You've got it. Fever B-17. Let me feel your pulse."

"I'm all right."

"There's no doubt about it. B-17. Percipient influenza. Where could you have picked it up?"

"Oh, let me alone!"

"Take your choice, immediate recovery or two weeks in bed— and not in this house, either, by God!"

"Aw, just leave me alone, Louie! What's the remedy like?"

"Get over on your own bed—polluting my pillow! You're a stink-hole of germs. I ought to report you."

"What's the remedy like?"

"When did you begin to feel funny?"

"I don't know. Today, yesterday."

"Had any lunch?"

"No."

"Lie down; lie down. I'm going back to the hospital to get the medicine. Queenie'll bring you up a big lunch. Eat as much as possible. You're not supposed to take this medicine on an empty stomach."

"I don't think I've got anything the matter with me."

"What do you know about it? I don't spend my life in hospitals for nothing. Here I am trying to do you a favor, and you go yipping around that you're all right. You're a sick man."

Louis fell down the stairs to the telephone. He was very excited and began calling joyously in all directions. He shared his plans with Herb and Morrie and Bat, and then tore over to the hospital. The idea grew and flowered. By three o'clock several doctors in white coats had climbed Queenie's stairs and held long conversations in German and Latin. A temperature chart had been hung on the wall. Sputum and urine had been put through precipitates. At half-past three the patient, awed and flushed, was sitting up in bed, eating T-bone steaks and creamed potatoes. From time to time he was told to hold his nose and take a swallow of the medicine which stood beside him in a large jar.

"You fellows are princes to go to all this trouble," he said, grinning shyly; then catching sight of Queenie, who was peering anxiously into the room from the landing, he called out: "That's all right, Queenie. I'm better already."

"Now hold your nose again, and drink a lot," commanded Louie. "Dr. Schnickenschnauzer, of Berlin, says you should drink it slow, but the Vienna fellas say you should drink it fast. How do you like it?"

"I guess it's all right."

"Now lie down a minute before you finish it."

"Will I sweat much?"

"Sweat? Baby, your very toe nails'll sweat. You'll steam like a lake in the morning."

"That's good, because I think I'm full of poisons. Up to a month ago I never had a sick day in my life, but lately I haven't been right. It's doing me good already, Queenie."

"I hope so, I'm sure, Mr. Brush."

Queenie had been forbidden to enter the room, but she now managed to sidle in. She went to the medicine-jar and sniffed at it. She turned abruptly and cried out with indignation: "You boys ought to be ashamed of yourselves. I'm ashamed of you doing a thing like that. I suspected you was doing something all along."

"Queenie," said Herb, "you get outa here or we'll break every bone in your body."

"Don't you touch me! I'm ashamed of you all. I've a good mind to put you out of my house."

Herb and Louie picked her up in a sitting position and began to carry her to the stairs. Brush gave a roar and jumped out of bed. He seized hold of her and began to pull her back. For a moment Queenie was being bandied about like the star of an acrobatic troupe. Brush was blazing with energy and vigor. He hurled Louie into a corner and restored Queenie to her feet.

"I'll kill the first person that touches Queenie!" he cried. "Speak up, Queenie. What is it you want to say?"

"You don't know it, Mr. Brush, but just for a joke those boys . . . those boys have gone and made you drunk."

"What!"

"That's not medicine; that's just liquor. That's rum."

Brush let his breath out slowly in astonishment. He lowered his voice: "Am I drunk, Queenie?"

"You go put your head under the tap and it'll pass, most likely."

He sat down on the bed and tried to think. He glanced up somberly at his tormentors; "It's lucky for you I'm a pacifist. If I were a different kind of person I'd break every bone in your body. So this is being drunk. . . . When am I going to begin to do queer things? . . . Herb, you stand out here and tell me about it."

"Aw, George, it's nothing. You'll like it."

"When am I going to see things double? When am I going to start breaking things—banisters and things?"

"You're not going to break things, you poor fool! What d'ya mean? You're not drunk."

"Well, I'm something."

He rose and began striding about the room, shaking his head sharply. He stopped and stood looking at himself in the mirror, frowning. Then turning, he declared, in a loud voice: "Anyway, I can't just stand here and be drunk. Now it's done it can't be helped. I'm even glad it happened, so long as it was accidental like this, because now I'll know what they're talking about all the time. So now let's go somewhere and do something." Here for the fun of it he began lifting tables and chairs with one hand, exclaiming: "Look't this. Look—Herb, come on and try and throw me. I feel like a rough-house. I won't hurt you, any of you. I'm a pacifist, but I feel like a rough-house. I'm the strongest man ever tested in our gym back at college, and I can polish off any cigarette-smoker in ten minutes. Come on! Why don't one of you call me cuckoo? Tell me I'm crazy."

"Aw, dry up, dry up! Let's get the hell out of here. This guy makes me sick," said Bat.

"Let's go out and go places," said Brush. "Let's do something." Suddenly an idea struck him; he turned majestically to Queenie. "Queenie—Queenie Craven—here's five dollars. We are going out. While we are out you get Mrs. Kubinsky who resides next door, and you two clean these rooms like they were—was—offices in a bank. This place is going to be clean for once. You fellows live like hogs and it's gotta stop. You hear me? It's gotta stop! You're the most aimless, shiftless sons-a-bitches in the world. Drink, drink, drink, that's all you do. No wonder you get your salaries cut. Now get out and leave these rooms for a cleaning, because tomorrow you bastards are going to begin your lives all over again."

"Poops to you!" muttered Louie. "Herb, I'm clearing out."

"Stick around. He's only begun. . . . Queenie, if you do, I'll kill you."

Brush leaned forward and lifted Herb by the seat of his trousers. Herb fell on his face. Brush placed his heel on his shoulder blade and began turning it. "Take that back," he ordered. "Go on! Go on! You give the order to Queenie yourself."

Herb caught him by the ankle and threw him. The building shook. All five were in the whirlpool now, but Brush only blazed the more with strength and confidence. He worked his way to his feet and began tossing the tenants against one another, kneading the pile playfully.

Bat struck his funny bone against the floor and fainted. He was resuscitated in great pain. "Gee! I'm sorry," said Brush. "Honest, I apologize. I apologize for all those things I said, too. I didn't mean to hurt your feelings. I guess I'm . . . drunk, you know, or I wouldn't have. . . . Is it getting better?"

Bat lay down on the bed, holding his elbow.

"Let's sing to him," said Brush, and soon the quartet was leaning over the bed, their arms about one another's shoulders, closing in on some diminished sevenths.

"No more harmony for me," said Herb, "until I get some more of Dr. Schnickenschnauser's in me."

"Then hurry," said Brush. "And I guess I'll have a little more, too. This is the only time in my life that I'll ever touch alcohol, so I'd better be sure I really touched it. I'm going to get it over with, once for all."

They had already had a good deal, but now they fell to for good measure.

"We'd better go down to Queenie's sitting-room, so as not to be in the way of the cleaning." For Queenie and Mrs. Kubinsky had entered with a battery of mops and pails and had begun stacking the furniture. The men gave three cheers each to Queenie and Anna Kubinsky, "the belles of Eighth Street," and went out.

Some sort of great journey took place that night. Rain came on and then the evening, but the party tramped up and down the hills of Kansas City, ran through the parks, and fell rattling over the cliffs. They climbed monuments. They entered newspaper offices and rebuked the press. They swept like crusaders through the lobbies of motion-picture houses. They defiled the City Hall.

The next morning Brush woke up and lay for a long time staring at the ceiling. He felt wonderfully well.

"Louis," he said to his roommate, "did I break anything yesterday?"

"No. Why?"

"Did I insult any passers-by—any women?"

"Not that I know of. Why?"

"I just wanted to know."

He got up and began to shave. It was his custom while shaving to prop up before him a ten-cent copy of *King Lear* for memorization. His teacher at college had once remarked that *King Lear* was the greatest work in English literature, and the Encyclopædia Britannica seemed to be of the same opinion. Brush had read the play ten times without discovering a trace of talent in it, and was greatly worried about the matter. He persevered, however, and was engaged in committing the whole work to memory. Now while shaving he boomed away at it.

Herb came in.

"What's the matter, big boy?"

"Herb, was I really tight last night?"

"You certainly were."

"Was I all those things? Was I stewed and boiled and pie-eyed?"

"Yeah. Why?"

Brush examined himself in the mirror, rubbing in the lather. "I've heard about them so much. I just wanted to know."

"Well, what did you think of it?"

Brush leaned against the wash basin and examined the floor. "I don't quite know yet," he said. "All I can say is, no wonder they made prohibition. I didn't know liquor was like that. You know, I felt I was the greatest preacher in the world and the greatest thinker in the world. It made me feel as though I was ready to be the greatest President of the United States. I forgot I had any faults in my character."

"Sure, that's the idea. Baby, you've only just begun. You'll have lots more yet."

"Mmm!"

"Well, listen, big boy. I've got a date for you. Yeah, just the kind of date you like."

"What do you mean?"

"You're always looking for a fine girl, aren't you? You know, to be the mother of your children?"

"You're just wasting your time, Herb. It doesn't get you anywhere to make fun of such things with me. Save your breath, Herb."

"I'm not kiddin' ya. I'm not kiddin' ya. What the hell are you so damned sensitive about?"

"I don't trust you when you try to be serious, Herb. Save your breath."

"Oh, all right, then. Here I come with a perfectly good invitation to go out to Sunday dinner in a nice home with a lot of beautiful girls in the house and you poop all over me. They've got money, too. The nicest girls in Kansas City."

"How'd you meet'm, Herb?"

"Insult me, will ya? Insult me."

"I didn't mean that as an insult. I just asked you."

"You don't know me, George. I've reformed. I'm a serious fella. In fact, if you must know, I'm courting one of these girls. I want to marry and settle down."

Brush kept his eyes on Herb's reflection in the mirror and went on shaving. "Where do they live?"

"MacKenzie Boulevard. Swell mansion. They've got money. Louie and Bat and I got asked to Sunday dinner today, and I told'm about you and they said bring'm along. It's Sunday dinner, big boy, and there'll be lots of eats . . . Well, make up your mind. It's twelve o'clock now and I gotta phone Mrs. Crofut how many's coming."

Brush watched him in the mirror. "Herb, do you promise before God that there's no catch in this?"

"Oh, you give me a pain. Stay home; stay home! Go and eat at the wagon. I hope it chokes ya. I told Mrs. Crofut we'd sing for them. Stay home and spoil the quartet if you like."

"I'll come," said Brush and returned to his *Lear*. *"When thou clovest thy crown i' the middle, and gavest away both parts,"* he cried, *"thou borest thine ass on thy own back o'er the dirt."*

"What?" asked Herb. "What's that?"

"I wasn't talking to you. *Thou hadst little wit in thy bald crown when thou gavest thy golden one away.*"

A few minutes later Herb returned. "Well, since you made me promise, George, perhaps I ought to tell you there's a little catch in this . . . just a harmless joker, see? . . . I told'm you were a famous singer, see? They're all excited about it. They think you're a famous singer, like on the radio. A concert singer, and famous."

Brush's answer was composure itself. "That's not a lie," he said. "There must be five thousand people in this country who've been thrilled by my singing at one time or other. That's not a lie."

Herb fled from the room, but Brush followed him to the door, razor in hand, and shouted after him: "Why, just the other night at Camp Morgan they were spellbound. I didn't know the human hand could clap so long. I don't say that because I'm conceited, because a fine voice is just a gift. Tell Mrs. Crofut I'll be glad to come."

6

Kansas City. Sunday dinner at Ma Crofut's. More news of Father Pasziewski. A moment of dejection in a Kansas City hospital.

Mrs. Crofut certainly lived in a very fine house. If it had any faults at all, it was that the paint lacked freshness and that it was too closely hemmed in by a business college on one side and an undertaking establishment on the other. But apart from that, Brush agreed, it was a very fine home. It rose above the street in a mass of towers and gables and bays and porches. It had not always belonged to Mrs. Crofut—though the Crofuts were a very old family—because the horse-block on the curb said Adams. For some reason a dilapidated electric signboard lay half hidden in the rhododendron bushes; it said: THE RIVIERA. CUISINE FRANÇAISE. The boys entered without ringing the bell, and Brush found himself in a dark hall. He was curious about everything and, pushing aside some reed portières at the left, he saw a large room filled with small tables, as though it had once been a restaurant.

"Well, boys, how are you?" said a large, honest voice emerging from the back of the hall. "This is fine."

"Mrs. Crofut," said Herb, "I want you to shake hands with George Brush, the singer."

"It's a pleasure; and let me tell you we've been looking forward to it a lot. I declare, my daughters have been dolling up for hours. Let's go and sit in the day parlor until my girls come down," she said, alluding to a whispering and twittering of joyous young voices upstairs. Brush glanced up the great staircase, past the stained-glass window, and saw a laughing face peering down between the posts of the balustrade. "Come in here and tell me what you've all been doing with yourselves."

Mrs. Crofut sat down with casual elegance in a huge rattan chair and beckoned them to seats about her. She had a fine large red face surmounted by a carefully built up head of yellow hair. A row of small yellow curls crossed her forehead. She wore a black silk shirtwaist covered with jet beads, and a gold watch was pinned over her lungs. She was an enormous woman, but her waist was remarkably small and she carried her vast bulk with a constant attention to grace. Brush liked her at once and could scarcely take his eyes off her. She was joined a few minutes later by a tall thin girl, likewise with yellow hair.

"This is my girl Lily. . . . Aren't you the bold one! . . . This is Lily, Mr. Brush."

Lily stood squirming and giggling by her mother's chair, staring at Brush.

"Lily's the musical one," continued Mrs. Crofut. "Very sweet voice."

Serious conversation was interrupted by the entrance of a military parade of five more young ladies. They were all of about the same age, sixteen to eighteen, and were very shy and modest. One was a tall dark girl of foreign origin. All of them had one trait in common, a certain vagueness in the eyes, as though it were difficult to focus the glance on a single object. Introductions were not easily gotten over with. There was much staring and blushing and suppressed giggling.

"You have a lot of daughters, Mrs. Crofut, I'll say," said Brush.

"Lord! have I! And this isn't all, by any means, is it, Herbert? The fact is the older girls are eating by themselves upstairs; this is just what I call my kindergarten. You see, Mr. Brush," she said, with intimate complicity, "perhaps they aren't *all* my daughters; some of them merely make their home with me for the time being. Dolores there is a Cuban girl. Dinner's ready now, so let's go in. Go in, go in, girls. What's the matter with you today? They're as nervous as witches about meeting you, Mr. Brush, that's a fact. They're not themselves."

The company passed through several sitting-rooms and came to a large dining-room at the back of the house. Mrs. Crofut stood behind her chair and directed matters in a large way. "There are thirteen of us," she said, "so May has to sit at a table by herself. We drew lots and May's the goat." May, blushing with confusion and pleasure, seated herself in the bay window and took a drink of water. "Now, Mr. Brush, by rights, you ought to sit by me, but I'm just an old woman and I'm going to set you down among my girls. The girls all want to sit by you and I'm not going to show any favoritism, so suit yourself. I see Herb's going to sit by Gladys, as usual."

Brush did not stop to pick and choose. He found himself between the Cuban girl and a girl called Ruth. Ruth was a soft-eyed girl with brown hair. She wore a simple white dress and scarcely dared raise her eyes from her plate. A number of awkward silences fell during the soup. There was a good deal of unabashed staring. Brush felt he had never seen so many beautiful, quiet girls in one place before. Mrs. Crofut drank her soup with great refinement; with one bejeweled hand she pressed a corner of her napkin to her bosom. From time to time she sipped from a tumbler containing a tonic. As the plates were being removed, anticipation could no longer contain itself and the quartet was called upon for a number. They linked their arms about one another's necks, cleared their throats, frowning, and entered upon "How can I bear to leave thee?" The reception was all that vanity could desire. They followed it with "Wasting in despair," leading up to the famous specialty cadence. The hostesses were lost in admiration and were greatly solemnized. There was no giggling after that. The quartet sat down, itself filled with awe, and the girls almost shuddered to find themselves seated next to so much achievement. Mrs. Crofut collected herself first:

"Have you lived long in these parts, Mr. Brush?" she asked.

"No. My home is in Michigan."

"You don't say! I had a friend ... Did you ever know a Mr. Pasternak there? He was engaged in the lumber business. He was very well off, really very well off."

"I ... I don't remember him now."

"You don't? Well, he was a perfect gentleman and I believe, as I say, very well off. It was lumber, I remember now. His name was Jules,—Jules Pasternak." Whereupon she leaned far back in her chair and laughed long and heartily. "Oh," she concluded, wiping her eyes, "I hadn't thought of him for years."

No further information was offered about Mr. Pasternak, but his warming image had passed through the room and henceforth there were no more alarming silences at the table. Lily was sent to push back the curtains at the window.

"Very lovely girl, isn't she?" said Mrs. Crofut.

"Yes indeed," said Brush.

"Lovely girl. She was on the stage for a while."

"Was she?" asked Brush, looking at her with even greater interest. "Was she ever in anything by Shakespeare?"

Lily looked timidly at Mrs. Crofut. "Speak up, dearie. Were you?"

The answer was almost inaudible, but it was "No."

"I guess Mayme would know more about that," continued Mrs. Crofut. "Mayme's a great reader. Nose always in a book. Mayme's our red-head."

Mayme's red head was turned by this praise; she was suddenly seized by a desire to show off. In a high voice rendered hoarse by nervousness she screamed, "I read a story by him just the other day."

"Really," said Brush. "Did he write other things besides theater plays?"

"Shakespeare?" cried Mrs. Crofut, eager to support her daughter. "Why, he wrote every kind of thing. We've got one of his upstairs. Gladys, you're by the door. Run upstairs and get the books."

Her glance rested on Gladys' back as she left the table. "I like that type don't you? Very pretty girl."

"Yes, indeed," said Brush.

"Lovely girl," repeated Mrs. Crofut.

Gladys returned with the books and went back for another that had fallen on the stairs. Their title pages were anxiously consulted. Everyone laughed at the thought that Shakespeare could have had a hand in "The Care and Feeding of Infants" or a bound volume of *Ainslee's Magazine* for 1903. *September Morn at Atlantic City* gave no author's name and *Barriers Burned Away* was attributed to E. P. Roe.

"There!" cried Mrs. Crofut, tapping the back of the novel with a jeweled forefinger. "I could have sworn that was by Shakespeare. I don't know how we could have come to make a mistake like that." Whereupon she went into gales of laughter, politely flinging her napkin over her face while she laughed. The girls laughed softly, proud to see their mother thus at her best; their doe's eyes passed softly from face to face, making sure that everyone was appreciating it.

"Well," she said, finally, "I guess we all like a good play. Mr. Shore, did you ever see Lillian Russell? . . . Sit up straight, Pearl."

"No," said Brush, as soon as he realized that he was being addressed, "I don't think I ever did."

"Oh, she was fine! *Beautiful* girl."

Lily's voice was raised in a sudden scream. "Ma looks just like her." The other girls burst out into shrill corroboration. Lily continued: "Her room's-covered-with-pictures-of-her. Ma-tells-us-all-about-her. Ma looks-just-like-her."

Mrs. Crofut lowered her eyes. "Well, people did use to say . . . but, of course, it was just foolishness. But let me tell you she was a very fine actress, and I may say, a very fine woman." Then lowering her voice and looking solemnly into Brush's eyes, she added, in a tone implying that only he would understand all the implications of her remark, "I never heard a word, not a word, against her reputation."

"That's fine," said Brush, deeply impressed.

Mrs. Crofut made a rapid transition to the conversational tone. "Herb," she said, "you haven't been around to see me lately. Where've you been keeping yourself?"

"It's the depression," said Herb. "Now I have to go to George Washington Park."

Mrs. Crofut threw up her chin loftily. "Well, be common if you want to. It's none of my business."

Herb made an answer that Brush did not understand.

"Now, boys, none of that," replied the hostess. "Eat your dinner. Just good clean fun today. We're having a good time. Just eat your dinner."

This was the first of a number of strange things that began to happen. Brush became more and more confused, but pinning his faith on Mrs. Crofut, whom he liked with increasing force, he bore up as best he could. A policeman sauntered into the room without removing his hat. He was greeted by cries of "Hello, Jimmy." He took a certain liberty with one of the young ladies sitting near him.

"Now don't go behaving like that, Jimmy," said Mrs. Crofut. "There's a surprise package for you in the kitchen."

"You don't say," said Jimmy, and disappeared from the scene.

The next unexpected thing was caused by Dolores. Brush had tried to engage her in conversation several times. On each occasion she had raised sullen eyes to his face for a moment, muttered a few words, and returned to her meal. The third time, however, she rose abruptly to her feet, overturning the chair behind her, and slapped him smartly across the face. She then ran to the door, turned, hissed and spat in his direction, and ran down the perspective of drawing-rooms.

Mrs. Crofut was horrified. She rose and followed Dolores through the room, screaming: "Go upstairs, Dolores. Go upstairs, you slut. You're a nasty slut. I'll give you something to learn you a lesson!" Then returning breathless to her place, she said: "Why, Mr. Shore, I'm so ashamed I don't know what to say. Imagine a thing like that! Here we were, having a nice home-like Sunday dinner, and that girl has to behave like that! However, don't give it another thought. These things will happen. Now we'll forget all about it. Tchk-tchk! You see, Mr. Shore, I have my troubles, like every one else."

"Yes," said Brush. "But you have what they call a silver lining. I never saw a home with so many nice and good-looking girls in it."

"Thank you," said Mrs. Crofut, sitting up very straight and getting a little more ruddy. "That's a real compliment coming from a great singer like you. I do think they're pretty nice girls, if I do say so myself."

"Wow!" cried Morrie, and bent his head to the floor, coughing and choking.

Mrs. Crofut rose, trembling with rage. "Now you behave yourself, young man. I don't care what you think and I don't like the way you're laughing. I don't care *what* you think. Answer me! Do I, or do I not, keep a careful eye on my girls? Do I, girls?"

"Yes, ma," said six tinkly voices.

"Answer me, Morrie!"

"Aw, ma, you get me wrong," said Morrie. "I wasn't laughing at you. I was laughing at Brush here."

"Well, if you had the gentlemanliness that he has, you wouldn't be making a fool of yourself in public places. Here we are, all friends, eating together and . . . and you have to bring in ideas like that. It doesn't give a very good idea of the home you come from, I must say."

"Mrs. Crofut," said Brush, "I'm sure he didn't mean to hurt your feelings. He's a very fine fellow, and I don't mind if he laughs at me."

Mrs. Crofut sat down slowly, still glaring at Morrie. A shocked silence fell upon the group. The girls sat with lowered eyes; one of them cried for a moment and then hurriedly brushed away her tears. But the affair had not blown over. Mrs. Crofut rose again and, pointing emotionally at Morrie, said:

"Come, tell me! What did you mean by that laugh? I won't have things like that said about me. I won't have it. Either I'm like a mother to these girls, or I'm not. Do I keep an eye on them, or don't I?"

Suddenly Herb's voice, flat and contemptuous, said: "Quit the high horse, ma. Who do you think you are?"

Now Brush stood up in his place, white with rage: "Herb, if you try that kind of thing I'll take you right out and turn the hose on you. I didn't know you were so crude. You've got a long way to

go before you're fit to associate with people that live in homes.—
Excuse me, Mrs. Crofut, and I apologize for *him,* too."

"That's all right, Mr. Shore," said Mrs. Crofut, who had sunk
back into her chair and was sniveling into her tonic. "I don't expect
any decency from a fellow like that, I'm sure."

"Come on," said Herb, "come on and fight it out, you goddamn simp, you. Come on outdoors and fight it out."

"There's no use your fighting with me, Herb. You're as weak as
water. Your cigarettes have done for you. You saw that last night."

Bat went over to Herb. "Sit down, Herb. Sit down. We'll tell
him later. It's all right. We'll tell him later."

This altercation was followed with the liveliest interest by the
young ladies. It brought the colored cook to the door, where she
stood meditatively picking her teeth. When it blew over there was
a general air of disappointment in the room.

Brush said, gravely: "I guess the best of friends quarrel every
now and then. It doesn't mean that they're any the worse persons;
it only means that human nature isn't raised up yet to what we
hope it's going to be. I'm really fond of Herb and I'm sorry I spoke
to him that way. Sometime the day's coming when there aren't
going to be any quarrels, because in my opinion the world's getting
better and better. And in spite of this little thing that's happened,
today has been an example of it. I want to thank you very much for
taking me into your home this way. Most of my life is spent on
trains and in hotels and I appreciate it; so I want to do something
for you in return. Generally, I don't believe in going to the theater,
and especially not on Sundays. But I think I know when to make
an exception, and can see when nobody's really harmed by it. I
want to invite you all as my guests to the movie around the corner
that opens at four o'clock."

"Well, now," said Mrs. Crofut, "that's real nice of you. Girls,
would you like to go to the movies with Mr.——"

"Brush."

"With Mr. Brush?"

There were squeals of enthusiasm.

"Now, Mr. Brush, I can't go myself, but my girls accept with pleasure. Let me whisper in your ear a minute. Mr. Brush, I don't want the girls to be any expense to you. I'll give them each some pocket money and they'll pay their own. You can pay for one, if you like."

"But, Mrs. Crofut, I *asked* them. I *want* to pay for them."

"No, no. I know better. All boys your age have quite a time making two ends meet. You save your money."

Brush submitted to this arrangement and presently he was proceeding down the street in a twitter of young feminine voices. His companions walked with an exaggerated primness, waving their hips delicately from side to side. They all talked at once, each trying to get his agreement to any thought that occurred to her.

Everything interested them. They followed closely an educational reel depicting the Vale of Cashmere, and another that showed a Boy Scout congress and a train wreck. The President of the country spoke a few words and they all agreed he was a very nice man. The principal picture on the program was pathetic, and they all cried happily and generously. Brush's handkerchief passed back and forth among them. It was about a beautiful girl threatened by the dangers that lurk in great cities. It was full of suspense. The girls sitting beside Brush insisted on clinging to him; he found himself holding two hot convulsed hands on his knees. When Brush returned the girls to their home each one in turn flung her arms about his neck and printed rouge on his cheeks. Each declared she had enjoyed it very much and would be waiting for him to come again. She'd be waiting.

Brush was so dizzy with well-being that he was obliged to take a long walk to calm himself. "It just goes to show my favorite theory that the world's full of wonderful people," he said to himself, "if you know where to look." When he returned to Queenie's it was almost nine o'clock. The disarray on the scrubbed top floor had begun again. The rooms were billowing with Sunday papers. The tenants sat about with their heels above the level of their heads. They were in a sour humor.

"Well, baby," said Herb, "you had a great time, eh?"

"I certainly did."

Herb asked an obscene question. It was taken up and furthered by the others.

Brush stared at them in consternation: "You fellows promised not to pull that kind of thing."

"All promises are off," said Herb.

Brush stood still for a moment, then dragged his suitcase out of the cupboard and began packing.

"You've had a pretty good two days," said Herb, "all told. Pretty good for you. You got so cock-eyed drunk on Saturday that you puked on the War Memorial, and on Sunday you raped a whole cat-house. Pretty fast, kid, pretty fast."

Brush raised his eyes and looked at him, but said nothing. Herb let him have it again.

"That's not true," said Brush.

"Not true? What do you know about it? Gad! you're the simplest galoot in the world. You're so simple, you stink."

Kneeling by his suitcase, Brush scarcely raised his eyes. "Were those . . . fallen women?"

"Fallen? You couldn't get'm more fallen."

"Herb, you promised there was no catch in it!"

"All promises went out with daylight-saving time," said Herb, dryly. He flung out the pages of his newspaper and went on reading. The room was silent. Brush, began to cry. He jumped up with sudden passion: "It can't be true. They weren't. You fellows don't know what you're talking about. I say they're perfectly all right and that's the kind of thing I don't make any mistake about. You fellows can't say things like that to me, just because you . . . Listen, Herb, it can't be true."

"It's gotta be true," said Herb, coldly scanning the headlines.

Brush marched wildly up and down the room. Suddenly, with a shout, he picked up a chair and, pointing the four legs horizontally before him, crashed them through the window-pane.

Louis whistled. "Tz-tz-tz! Naughty!" he said.

Brush stood by the window, looking out over the housetops. "You fellows pretend you don't know what it's all about, but you know. You're just pretending. You spend your whole life pretending it's not serious. . . . I wish I were there talking to them now. . . . I'm glad I went, I thank you very much."

Herb arose and, hitching up his pants, took his place in the middle of the room. "Take off your coat," he said. "I've got an account to settle with you. Come on, take off your coat and fight it out."

"I don't fight, Herb. Hit me, if you like."

"You'll fight. You'll fight, all right," said Herb, advancing.

Brush raised his arms passively to defend himself. The others joined in. They drew him down and stamped on him. In a paroxysm of hatred they kicked him and threw him downstairs and left him on the pavement. Louie curtly telephoned his hospital, and the ambulance took him away, unconscious.

The next morning Queenie called on him in his ward. She entered, ill at ease in hat and gloves, and casting alarmed glances about her. Catching sight of Brush's head, almost entirely bound with bandages, she crossed herself, then sat down and gazed at him. Brush smiled at her, sadly.

"Here's your suitcase and purse, Mr. Brush. It musta fallen out of your pocket some way. They told me to bring it to you."

"Thanks, Queenie."

"Are you in any pain, Mr. Brush?"

"No."

"Why, you look all knocked about. What did you do to'm to make'm all set on you like that? I knew they were wild boys, but I didn't think they'd try to break your bones, Mr. Brush."

Brush did not answer.

Queenie began to cry. "I told'm to pack up their things and go. I told'm I didn't want no hoodlums like that in my house. I told'm to get right out."

"No, no, Queenie. You let them stay. I'll explain to you some day." There was a pause. "Are they packing, Queenie?"

"I told'm to, but I guess they aren't packing very fast. They just told me to shut up and get out. But I'll let 'em stay if you say so, Mr. Brush. With these hard times I don'o' who I'd find. Mrs. Kubinsky—lives next door—'s had four rooms empty ever since August."

Queenie's tears were drying already. A giggle began to appear. "I declare you look funny with that rabbit's ear on your head, Mr. Brush. I'm glad you're in no pain."

"This is the hospital Louie works in, isn't it?"

"Yes. I saw'm in the hall when I come in. I declare he didn't look natural in white pants and coat."

"What did he say to you?"

"Oh . . . mostly hello."

"When you go out I wish you'd tell him to come and see me for a minute."

There was a pause.

"How's Father Pasziewski, Queenie?"

"I told you, Mr. Brush. He seems pretty well again. Funny, your asking about him so much, because he always asks about you, too."

Brush almost sat up. "Does he? . . . How?"

"Yes, I told him a lot about you once and he's very interested in you."

Brush lay back and looked at the ceiling. "The kidney trouble just got better of itself?" he asked, softly.

"They think now it was gall stones and they were melted down by drinking tea with some drops of the River Jordan in it. Mrs. Kramer was saving it for the christening of her grandchildren, but we think now maybe there aren't going to be any grandchildren, so Father Pasziewski got the benefit of it."

"Some day . . . tell Father Pasziewski I . . . I think of him a lot."

"Yes, I will. Can I write a card for you to somebody, Mr. Brush?"

"No, Queenie . . . there's nobody."

Queenie went out. Later in the day Louie passed through the ward. Brush whistled to him.

Louie drew up beside the bed and whispered in his ear: "You give me the belches. Hurry up. What do you want?"

"Louie, sit down a minute. I want to ask you a question."

"Well, hurry up about it. I've gotta go and get some arms and legs."

"Louie, tell me what's the matter with me?"

"You've no brains, that's all. God didn't give you any brains."

"I know." After a breath or two he looked at Louie. "What ought I to do about it?"

"Sure. Snap out of it. Get awake. Get wise to yourself."

"Sure, I want to. I don't know how to go about it, that's all. . . . There must be something serious the matter with me, because that's the third time people have suddenly hated me. . . . I must have some kind of brains, though, because I just got a raise, even in a panic year . . . and my grades were good at school; they were the best."

Louie put his face close to Brush's ear. "You'll learn in time. I guess you'll find your place in time, see? Only don't come around us any more. We got our own ideas and our own lives all arranged, see? and we don't like to be interrupted."

"Did the fellows say that?"

"Yes. Yes."

"All right. . . . So I suppose this is good-by. Only, listen. If ever you fellows change your minds and want to sing some more, drop me a line, will you?—Caulkins and Company."

"Listen, George. You asked me what you could do. All right, listen. Get to be one of the fellas. Learn to drink, like anybody else. And leave other people's lives alone. Live and let live. Live and let live. Everybody likes to be let alone. And run around with the women. You're healthy, aintya? Enjoy life, see? You're going to be dead a long time, *believe* me."

Louie had not noticed that Brush was slowly rising to a sitting position. Brush's voice now rose in an answer that grew to a shout in the full open ward:

"You can get away and stay away," he cried. "If I ever became like you fellows I'd expect to be dead a long time. I may be cuckoo, perhaps I am; but I'd rather be crazy all alone than be sensible like you fellows are sensible. I'm glad I'm nuts. I don't want to be different. Tell the fellows I'll never change—"

"All right. Pipe down!"

"And if they want to have me back, they must have me as I am, only worse."

By this time the nurse had run up with a hypodermic. "This is a mental case," she exclaimed. "Help me, Louie. He ought to be in the annex. Hold his arm, Louie."

"I'll take it quietly, nurse. I'm sorry I lost my temper."

"You've gone and upset all the patients. Look at them staring at you!"

"I want to say just one more thing, nurse," he said, and shouted after the departing Louie: "And if you must know, I'm not crazy. It's the world that's crazy. Everybody's crazy except me; that's what's the matter. The whole world's nuts."

7

*Three adventures of varying educational importance: the evangelist;
the medium; first steps in* ahimsa.

On being discharged from the hospital Brush set out again on
that long swing of the pendulum between Kansas City and Abilene, Texas, that was his work. At Abilene he waited his turn in
the halls of Simmons University, McMurray College, and Abilene Christian College. He visited Austin College at Sherman,
Baylor College at Belton, and Baylor University at Waco. He visited Daniel Baker College and Howard Payne College at Brown-
wood; he visited the Texas Teachers College at Denton, Rice
Institute at Honston, Southwestern University at Georgetown,
and Trinity University at Waxahachie. He looked in at Delhart
and Amarillo. He went down to San Antonio to see Our Lady of

the Lake and to Austin to place an algebra at St. Edward's University. Returning through Oklahoma, he visted the state university at Norman, the Baptist University at Shawnee, the college at Chickasha, the Agricultural and Mechanical College at Stillwater. He digressed into Louisiana and called at Pineville and Ruston; he spent a solitary Christmas in Baton Rouge. Arkansas tempted him to Arkadelphia and Clarksville and Onachita. And everywhere on his journeys he selected certain high schools in strategic positions where the employment of his textbooks could serve as influential examples for smaller schools in the neighborhood.

Many unusual adventures befell him during these weeks. Of the great number we select three that illustrate certain stages in his education.

On the train that carried him from Waco to Dallas he occupied himself with reading a second-year algebra that had recently been placed upon the market by a rival publishing-house. Such reading held for Brush an element of suspense. He lived in fear lest some other firm bring out a better series of textbooks than those issued by Caulkins and Company, a contingency that would greatly impair the energy and serenity of his sales talk. He knew that his books were the best books obtainable, because he had himself read them, done all the problems, verified the answers, translated the sentences, and compared the methods with the methods employed by all the rival books in good standing. At this moment he was discovering with considerable relief that Dr. Ryker of the Worcester, Massachusetts, high schools was fumbling badly with the problem of rendering negative fractions comprehensible to fifteen-year-old boys and girls; that Dr. Ryker had no skill in contriving attractive and stimulating problems about racing airplanes and the hands of clocks; and that Dr. Ryker had all too clearly helped himself to the superior inspirations of Dr. Caulkins. Brush was deep in these matters when he heard a voice say:

"Young man, have you ever thought seriously about the great facts of life and death?"

He looked up to see leaning over him a tall unshaven man of fifty, wearing a soiled linen suit. A handkerchief was stuffed into the band of his collar and his cuffs were protected by black cotton guards. He had a white-and-yellow waterfall mustache and black steely eyes.

"Yes," said Brush.

The man removed a newspaper from beside Brush and sat down. "Are you right with God—this very minute?" he asked, putting his arm along the back of the seat in front of him and his nose very close to Brush's face.

"Yes," said Brush, beginning to blush violently, "I try to be."

"Oh, my boy," said the other, with a strong vibrato and an odor of decaying teeth, "you can't answer that question as quickly as that. No one can. Being saved,—oh, my boy!—isn't as easy as being vaccinated. It means wrestling. It means fighting. It means going down on your knees." He took hold of the lapel of Brush's suit and fingered it disparagingly. "I can see that you're still entangled with the world's snares and shows. Boy, do you touch liquor?"

"No."

"Do you use filthy tobacco?"

"No."

The man lowered his voice. "Do you frequent loose women?"

"No," said Brush, expelling the poisoned air from his nose.

"Do you indulge in lascivious thoughts?"

Brush coughed.

"Yes, sir," cried the man. "'Let him who thinketh he stand, beware lest he fall.' The trouble with you is you're puffed-up. You're stiff-necked. Do you know the Good Book?"

"I study it."

"What's Romans five one?"

"'Therefore, being justified through faith, we have peace with God, through—"

"No. No, it's not."

"I . . . I think it is."

"No. By faith. . . . Therefore, being justified *by* faith. . . ."

"Yes, I guess it is."

"You *guess* it is," said the other, producing a Bible and striking Brush sharply on the knee with it. "Is that the way to talk about God's word? You *guess* it is?—Philippians three thirteen?"

"'Brethren, I count not myself to have apprehended: but this one thing I do . . .'"

"Yes, go on."

"'Forgetting the things which are behind . . .'"

"'*Those* things.'"

"'And reaching forth to those things which are before, I press toward the mark . . .'"

"I didn't ask for the fourteenth verse. Brother, you don't know it. You think you know it. You *guess* you know it. The trouble with you is you're shallow. You haven't even *begun* yet. Oh, brother, I've had great experience with suffering, sinning men and women, and I want to tell you it's not enough to say that you've been saved."

Brush's eyes began guardedly to look about him for another seat. The man raised his voice and waved his arms about:

"I've been in the vineyard twenty-five years, wrestling with the devil. Yes, the world's full of suffering, sinning brothers and sisters. But there's a way to peace and mercy. Why don't you take it? Why don't you stretch out your hand and take it, instead of sitting around in city clothes like a Pharisee . . ."

The man had now risen and was addressing the car. Brush started to edge out by his knees. "Running away from conscience, eh? Can't face it, eh? You'd rather sit there and pass for perfect, I know."

Voices from the back of the car broke in on him. "Aw, shut up! Go to sleep!"

"Brethren, fire and sword can't frighten me as long as I have a message."

Brush took another seat and opened the algebra. He was blushing and his heart was beating quickly. The evangelist, under a gathering storm of resentment from his fellow passengers, continued to harangue the car, using Brush as an example of moral cowardice. He began striding up and down the aisle, retorting to the jeers of his listeners. Brush, furiously biting the inner sides of his cheeks, finally rose and, taking the evangelist's arm, firmly directed him to a seat.

"You don't do any good making them mad," he said, and sitting down by the aisle, penned the other in beside the window. The evangelist continued with fiery eyes to fling some charges over his shoulder, but the controversy died down and he fell to muttering and grumbling to himself.

At last Brush said, "May I ask you some questions?"

"Brother, I'm here to help you."

"Have you a church somewhere?"

"No, brother, I'm a wandering witness for the Lord."

"Do you set up a tent?"

"No. I help my laboring brothers out. I use their churches. I take services for them."

"What do you—what do you live on?"

The other turned and peered at him with great displeasure. "What kind of a question is that? Brother, that's none of your business."

Brush stared gravely back at him.

"However," continued the other, "I'll tell you. The Lord doesn't neglect his workers. No, sir-reee, no, sir. He touches the hearts of people here and there, sometimes one place, sometimes another. Money? What's money? Brother, I don't believe in money.

Matthews six twenty-five. This minute, boy, I have one dollar between me and the birds of the air," he said, emptying his pockets and producing two dollar bills, a clergyman's railroad pass, and a soiled letter addressed to the Reverend James Bigelow. "Two dollars between me and the fowls of the air. But am I afraid? No. I live by faith and prayer. Psalms thirty-seven twenty-five."

"Have you a family?"

"Yes, boy, I have a noble wife and six fine children."

It seemed, however, that Dr. Bigelow's wife had found it best to take a place as laundress in a Dallas hotel. At first it appeared that the six children were doing well in school. But gradually it came out that the oldest two boys had run away, another had joined the navy, and that one daughter was bedridden; that left two children doing well in school.

Dr. Bigelow's assurance was considerably diminished under Brush's questioning. When they arrived at Dallas, Brush gave him ten dollars and, with lowered eyes, shook hands with him and took his leave.

Another adventure of this order took place at Fort Worth. Brush was taking an evening stroll through the residential section of the city, preparatory to settling down at the Public Library over the Encyclopædia Britannica, when he noticed a sign in the window of a faded brick apartment-house: "Spiritualistic Readings. Mrs. Ella McManus, medium. Tuesday and Friday evenings or by appointment. Fifty cents." It was a Friday evening. Brush wandered about the house for a time, hesitating. Around the corner, in another window of what appeared to be the same apartment, he saw a card that read: "Varicose Veins Reduced: Consultation Free." Finally he decided to go in. He was ushered into an overfurnished parlor in which a number of women were already seated. Mrs. McManus introduced herself; she was a short, stout woman with an air of importance and bad temper. After a prolonged conversation about the weather the company adjourned to the dining-room and sat down about the table, holding hands. The lights were turned off and a gramophone played "The Rosary." Presently Mrs. McManus began to shudder violently, and an Indian chief named Standing Corn addressed the company through her lips. He gave a stirring description of the next world, following it with some words to earthbound spirits exhorting them to courage and patience. He rapped on the table at command, threw a tambourine across the room and caused a picture to fall from the wall. He then offered to answer any questions put to him. Mrs. McManus had already secured the names and birthdays of the visitors, and now required to hold in her hand some object belonging to each of the questioners. She took the wrist watch of the woman at Brush's right, a Mrs. Caufman, and clutching it passionately to her bosom, gave her messages of the most convincing nature, referring by name to a host of departed relatives, giving the hiding-places of lost objects, and offering advice on intimate matters. The next interview was of a more general nature. A widow wished for a few words from her husband. The message was comforting in the extreme, but the widow wept the whole time so heartbrokenly that she was scarcely able to muster sufficient voice to return thanks to Chief Standing Corn and Mrs. McManus.

Brush sat with lowered head and furrowed brow.

Mrs. McManus asked: "Have you a question to put tonight, Mr. Brush, across the veil that separates but for a time the living and the dead?"

Brush hesitated. Then he said, "I'd like to speak to Dwight L. Moody."

There was a long pause. It was broken by Mrs. McManus intermittently assuming a voice even farther in the bass than that employed by Chief Standing Corn. Mr. Moody said that he was happy. "'Oh, so happy. Where I am all is peace. Peace like the world cannot give.' What would you like to ask Mr. Moody?"

Brush gazed darkly before him and did not answer.

"I have another message from Mr. Moody for you. He says: 'Take care of your health.' And he seems to wish to send you a word about some one you love . . . I think it's a woman. . . . Yes, it is, and her name begins with an M—an M, I think. Do you know who that would be?"

"No."

"Well, perhaps it's an R. It will come more clearly directly. He says do nothing hasty just now. Especially the money way. Save, or put away in very conservative investments, he says. And wait. He says—I know our other friends here won't mind my repeating this personal word—there's a certain woman that's come into your life lately . . . rather on the blond side, I should say. . . . You should find out slowly whether she's a *true* friend or not. He says to be cautious in all letters you write. Now he's gone. No! he says to keep up your courage. He's waiting for you up yonder. It won't be long, he says, because up there fifty years is like a minute."

"If that was anybody," said Brush, somberly, "it wasn't the Moody I meant. I meant Dwight L. Moody."

"I hope Chief Standing Corn didn't make an error," said Mrs. McManus, a little sharply. "Of course, there are thousands of the dead by the name of Moody."

The telephone rang in the parlor.

"Will you answer the phone, Mrs. Caufman," said Mrs. McManus, dreamily, "and ask the party to call later?"

"Mrs. McManus is in the spirit world," reported Mrs. Caufman. "and asks that you call later." Then after a pause, in a lowered voice: "Not now! Anyway, not now! Don't y'understand? . . . First lukewarm, then cold. Yes. And massage downward, not up; *down.* Yes. Yes." Then returning to her chair, Mrs. Caufman said, deferentially, "The gentleman says he will call later, Mrs. McManus."

Brush sat up straight.

At the close of the meeting the others brought out their half-dollars and were emotionally thanking Mrs. McManus, when Brush said:

"I can't pay you for this evening, Mrs. McManus."

"What do you mean you can't pay me?" asked Mrs. McManus, turning very red and marching toward him.

"I mean: I have the money and everything, but I can't pay you for something you haven't earned. If you tell me the name of some church you go to, I'll send the money to that church, but I can't give it to you."

"Now wait a minute," she replied, going to the door, shutting it firmly, and standing with her back to it. "Girls, I want you to wait a minute and hear this with me."

"I can't pay you for a fraud, Mrs. McManus. It wouldn't be fair."

"Did you say I was a fraud?"

"Well, Mrs. McManus . . . you know you are. I couldn't help hearing Mrs. Caufman at the telephone. That showed she was an old friend of yours. And all that about Dwight L. Moody. I couldn't pay you for that."

Mrs. McManus turned coldly to Mrs. Caufman. "Cora," she said, "phone for the police. Mr. Brush, if you try to leave the room I'll scream so the whole house'll be in here. . . . One minute, Cora, I'll phone, myself. It's too late to get out of it now, young man. I'll sue you. I'll sue you for everything you've got. I *thought* you were phoney, sitting there with that . . . that pie face of yours. I thought it was funny, a man of your type coming to a meeting like this, instead of tending to your own business. The minute you came in that door, I said to myself you were phoney. You and your Moodys! Well, it's the last time you'll insult me."

"I want you to call the police, Mrs. McManus," said Brush, "so they can warn other people against being given wrong ideas."

Mrs. McManus flung open the door majestically. "Now go!" she cried, "and never put your silly head in my door again. Girls, I want you to look at this man closely. If ever you see him again interfering with anybody, I don't care who it is, I want you to have him arrested. Look at him well! Do you see him?"

"Yes," said the terrified girls.

"Here I am doing a good work . . . as best I can, to the limit of my abilities . . . and that doubter, that atheist,—for that's what he is, an atheist. . . ."

Still Brush did not go. He stood in the doorway, lost in deep thought, his eyes resting on Mrs. McManus. At last he slowly put his hand in his pocket and drew out half a dollar.

"I guess I'd better give you this, after all," he said, slowly, "since I stayed. But I don't see how you can do it, Mrs. McManus. What I don't see is, what goes on in your head while you're making up these things. I mean, I don't understand how people *can* tell lies for long at a time. . . . I guess it's just human . . ."

"I don't want your money!" screamed Mrs. McManus.

Brush laid the money on the table and continued talking, half to himself, "I've got a lot to learn yet, I see."

He said good night to each of the ladies by name and took a long walk through the suburbs of Fort Worth, thinking the matter over.

The third adventure took place in a small town in Arkansas, Pekin. Brush called in the evening on a family, the Greggs, whom he had met on a previous trip. He arrived just as the younger members of the family were setting out to attend a church social. He accepted their cordial invitation to go with them, and he and Louise Gregg started off, stopping on the way to pick up a former English teacher of Louise's in the grade schools, a Miss Simmons. Miss Simmons turned out to be a vivacious elderly lady, given to more affectations than Brush could have wished. Their destination lay on the other side of the railroad tracks, and crossing the waste of rails, they could see the brightly lighted windows and wide-open door of the Sunday-school rooms. It was a bright moonlight night and the three of them stopped among the switches to admire the red and green signal lights in the near and far distance and to catch the sound of some singing voices that were approaching along the ties.

"Let's go along," said Miss Simmons. "It's those Cronin boys."

The Cronin boys recognized their former teacher and began inserting into their song a muffled version of an obscene nickname that had been attached to her for thirty years.

"Good evening, Bill. Good evening, Fred and Jarvis," said Miss Simmons.

They returned a mock deferential "Good evening, Miss Simmons," but, suddenly aware of their recent release from the long and hated years of schooling, they grew bolder and began in falsetto to address one another as Miss Simmons, with the epithet, and with the invention of new material.

Brush walked over to them and in a changed voice said, "You fellows have got to apologize for that."

"Who says so?" asked Bill Cronin, putting his hand in his belt.

Miss Simmons called: "Oh, Mr. Brush! Oh, Mr. Brush! D-don't speak to them. The Cronin boys have always been impolite, rude boys."

"I do," said Brush. "You apologize to Miss Simmons right now."

Bill Cronin made a further remark, and Brush with a wide sweep of his arm struck him behind his left ear and knocked him down. The other two drew back a few steps and stared at their brother. Bill groaned and twisted on the tracks. Then rose on all fours.

"Apologize to Miss Simmons, all three of you," said Brush.

Bill Cronin mumbled an apology and the other two joined in.

Brush rejoined his companions. "I'm sorry about that," he said.

Miss Simmons was hysterical. "I think they're *terrible*. They always were terrible. . . . I think I must sit down."

Whereupon she sat down on the tracks. Brush fanned her with his hat. Over his shoulder he looked at the Cronins.

Bill was sitting on the ground. His brothers were leaning over him, whispering. Finally they lifted him up, and supporting him between them they guided him unsteadily toward the town.

"I'm all right now," said Miss Simmons.

"Are you sure?" asked Brush.

"Oh yes, I'm all right now."

"Then if you'll excuse me, I'll . . . be back in a few minutes," said Brush.

He caught up with the Cronins, who had sat down to rest on the platform of the freight station.

"How do you feel?" he asked. "I didn't mean to hurt you bad."

They were silent, avoiding his earnest glance.

"I don't believe in hitting people," he continued. "Do you think you're hurt any? . . . . Did it give you a headache?"

There was another silence. Bill Cronin grunted and put his feet on the ground; the other two put their shoulders under his arms and the three began hobbling off.

"After all," continued Brush, "that was a pretty dirty thing you said about Miss . . . Miss What's-her-name. You know you ought-n't to do that. Won't you shake hands, Cronin?"

Bill Cronin, with bent head, mumbled something, and the march continued.

Brush called out: "If there's any doctor bills, I'd like to pay them. You can get my address from Louise Gregg."

When Brush entered the Sunday-school rooms he was met with great acclaim. Miss Simmons had fainted away on her arrival and the whole story had been retold many times. Everyone was talking at once: "It's time someone gave those boys a lesson. . . . They're just the biggest rowdies in town. . . . He's been sent to the penitentiary once already and now he ought to go again."

Brush accepted the tributes in silence. His face had turned

very red. The minister could not put the chivalrous act out of his mind. An hour later, during the refreshments, he made a speech, calling attention to the qualities in George Brush of a "true gentleman." He concluded by saying:

"Mr. Brush, won't you say a few words to us?"

Brush, deeply troubled, stood up and fixed his gaze on a light at the end of the room. He was thinking so hard that he seemed to forget where he was. At last he said:

"If I can help it, I don't like to contradict anything that a minister says . . . but I've been thinking about what happened out on the tracks, and I ought to say to you all that I'm sorry I did it. I'm really a pacifist and I don't believe in striking anybody. In the first place, it's too easy. And now that I hear that the Cronin boy has been to the penitentiary, I feel still worse about it."

"But—but, Mr. Brush! The man was rude to Miss Simmons. I understand that what he said was almost an insult."

Brush kept his eye on the light and said, slowly: "It's a hard thing to think clearly about. . . . I guess we ought to have let him insult her. You see, Mr. Forrest, the theory is this: if bad people are treated kindly by the people they insult, why, then they start thinking about it and then they become ashamed. . . . That's the theory. That's Gandhi's theory."

Mr. Forrest said, sharply: "When a lady's insulted, Mr. Brush, it's no time for a gentleman to talk about theories. You know what we think of Southern womanhood down here. We don't agree with you."

Brush brought his eyes back from the distance and fixed them on the minister.

"Well, I think the world's in such a bad way that we've all got to start thinking all over again," he said, with mounting force. "I think all the ideas that are going around now are wrong. I'm trying to begin all over again at the beginning." He turned to Louise

Gregg, and said: "I've hit somebody today and I'm not fit to be here, so I'll say good-by, Louise. I guess I'd better go."

He took his hat off the rack in the hall, and crossing to the middle of the railroad tracks, he stood for a long while at the scene of the crime, thinking.

8

Kansas City. The Courting of Roberta Weyerhauser. Herb's Legacies.

During the days following his discharge from the hospital in Kansas City Brush had given much thought to the problem of finding Roberta. One day his eye had fallen on the advertisement of a private detective agency. He called upon the manager and laid most of the facts before him. Now after many forwardings a letter from the agency reached him. It gave the address of the farmhouse and added that one of the daughters in the home, a Miss Roberta Weyerhauser, had left the farm over a year ago, coming to Kansas City and had found employment as a waitress at the Rising Sun Chop Suey Palace.

On the first noon following his return to the city, Brush hurried to the restaurant for lunch. He climbed a narrow staircase, and on the second floor entered a large room hung with Chinese lanterns. The floor rose in gradually ascending levels about a central space reserved for dancing. On each tier there was a ring of tables for the diners. Brush seated himself at one of the tables on the highest level and looked about him. There were five waitresses standing about, and looking at them closely, he decided that any one of them might be Roberta Weyerhauser. They were dressed in a vaguely Chinese costume that included red satin trousers. A disc of rouge had been drawn on each cheek and their eyebrows had been painted in an upward curve at the outer edges. The waitress who came forward to take Brush's order was a tall bony girl with a mass of disheveled hair and a sullen expression.

"What'll you have?" she asked.

Brush scanned the card. "What's specially good?" he asked, slowly.

" 'T's all wonderful."

"Is there anything here that's a favorite of yours?"

"I like'm all. I'm crazy about'm all," replied the girl, coolly, scratching her head with the pencil. "Everyone of'm'll give you a great big thrill you'll never forget."

Brush looked up. "Might I ask you your name?" he said.

"Sure. You can know everything. My name's Whosis. I live with my mother and we don't keep a phone. I get out at four o'clock, but I only let my boy-friend see me home. I don't like to dance and the pictures hurt my eyes; so what else would you like to know?"

Brush turned red. "I didn't mean anything like that," he said, in a low voice. "All I wanted to know was, was there one of the waitresses here named Roberta Weyerhauser."

"What is this, anyway?" she replied, angrily. "What's it *to* you? Who are you?"

"I . . . I'm just a friend of Miss Weyerhauser's."

"Say, who are you? Did somebody send you?"

"Are *you* Roberta Weyerhauser?"

"No, I'm not. My name's Lily Wilson, if you must know. And looka here: you tend to your business and I'll tend to mine. That way we'll get on better. See?"

Brush looked at her earnestly. "I asked you a question, that's all," he said.

"Hurry up. What'll you have?"

Without looking at him she took down his order, then cast a contemptuous glance at him and started to go. She had scarcely taken ten steps when she was suddenly struck with recognition of who he was. She gave an exclamation of astonishment and hatred and turned to look at him once more. He had been following her with his eyes and their glances met. She hurried off and his dishes were brought to him by another waitress.

He returned that evening for dinner. Dancing was going on. Most of the tables were filled and he was unable to find a place in Roberta's territory.

At lunch the next day he was back at his former table. Suddenly she was saying angrily in his ear:

"If you keep coming around here any more, I'll tell the manager and he'll tell the police. Now that's the truth."

"Roberta . . ."

"Don't you call me that!"

"Won't you give me ten minutes to talk to you?"

"I never want to see you again. I don't *ever* want to."

"Roberta, I have a right to talk to you."

"No, you haven't."

"Listen, for months and months I looked for your father's house. I tried every road. I didn't know how to find you."

"I'm glad you didn't. Hurry and give me your order and then never come back again. Now I mean it."

Brush gave an order.

When she laid the dishes before him, he said: "I'll have to keep coming back here until you set a place where I can meet you for a short talk."

"Well, I won't. I'll leave this job and I'll change my room and I'll go somewhere where you can't find me. I hate you more than I hate anybody in the world. I never want to see you again and I don't want to talk to you again. What happened was *terrible* and I never want to *think* about it again. Now that's all."

The Chinese manager of the restaurant seemed to have become aware of these conversations. He strolled about in the neighborhood with affected indifference. Roberta saw him approaching and fled. He stopped at Brush's table and asked:

"Is everything all right?"

"Oh yes," said Brush, hastily, "fine. Everything's fine."

When Roberta returned with the dessert, Brush whispered, "I want you to marry me, Roberta."

"You're crazy."

"Anyway, we're married already."

"You're crazy as a coot," repeated Roberta, crying as she punched his check. She hurried away. Brush put thirty dollars into an envelope, solemnly licked the flap and wrote his name, address, and telephone number on the cover.

At a few minutes after four his landlady called him to the telephone.

"I don't want your money," said Roberta, "and I won't take it."

"Can I see you somewhere?"

There was a short pause. Then, "If you promise not to come to the restaurant any more, I'll see you for a minute."

"Now? Can I see you now?"

"I have to go back to work at six."

"Where are you?"

"I'm in a drug store, center of town."

"Can you be by the steps of the Public Library in about twenty minutes?"

"I guess so. Where's it at?"

"Why," said Brush, "it's still at Ninth and Locust."

"If I come," said Roberta, "you've got to promise it's the last time. You've got to promise to leave me alone."

"Roberta, I can't promise that. But I promise to do everything I can not to trouble you."

There was a silence, then both furtively hung up.

Roberta was already waiting at the corner when Brush arrived. It was growing colder and a strong wind had risen. She was holding her hat with one hand: the other held Brush's envelope. She kept her eyes on the distance.

"Hello, Roberta!" he said.

She held out the envelope. "Here—I won't take it," she said.

"I won't take it, either," he replied. "I owe you money all my life. I'm going to support you until you die."

She threw the envelope upon the ground. Brush picked it up.

Still looking into the distance, she began speaking in low, angry tones: "I know you think you have me in a corner. Well, you haven't."

"Oh, Roberta, you don't understand!"

"Then what *is* it? What do you *want*?"

"Don't you see? I can't bear to have you be my enemy. I can't bear living on in life while there are things in the past that haven't been put right and fixed up—fixed up with friendship. Roberta— don't you see that? So that if you'll only let me call on you now and then, I think you'll get to know my character better and I think you'll get to like me. Because the most important thing in my life is that you and I be friends."

"All right! All right! I haven't anything against you. Call it friends, if you like, only don't ever come to the restaurant again. Don't keep hunting me all the time this way."

Brush was silent a moment. Then he said, solemnly:

"Nothing can change the fact that you and I are married already."

"There you go again. That's *awful* to say a thing like that. You're crazy."

"Roberta, can I go and talk to your father about it?"

At this she became distraught. "Now that's enough," she cried. "If you do that, I'll kill myself. I'm not joking—I tell you plainly I'll kill myself."

"Sh! Roberta, I promise I won't do anything you don't want me to."

"Oh, you won't?"

"No, of course not. Now listen and don't get mad at what I am going to say: I have to be in and near Kansas City for about a week and a half. Will you let me come and see you once a day, or once every other day? just for a talk or a meal or even a movie?"

"What good is talk if all you do is to get back to that . . . that crazy idea of yours?" There was another pause. Roberta shivered. "I'll be catching cold here," she said. "I'm not supposed to stand out in the cold this way. . . . I'll tell you what you *can* do. My sister Lottie is coming to Kansas City next Sunday to see me. You can talk to *her*."

"Will you be there, too?"

"Yes. Yes."

"Where?"

"We'll meet you here on this corner at four o'clock."

"Today's only Tuesday."

"I don't care. I can't see you before Sunday or I'll go crazy, too."

"Can I write you letters?"

"Yes, only don't come to the restaurant. Now I'm going."

"Roberta, will you . . . accept this present from me?"

He took from his pocket a mass of tissue paper and unwrapped the wrist watch which had last been offered to Jessie

Mayhew. Roberta looked at it, then burst into tears and cried: "Don't you realize I don't want to have anything to do with you? Don't you see that my life's all arranged and I don't want anything new coming into it and that I don't want to think about anything that took place a long while ago? Don't you *understand* that?"

"No," said Brush, sadly.

"Well, I've got to go now," she said, and went down the street.

Left alone, Brush went into the Library and settled down to read the article on Confucius in the Encyclopædia Britannica. His mind wandered from the subject, however, and presently he took a piece of paper from his pocket and began the first of his daily letters to the woman he meant to marry.

That evening he walked by Queenie's boarding-house, staring at the lighted windows on the top floor. The lights went out and a few minutes later Bat tore down the front steps and hurried away along the street. Brush rang the bell.

"Hello, Queenie! How are you?"

"I'm fine, Mr. Brush. How are you?"

"Can we go in here and talk where they won't see us? How are they, Queenie?"

"Didn't you know? Mr. Martin's terrible sick."

"Herb?"

"Yes. He isn't here any more. He's out to a hospital ten, fifteen miles in the country. . . . Yes. Mr. Baker says the doctors say he's going to die soon. Course, I don't know."

"Have you seen him there?"

"Yes. I went out with some laundry that come back late. The car fare's twenty cents each way."

"Queenie, will you go there with me tomorrow?"

"Well, . . ."

"You can go in and see him first, and when you've finished visiting, ask him if I can come up and see him. I won't say anything to make him mad, I promise. Will you do that?"

"I suppose I could go in the morning—I suppose I could. Mrs. Kubinsky's daughter—lives next door—could come in and answer the bell."

The next morning Brush appeared with a bunch of carnations and they started off.

"It's a nice ride," said Queenie. "There's nothing I like more than a good long street-car ride in the country."

"How's Father Pasziewski, Queenie?"

"Well, you know he was sick, and hardly had he got better than he began doing everything again. He went on hikes with the Knights of St. Ludowick and he took Mary's Flowers to the Zoo, like he used to do in the old days. He did all those things and the gall stones come back. Yes, sir, sure as you live."

"Did they?"

"Yes. You know, I don't think he'll ever get well. He's awful disappointed, Mr. Brush. Way down deep he's an awful disappointed man."

"What about?"

"About the way his young people have turned out. You know all those Knights of St. Ludowick he took so much trouble with two years ago? Well, they've turned out to be practically gangsters. Yes, sir, they hold people up in the park and they steal automobiles and everything. And a lot of Mary's Flowers have become taxi-dancers."

"M-m-m! What's a taxi-dancer, Queenie?"

"Well, now you ask me, I don't quite know, myself. Only when at a dance a man hasn't got a girl himself, he pays other girls to dance with him. Something like that. Father Pasziewski says he might as well hold the meetings of Mary's Flowers at Billy Kohn's Roseland Glades."

"It's not immoral to be a taxi-dancer, is it, Queenie?"

"No, I guess not; but it's not as good as a trip to the Zoo. He just don't know what to do about it. They want to make a little money on the side, what with the depression and everything. Another thing: none of those Polish workmen that used to do bowling in the basement—none of them have jobs any more. They all live on cabbage; that's all they live on. Let's talk about something else, Mr. Brush. I declare I can't talk about the depression for very long at a time. I get dizzy."

Brush shyly glanced sideways at Queenie: "Does Father Pasziewski . . . does he still ever say anything about me?"

"I told you—Didn't I tell you?—he prays for you."

Brush turned pale. His heart stopped beating.

Queenie added: "You're on the Friday list. I'm on the Tuesday list; that was yesterday."

After a pause Brush asked, in a low voice: "You didn't just say that to be nice, did you, Queenie? Is that true?"

"Why, of course it's true! I thought I told you before."

At the end of an hour's ride they reached the hospital. It was one of a number of institutions set in a great park. Brush waited downstairs while Queenie, bearing the carnations, went into the wards. When she returned she said:

"He says you can come up. I'll wait for you here. . . . And, Mr. Brush, he says . . . he was kinda violent, Mr. Brush . . . he says, you're not to preach to him. He feels so strong about it, I guess you'd better not."

"Oh, I won't. Honest, I won't. I've learned not to. That's one of the things I've learned. Is he in pain, Queenie?"

"I don't know, but he looks terrible. I want you to be ready for it; he don't look at all well to me."

Brush entered the ward on tiptoe and looked about. He saw Herb's eyes resting on him sardonically. He sat down by the bed, appalled.

"Hello, nuts! How are you?" said Herb.

"I'm all right."

"I know. You're perfect. You're always perfect. It's great."

Brush kept his eyes on him, but made no answer.

"Well, since you've come here, I've got something to say to you," continued Herb. "I didn't send for you. You came all by yourself. See? And I'm going to do the talking. If there's any talking going on I'm going to do it. Do you get that?"

"Yes."

"Well, in the first place, you might as well know that I'm on the point of croaking, and I don't care if I do. And since that's settled, I'm going to ask you to do me a favor. All you've got to do is to say yes or no."

"Of course, I will, Herb."

"Wait 'til you hear what it is, damn you. . . . That's all, just yes or no. It's all one to me, if you can't do it. Yes or no, and then quits. Oh, don't sit there like a cock-eyed idiot with your mouth open. Shut your mouth, anyway; you never can tell what'll fly in. . . . It's not even a favor I'm asking you; it's just a proposition. I'm not going to thank you, either. It's just one of those things; take it or leave it."

A nurse who was leaning over an adjacent bed turned and said: "You mustn't get excited, Fifty-seven, or I'll have to send your caller away. Just a few minutes, that's all."

Herb groaned: "Oh, go to hell. . . . God! I hate hospitals! . . . Now, listen, Jesus, it's this way. . . . Hell, what *is* your name?"

"Brush—George Brush."

"Brush, then. I've got two hundred and forty dollars in the bank and I'm going to leave them to you so that you can do something for me. Now, I'm going to make this story short and snappy, see? I don't know whether you knew about it, but I had a wife and kid. I lived at Queenie's, and she lived with some friends of hers. We hadn't quarreled or anything . . . we weren't separated . . . it was just that way, that's all. I didn't see the point of living in the same house with her. I didn't see myself coming home to eat at regular hours, and wheeling baby-carriages about the streets and all that tripe—I'm not that kind of fella, that's all. Well, one day she beat it. She's never been seen since, so I guess it was with somebody that was passing through town. And she left the kid behind. The people she was staying with were awful sore, so I took the kid and parked it in another house where I knew some people. I pay them three dollars a week for it. So I'm going to leave you this money and, if you want to, you can see they get their three dollars a week. I couldn't give them the money in a lump or God knows what they'd do with it. Do you get the idea?"

He paused for breath. Brush started to say something, when Herb called out in anguish: "Now don't say anything. You always make a fool of yourself when you say something. If you go into that soft stuff of yours I'll kill you."

"I won't, Herb, I won't. I want to ask if I can adopt the kid . . . I mean, forever."

"Oh, I don't give a goddamn."

"What's its name, Herb? How old is it?"

"I don't know its name. . . . Oh, I guess it's called Elizabeth. It's four or five years old."

"Herb, can I have it for my own, legally?"

"Oh, I wish I hadn't brought the thing up! Drop it! Drop it! Forget it!"

"Well, say yes or no, Herb. I could bring a lawyer . . ."

"You don't need a lawyer. Just take it."

"That's fine, Herb. There's nothing I'd like more."

"Poops! Well, don't say I saddled you with anything. It's just a proposition. It's all one to me."

Herb began fumbling under his pillow. He brought out a bankbook and some blank checks.

"Herb, I don't need the money," said Brush, hastily, "I've got more now than I know what to do with."

"Shut up! Write what I tell you!"

Brush made out two checks, one for twenty dollars to Herbert Martin; one to himself for the remainder. With great difficulty Herb signed them. "In the back pages here," he added, "you'll find the kid's address. Mrs. Barton, something Dresser Street. Get that?"

"Yes."

"And underneath it's my mother's address. I give her four dollars a week. She hasn't been getting any for these last few weeks since the time when I was taken cuckoo, so I don't know what she's doing. She don't know, either, she's so full of gin. Some day when you think of it you might slip her twenty, thirty dollars, see? I don't care, though. They can all go to hell, for all I care. I'm glad I'm clearing out."

There was a long pause during which he glared angrily at the top of the windows. Brush sat stiffly beside the bed.

Herb's eyes slid toward Brush. He said, "I see that the tricks the fellows played on you didn't do you any harm."

"No, no," said Brush quickly. "I was all right next day."

"They oughtn't to put the window-curtains up so high. They don't know how to run a hospital, that's all. You'd better go now before you say something wrong, Brush. You'd better not say anything, but just go. Only, leave your address, and if I think of anything else I'll have them write it to you."

Brush went. He turned at the door and looked back. Herb had covered his face with the sheet. Brush rejoined Queenie without speaking. They walked through the grounds in silence and stood by a marked telephone pole, waiting for the street car. Suddenly Brush flung himself face downward on the grass.

"Why, Mr. Brush, what's the matter?"

"I don't want to go on living, Queenie. I don't want to go on living in a world where things like that can happen. Something's the matter with the world, through and through."

At first, Queenie did not answer. She pressed her knuckles against her mouth. Then she said, "Mr. Brush, I'm ashamed of your talking that way."

"I believe there's a God, all right; but why's he so slow in changing the world? Why does he deliberately disappoint people like Father Pasziewski, and why does he let fine fellows like Herb get so mixed up?"

"Mr. Brush, it's awful to think things like that. I won't listen to you."

"But isn't there an explanation?"

"I won't listen to you?"

Queenie covered her ears with her hands. Suddenly Brush rose and, taking hold of Queenie's wrists, firmly peered into her eyes. He said, softly, as though to himself, "Queenie, wouldn't it be terrible *if I lost my faith?*"

Queenie had no protests left in her. She stared back at him. He continued, slowly: "Even . . . then . . . I'd go on . . . just as I am, I guess . . . wouldn't I? . . . Only, I wouldn't get any pleasure out of it. The world isn't worth living in for its own sake. Anyway, I haven't lost my faith, but now I know it's not so easy as I thought it was. . . . Queenie, here's your twenty cents. I can't go back with you. I've got to walk back and think these things over."

The street car was hurtling toward them. Queenie screamed out: "You're not going to walk all that way!"

"Oh yes, I am."

Queenie was already on the step when another thought occurred to him: "Queenie, have you ever had anything to do with babies?"

"Yes."

"I'm bringing you one tonight."

"What?"

"I say that—"

"Step lively," said the conductor.

"I'm bringing you a baby about three o'clock. Herb's."

"Conductor," said Queenie, sharply, "will you hold this car a minute. . . . You'd better come and ride on this car, Mr. Brush. You're not well."

"I'm bringing an old lady, too—Herb's mother."

The conductor rang his bell. "Get on or off, lady," he said. "This car's gotta go places."

The car bore off an anxious Queenie, but not before she had leaned out of the window and called, "Now take care of yourself."

Brush walked to Kansas City. Gradually the exhilaration of the exercise and the interest of making plans for his new dependents drove away his dejection. He called on the Bartons and carried Elizabeth off to her new home. Herb's mother refused to put her foot out of her room, or to permit Brush to enter it, but she listened through a crack to the arrangements he was making with her landlady. He then sent a telegram of reassurance to Herb and sat down to tell Elizabeth the story of the Flood.

9

Ozarksville, Missouri. Rhoda May Gruber. Mrs. Efrim's hold-up man.
George Brush's criminal record: Incarceration No. 3.

In spite of the absorbing occupation that entered his life with the appearance of Elizabeth and the problems of her education, George Brush's mind was filled with the coming interview on Sunday. In order to quiet his anticipation he decided to fill in the time with work. There were a number of professional calls in the vicinity waiting to be made, but first he decided to journey some distance and confer with a certain mathematics teacher and high-school principal at Ozarksville in lower Missouri. Arriving at the town, he discovered that he had more than a day's free time on his hands—the man he had come to see was away on a tour of inspection in the rural districts—and he decided to put into practice a plan that had long appealed to him. He resolved to pass a day in silence, following the example of his master, Gandhi. From four o'clock on Thursday until four o'clock on Friday not a word would pass his lips; and to mark the occasion still more solemnly he decided that not a particle of food would enter them.

He now communicated with the outside world by means of paper and pencil. The staff of the Baker Hotel was astonished to discover that its guest had been visited by so sudden an attack of laryngitis. On Thursday night, Mr. Baker, staring at the sky from the railing of his veranda, asked Brush whether he thought it was going to snow. Brush drew out his pad and gravely wrote the word, "No." He was mistaken. The next morning he woke up to find that it had been snowing during the night; it grew warmer, however, the snow changed to rain and presently cleared to a mild winter day. He spent the morning in his room, light-headed from hunger, but rendered strangely happy by what he took to be the spiritual benefits of the experiment. Soon after two o'clock he started out for a walk, having put some apples in his pocket in anticipation of the stroke of four. He was strolling down a street looking at the houses to right and left when his glance fell upon an arresting sight. A little girl was sitting on the front steps of a house and a few yards from the sidewalk; around her neck was a placard which read, "I AM A LIAR." Brush stared at the little girl and the little girl, pursing up her mouth importantly, stared at him. He hesitated only a moment, however. He walked up the path to the house and, drawing out his pencil and pad, wrote:

"What is your name?"

The little girl took his writing materials from him and wrote, "Rhoda May Gruber."

"You can talk?" wrote Brush.

Rhoda May insisted on being given the pencil and paper again. She wrote, "Yes."

"How long have you been here?"

"Ten years."

"Talk. You can talk," wrote Brush.

"Yes," wrote Rhoda May, "only I cannot talk now because I have been noty."

"Are your father and mother home?"

"Yes."

Brush hesitated, but it was too late. The Grubers had become aware of the unusual conversation on their front steps. They came out upon the porch.

"What's goin' on here?" asked Mr. Gruber, darkly.

Brush smiled reassuringly up at him.

Mrs. Gruber said, shrilly: "Rhoda May, git up off that step. Come here to me."

Mr. Gruber followed her with his eyes. "Take that thing off your neck," he said. "What did this man say to you?"

Mrs. Gruber gave Rhoda May a sharp pull and clutched her to her skirts. Rhoda May began to cry. Mr. Gruber turned back to Brush.

"What do you want? Eh? What is it you want?"

Brush began writing on his pad.

"You're deef-'n'-dumb, is that it?"

Brush shook his head, still smiling.

"You're not deef-'n'-dumb? Then what is it? . . . Rhoda May, what did this man say to you? . . . There's something funny about this," he said, raising his eyebrows significantly. "You'd better run over to the Jones' telephone and call Mr. Warren or the sheriff." Then he turned back to Brush. "What is it you want? Are you selling something?"

Brush raised his head from his work, shook it, pointed at Rhoda May, then at the placard, and went back to his writing.

Rhoda May's wails rose louder. Her father slapped her smartly and roared: "Git in the house. Git in there. . . . You git in there, too, Mary. I'll tend to this."

Mrs. Gruber put out one trembling hand. "Now do be careful, Herman."

Brush now presented his statement: "I will be back later to talk to you about that punishment. I think you'll see what I mean."

Whereupon, walking down the path backwards, with gestures of cordiality, he returned to the sidewalk.

"You show up here again," called Gruber, "and I'll lick the hide off you, d'ya hear? I'll get the police on you, d'ya hear?"

Brush nodded, making gestures of pacification with his hands.

"You come around here and I'll knock your teeth out!" bellowed Gruber, and went into the house, slamming the door on Rhoda May's howls.

Four o'clock found Brush several miles from town, stumbling about in the mud of the road. As he looked at his watch and found that the vow was accomplished, he was filled with a satisfaction that was almost ecstasy. He turned back toward the town and did a quarter of an hour's running, then slowed down and ate an apple. He gazed with affection at the squatters' frame cabins, at the hound dogs that hesitantly approached the gates in the wire fences, at the chickens that had ventured out in the pale wintry sunshine. The path amid the dried weeds at the side of the road gave way to a sidewalk of planks. In the distance he could see a few rusty automobiles drawn up before the long arcade made by the projecting fronts of the stores beside the post-office.

At the edge of the town he came upon a store, or rather two stores thrown into one, that bore a sign: "N. Efrim, Dry Goods and Notions." One door had been boarded up. In the windows lay a disordered mass of such objects as dress patterns, slates, kites, and licorice whips. It occurred to Brush that he might buy some milk chocolate here, and seeing a row of dolls in the window, that he might take one of them as a peace-offering to the Grubers.

Mrs. Efrim was sitting by the window, knitting, when Brush entered the store. She was a wrinkled old woman with the head of an intelligent and dolorous monkey. Over a thick woolen dress she was wearing a frayed sweater, and over the sweater a short greenish-black cape trimmed with rusty braid. She pushed her spectacles farther down her nose and looked over them at Brush.

"I'd . . . I'd like a doll, please," said Brush.

Mrs. Efrim laid aside her knitting and, putting her hands on her knees, painfully rose to her feet. They inspected the dolls together.

"It's for a girl ten years old," said Brush. "I guess you may know her. Her name's Rhoda May Gruber."

Mrs. Efrim nodded. Brush told her about the placard.

"Ain't that terrible, now!" said Mrs. Efrim.

They looked at one another and became great friends. Both were pining for conversation. They agreed that that was no way to bring up children. Brush, a little mysteriously, alluded to the fact that the bringing up of little girls had recently become a problem in his life. Mrs. Efrim had six children and Brush was glad to hear about their good and bad traits. He suddenly remembered that he was hungry, and offered Mrs. Efrim an apple, adding that he had eaten nothing for twenty-four hours, but that he felt fine. When he came to pay for the doll and the milk chocolate he laid a ten-dollar bill on the counter. Mrs. Efrim, making change, had a moment's hesitation before the cash register.

"I'll go and change it at the drug store," said Brush.

"No, no. I have it. You'll see. I have it fine, only it's hid."

"Hid?"

Mrs. Efrim looked at him and nodded mysteriously. "It don't do to have money in the till these days. No, sir. It don't hurt *your* knowing where it's kep'. Look!" Whereupon she put her hand behind a bolt of cloth and drew out a packet of one dollar bills and pushing aside some spools of ribbon came upon a store of fives. "That's the way we do it."

"I see."

The purchase was completed, but Brush lingered on, looking about the shop enviously.

"Young man," said Mrs. Efrim, who had again seated herself by the window, "do you know how to thread a needle?"

"I certainly do, Mrs. Efrim. I can sew pretty well, too."

"Well, my eyes aren't as good as they used to be. My children—every morning before they go off to school and to work—every morning they thread me up five or six needles, but sometimes they give out. Now, if you could thread me two or three needles . . ."

"I'd like to."

So it was that when the hold-up man entered Mrs. Efrim's store he came upon Brush standing by the window, threading needles.

"Stick up your hands," he roared. "Stick'm up, you two!"

"Ach Gott!" cried Mrs. Efrim.

"Stand where you are and keep your mouths shut. One peep out of you and you're dead. Do you speak English?—Eh? Spika Inglis?"

"Yes," replied Brush and Mrs. Efrim.

"All right, then. Now stay where you are."

This burglar was a nervous young man, new to the work and considerably hampered by the fact that the bandana handkerchief which he had tied about his nose was continually slipping and falling about his shoulders. He was given to crouching and glaring, and what he lacked in terrifying appearance he tried to make up for by shouting and by pointing his revolver squarely at the noses of his victims. He slowly crept over to the counter, keeping his eyes and his aim on Brush, opened the cash register and swept the silver change out of the drawer. Then he began uncertainly looking about for objects of value. Brush and Mrs. Efrim stood side by side with arms upraised. Brush's face shone with happy excitement. He glanced downward, trying to meet Mrs. Efrim's eyes in an exchange of intimate amusement.

"What are you laughing at, you big hyena," said the burglar. "Wipe that smile off your face or I'll plug you."

Brush assumed a grave expression, and the burglar continued his search. There was a long pause, filled only by the rumblings in Brush's famished stomach.

At last the burglar turned and said: "I didn't come in here for two dollars and a quarter, you two. There's some more money somewhere here and I'm going to get it." He addressed Brush: "Take off your coat and throw it on the floor,—here by me. One extra move from you and you get it in the belly. Do you hear?"

"Yes," said Brush.

The burglar rested the revolver on the counter, retied the bandana about his face, and carefully went through Brush's pockets. He found two apples, a purse containing two dollars, a nail file, copies of *King Lear* and other classics, some newspaper clippings about India and an application for a marriage license.

"Can I say something?" asked Brush.

"What the hell's the matter with you—can you say something? What is it?"

"There's hardly any money in that coat, but I know where you can find some. . . . I'll pay you back, Mrs. Efrim, when it's all over."

The burglar stared at Brush, pointing the revolver at his eyes. "Well, where is it?"

"I won't say anything if you point that gun at me like that," said Brush. "You ought to know better than that."

"What's the matter with you?"

"You don't really mean to kill us, but you might kill us by accident."

"I don't, eh?"

"No, of course not. Not *kill*. Never point a gun at a person. That's a rule everybody ought to know."

"Well, I *do* mean to shoot you, so keep your face shut. Now where's this money you were talking about?"

"I *want* to tell you about it, but I won't tell you until you point that gun at the window."

The burglar turned the barrel a fraction to the left and shouted, "All right now, spit it out."

"You'll find some money on the shelf behind the cash register," said Brush, calmly, "behind that roll of blue cloth."

"*Gott—enu!*" cried Mrs. Efrim. "How can you tell him that! You're crazy! Telling him that!"

The man was looking at the bolt of cloth suspiciously: "So you say! So you say! What's the trick, eh?"

Brush said in a low, urgent whisper to Mrs. Efrim: "I'll pay you back, Mrs. Efrim. He needs it a lot more than we do. I swear to you you won't lose a cent." Then he continued to the burglar, "And there's some more in five-dollar bills behind those spools of ribbon."

Mrs. Efrim wailed still more loudly than before. Brush entered into an earnest debate with her. The hold-up man, still distrustful of the hiding-places, tried to follow the argument.

"You see, Mrs. Efrim, this is very interesting to me, because I have a theory about thieves and robbers. I'll explain it to you afterwards. Really, I'll pay you it all back."

"I don't want your money. I want my own," said Mrs. Efrim.

The hold-up man finally outshouted them: "Say, shut up, you two. What's the idea? Who do you think I am, anyway? I'm not fooling. I'm serious. Now what's all this about money over here?"

Brush repeated the directions. The man extracted the money from its hiding-places.

"All right, now. Where's some more. Out with it."

"That's all I know about over there," said Brush, "but if you'll let me put my hand down I'll get you some I have here."

"Where?"

"In my . . . my watch pocket, here."

"Say, what is this?" cried the man, as though in pain. "You keep your hands up or I'll shoot you."

"Well, I'd like to give you twenty dollars I have here."

"Keep your hands up! Say, are you yellow or cuckoo, or what? Keep your hands up. Where's this money?"

Brush motioned with his chin toward the pocket.

There was silence for a moment while they stared at one another.

Brush said, quietly: "You want money, don't you? That's what you came for. Well, I want to give you some. You need it a lot more than I do. Only you won't let me put my hand down to get it."

At that moment a gust of wind flung open the warped door of Mrs. Efrim's shop and then slammed it shut with a tremendous detonation. The current of air rushed through the room, tossing the window curtains toward the ceiling and flinging a shower of the exposed objects over the floor. The burglar was so alarmed that the gun went off in his hand and the bullet shattered the window pane. Mrs. Efrim, wailed louder than ever. The burglar let fall the revolver, jumped across the counter, and sank on one knee, still crying: "What is this, anyway? What's going on here?"

Brush picked up the gun and planted himself in the middle of the room. With furrowed brow, he pointed the barrel towards a corner of the ceiling.

"Now *you* hold up your hands," he said. "I don't believe in weapons of any kind, but I want you to stay there while I say something."

The hold-up man, swearing softly, stooped so that only his eyes appeared above the counter. Mrs. Efrim began pulling at Brush's sleeve, "Now, you make him give back that money before you do another thing."

"No, Mrs. Efrim, no! Don't you understand? This is a kind of experiment. We're going to give this man a new start in life, don't you *see*? I'll pay you back every cent that he's taken."

"I don't want your money. I want my own money. That's all I want. And I'm going to phone Mr. Warren this minute."

"No, Mrs. Efrim."

"Yes, I will."

"Mrs. Efrim," said Brush severely, "you move over there and put up your hands."

"Ach, g'rechter Gott!"

"Put up your hands, Mrs. Efrim. I'm sorry, but I know what I'm doing. Burglar," continued Brush, quietly, "what's your name?"

There was no answer.

"Do you know a trade of any kind?"

More silence.

"Have you been holding up people long?"

"Oh, shoot me and get this over with," muttered the burglar, contemptuously, but remained in hiding behind the counter. Brush was not abashed. He continued:

"I'm going to see that you leave this store with about fifty dollars in all. That'll give you room and board for a while. You go somewhere where you can think things over. Now listen. Even I can see that you'll never be a very good hold-up man."

Brush was entering into a discourse on the rewards of honesty when an unfortunate interruption occurred. A customer opened the door of the shop, an old woman who promptly put her hand over her mouth and screamed through it:

"Why, Mrs. Efrim, what's the trouble?"

"I don't know, Mrs. Robinson," replied Mrs. Efrim, sullenly. "I don't know at all."

Brush turned his head a fraction and said, curtly: "You can't come in now because we're busy here. Come back in half an hour."

"Mrs. Efrim," gasped Mrs. Robinson, "I'll call Mr. Warren," and disappeared.

"That woman's coming in here has spoiled everything," said

Brush, lowering his gun with an impatient sigh. "I guess we'll have to hurry.—Mrs. Efrim, there's a way he can escape through the back of the house, isn't there?"

"Don't ask me no questions," replied Mrs. Efrim. "I'm not going to tell you a thing."

Brush walked up to the counter and laid some bills on it. "Here's your money," he said to the burglar. "The price of the gun's in it, too. Now you can go. You'd better go out through there."

The man snatched up the money and, sidling about the room, filled up his cheeks with air, made an explosive sound, and dashed out of the door.

Brush put down the gun carefully. "That was awfully interesting, wasn't it?" he said, with a constrained laugh. "Now I want to pay you what I owe you."

Mrs. Efrim did not answer. She crossed the room and closed the till with a bang.

"Mrs. Efrim, don't be mad at me. I had to act that way to live up to my ideals."

"You're crazy."

"No, I'm not."

"You are. You're crazy. Whoever heard of anybody going out of their way to give money to a burglar. Yes, and letting him go free, too. No, I won't take your money. Look at all that's been took from you already. Now go away before the police come and arrest you."

"I'm not afraid of the police."

"Now you mind what I say—go away."

"Mrs. Efrim, if I'd done anything wrong I'd apologize. I owe you about thirty-five dollars . . ."

Mr. Warren, the town constable, appeared at the door followed by some men and by Mrs. Robinson.

"Now come out quiet," commanded Mr. Warren. "Hold up your hands and come quiet."

Brush said to Mrs. Efrim, smiling: "He thinks I did it! . . . Here I am, Officer." Mr. Warren handcuffed him. "Oh—oh, Mr. Warren," said Brush. "I hope I can eat with those things on, because I haven't eaten anything but an apple for twenty-four hours and I'm very hungry."

"Lock up your store and come with us, Mrs. Efrim," said Mr. Warren. "We'll want your story of what's been going on."

"There's nothing to tell," said Mrs. Efrim, shrilly. "It was just foolishness. No, I'm not going to leave this store. No, I'm not."

The officer insisted, however, and presently the procession was making its way down Main Street. As luck would have it Mr. and Mrs. Gruber were standing under the arcade.

"Look! Herman, look!" cried Mrs. Gruber, catching her husband's arm. "That's the man!—The kidnapper!"

"Charley Warren," said Mr. Gruber, "I charge that man with attempting to kidnap my daughter Rhoda May."

"Follow in behind, Herman," said Warren.

When they reached the jail, Brush was shown into a cell. He ate another apple, sighed heavily and went to sleep.

10

Ozarksville, Missouri. George Brush meets a great man and learns something of importance about himself. The trial.

After breakfast the next morning the jailer opened the door of Brush's cell and said:

"You can go out into the yard if you want to. Judge Carberry can't see you till this afternoon. He's out fishing."

It was mild and sunny in the open air. The yard was surrounded on three sides by the jail and on the fourth by a high wire fence on the other side of which was the jailer's house and back yard. Beside the gravel path in the jail yard stood a number of rough benches. On one of these a man lay stretched on his back, wrapped in his overcoat, sunning himself. He turned his head and examined Brush. He had a thin, sardonic face and long silky mustaches.

"Well, well," he said, "another?" and sat up.

Brush went up to him and shook his hand. "My name is George M. Brush. I come from Michigan and I sell textbooks for Caulkins and Company."

"Any birth marks?"

"What?"

The man lay down again. "My name is Zoroaster Eels. I lie on benches for a living."

Brush looked at him in surprise, but Eels turned his back on him, so Brush continued his inspection of the yard. On the other side of the fence an enormous buff-colored cat was picking its way fastidiously among the weeds. Brush made a number of ingratiating sounds, but the cat ignored him and began washing its forepaws. A woman who was hanging clothes on the line called, "Here, Bitty! Here, Bitty!" stared at Brush with revulsion, and went into the house. Brush's thought turned to physical exercise. He strode energetically about the yard and did some hygienic bending. His fellow-prisoner turned and opened one eye. He yawned and sat up: "Relax, oh, relax," he said.

Brush went over to him. "Yes, I believe in relaxation, too," he said, "but the best relaxation comes after some kind of exertion."

Brush sat down. There was a silence; then he said, "They're real good to you in this jail."

"Wonderful," said Eels, and spat. "Wonderful."

Brush realized he had made an unconsidered remark. He blushed slightly and added: "The ham and eggs, I mean, and the use of the garden."

"They aim to please," said the other.

"They don't take your fingerprints here, though."

"I guess they would for you, if you asked them to. They can see you have the right spirit. You appreciate'm. You're the kind of prisoner they like to have." Whereupon Eels lay down and shut his eyes. "They'll be sorry when you go."

"Oh, I see," said Brush, laughing. "Everything you say is a joke. I couldn't understand you at first."

The other opened his eyes and regarded Brush narrowly, then closed them again. Brush, cut off from conversation, wandered forlornly about the yard, picking up rubbish and making a neat pile of it in one corner. Presently the other rose from the bench and with an altered manner came toward him.

"Why should we quarrel?" he said. "My name is Burkin, George Burkin. Shake hands, Brush, shake hands. I'm from New York City. I'm at present unemployed, but my profession is that of a motion-picture director. Come and sit down and let's discuss our shame. I've been stuck in here for a peeping Tom. What are you here for?"

"I'm here for two reasons. First they think I was trying to kidnap a little girl, and then they think I was trying to hold up a store, or at least help a hold-up man to escape."

"I see. It was all a misunderstanding, though?"

"Yes. Except the second one, but even then I knew what I was doing all the time. Would you like to hear about it?"

"Just a minute. Have you got a cigarette?"

"No, I don't smoke."

"You don't smoke?"

"No."

"Well, let's hear about it."

So Brush told him the whole story from the vow of silence to his arrival at the jail. He then added the account of his arrest at Armina, his theory of voluntary poverty, and his theory of robbers. After he had finished there was a long pause. Finally Burkin arose and, putting his thumbs in his belt, gazed, squinting meditatively, into the sun.

"Well," he said, "I've been hunting for someone like you for a long time. To think I had to go to jail to find you."

"For someone like me?"

"Yes. Do you know what you are? You're the perfectly logical man."

Brush, for delight, could scarcely believe his ears. "I? I'm *logical*?"

"The most logical man I ever met."

"Well . . . naturally I always claimed I was logical . . . but almost everybody I meet says I'm crazy." Then he added, hesitantly, "Is it a good thing to be logical?"

Burkin strolled away a few steps without answering. When he came back he said, "Well, at least, it's no fun."

"Oh yes, it is," said Brush, hastily. "I'm the happiest man I ever met."

"Have it your own way," said Burkin.

Brush hesitated again. "Will you tell me how . . . how the misunderstanding came up that made them put you in here?"

"Sure, I will," said Burkin. He stood with one foot on the bench in a pose of nonchalance, but his words emerged with increasing violence and a nervous twitch of the left side of his face which Brush had noticed earlier became more and more pronounced. "I was standing on the lawn of a house looking in the window. The people in the next house phoned for the police and I was stuck in here. That's all." There was a pause, then he broke out: "I never explain anything. I never regret anything. I don't care a goddam what they think. If they think I've been prowling around their streets, trying to catch their hags undressing, let'm think so. Let them keep me in jail here as long as they like. I don't care. I never explain. I never try to put idiots out of their misery. See? I am what I am."

Brush held his breath. Burkin leaned over him and shouted into his face: "Listen, now listen. The day'll come when they'll be glad for me to so much as mention their goddam town. I'm a movie-director. See? I'm the best that ever was or will be. I'm the greatest artist America ever had in any line. See? I'm a movie-director. It's my business to know everything. I knock about the whole country in a Ford, just looking. That's all. One night I'm in Ozarksville, Missouri. What of it? I'm walking down the street and I see a lighted window. What of it? A man and his wife and kid are eating supper. Now when you're looking through a window at people who don't know they're being looked at, you see a lot more than you see any other way. Can you understand that?"

"Yes," said Brush, in a low voice.

"It's terrible how much you see. You see their very souls. Can you understand that?"

"Yes."

"I stayed there for hours until the police took me away. That's all. Do you like it?"

Brush said quietly: "All you have to do is to tell them—like that. They'd believe you."

Burkin shouted, "I tell you I never explain."

"I'm going to tell the judge myself," said Brush. Then slowly raising his eyes with a smile, he added, "It's a pleasure to believe you."

"Who the hell are you, anyway?" said Burkin, and walked away as though in anger. When he came back he said: "Besides, don't you know that the judge in this place is a tight old bird? He's had the town in his pocket for forty years. He doesn't even go through the forms of the law, let alone listen to anything that's said to him. You haven't got any more chance than I have. What are you looking so damned pleased about?"

"I don't know," said Brush, in a low voice. "I guess it's because I like to have things happen to me."

"You're crazy," said Burkin.

"I know," he said, smiling, "but you said I was logical."

"Have you got anything to read in your baggage?"

"Yes, I have several things in the cell there. This is all I have on me," and Brush produced a New Testament, his paper copy of *King Lear* and a pamphlet on colonic irrigation.

Burkin took the *Lear* and gave the other two back. "You mustn't separate those two," he said.

Brush stood with lowered eyes, thinking this over. "I don't like you to say things like that," he said.

"It's a big free country," replied Burkin, airily, and lying down again read *King Lear* from beginning to end.

George Brush had already become a legend of terror in the town, and by two o'clock the courtroom was filled with spectators sitting in a church-going silence. When Brush entered and took his place the silence became even more profound; the room held its breath. Brush's lips were pressed tightly together and he was paler than usual, but he looked about him with an unabashed glance. Judge Carberry had been for thirty-five years the best-known citizen in town, but when he entered all eyes rested upon him as though for the first time. He looked about him wearily, blew his nose, and sat down. He was a bald old man with small black eyes and a pointed nose set in a myriad of wrinkles that read kindliness, disillusion, and boredom. He was vexed by the unaccustomed throng and today pushed even farther than usual his habitual contempt for the procedure of the law. He grunted a few instructions to the clerk, who began to expedite matters furiously. While the charges were being read he artfully adjusted the screen of books—a vast bulwark of Blackstone—behind which it was his custom to read during sessions. He was hurrying through George Eliot and looked forward to a review of *Waverly* in the spring.

"... attempted kidnapping," mumbled the clerk "... aiding and abetting larceny ... pleads not guilty ... undertakes his own defense ..."

Mr. Warren was called. "Wa-all, I got this here phone call from Mrs. Robinson that there was this hold-up goin' on over to Mrs. Efrim's store; so I . . ."

The judge stole a paragraph or two of *Adam Bede,* then raised his head. "Both these charges against the same person?" he asked, dryly.

"Yes, Your Honor."

"Same day?"

"Yes, Your Honor."

The judge let his eyes fall on Brush in a cool, contemptuous glance. Brush returned his gaze without flinching. There was a silence. Brush raised his hand. "May I speak, Your Honor?" he asked.

For a moment it seemed as though the judge had not heard him. "What do you wish to say?"

"Your Honor, I think you ought to know there is no case here at all."

"Indeed?"

"Yes, it's all a misunderstanding. And if you'll let me tell my account of it right now we can all be out of the court building in fifteen minutes. Also, Your Honor, I can explain the case of Mr. Burkin, who you're going to see after me, and that's just a misunderstanding, too."

"Have you ever been brought before a court before?"

"No, Your Honor." Then he added, with some difficulty. "But I've been arrested before."

"Oh, you have?"

"Yes, but they were misunderstandings, too. I was let go in an hour."

"Would you feel able to tell the court what you were arrested for, and where?"

"I'd be glad to, Your Honor."

"We should be glad to hear it."

"The first time was in Baton Rouge, Louisiana. I was arrested for riding in a Jim Crow car. I believe in the equality of races, Your Honor, in the brotherhood of man, and I rode in the Jim Crow car to show that I believed it. They arrested me. The second time—"

Judge Carberry stopped him with a gesture of the hand. The judge looked slowly and a little dazedly over the spell-bound audience, then turned toward the court stenographer as though to make sure that this testimony was being recorded. He then looked at the tops of the windows as though he were debating as to whether he should issue orders for new sashes. Finally his gaze returned to Brush. He blew his nose and said, politely, "Kindly continue."

"The second time was about a month ago in Armina, Oklahoma. I was drawing out my savings from a savings-bank and I told the president of the bank that in my opinion savings-banks are practically immoral. They arrested me for that."

"Had you any reason to think that the bank was unsound?"

"I didn't mean that, Your Honor. I meant that all banks like that are due to fear and breed fear in the people. It's a theory of mine and it takes quite a while to explain."

"I see," said the judge. "Your ideas aren't the same as most people's, are they?"

"No," said Brush. "I didn't put myself through college for four years and go through a difficult religious conversion in order to have the same ideas as other people have."

Again the judge allowed his astonished gaze to wander about the room. He saw Mrs. Efrim, sitting in the midst of her six children, all dressed in their best clothes and staring up at him with awe-struck eyes. He saw the Grubers and Rhoda May scrubbed to startling pinkness and wearing a starched white party dress. "You may be seated," he said to Brush, then mumbling a few words to the clerk, he left the room. He went to the telephone and called up his wife. He talked slowly with many pauses and with an affected indifference.

"Oh, Emma," he said, looking down his nose and scratching his cheek. "... euh ... euh ... better get your sewing and come down to the courthouse."

"What do you mean, Darwin?"

"Well ... well ... you might be interested in something that's going on here."

"Now, Darwin, if it's something improper, you know I don't like such things."

The judge slowly passed his tongue over his front teeth. "No ... oh, no ... perfectly proper."

"Well, what is it, Darwin?"

"... there's a type here ... little out of the ordinary. Better come down. Bring your sewing."

"Now, Darwin, I won't have you tormenting some poor prisoner. I know you. I know you and I won't have it."

The judge's shoulders shook. "Prisoner's tormenting me, Emma ... seems like. We're putting on a little show today. Call up Fred and see if he's free. You can bring Lucile, too."

Fred Hart had been mayor of Ozarksville for twenty years. Lucile was his wife. The Harts and the Carberrys had played bridge together three nights a week for a longer time than that.

"Well, if I come down I want you to behave, Darwin. I've told you a thousand times I don't like you when you're sarcastic."

The judge returned to the bench. He gave the prisoner an awe-inspiring glance. He saw to it that the court marked time until the arrival of his wife. Mr. Gruber was sworn in and told his story of indignant virtue ... only and treasured child. He dwelt upon the peekyuliar behavior of the accused, his pretense of being unable to speak. The whole court could see for itself that the accused could speak as well as anyone else. Brush raised his hand, but the judge sharply ordered him to lower it. Gruber droned on and the judge caught half a chapter of *Adam Bede*. Mrs. Gruber was called and gave a flighty, incoherent account of the affair. At last the judge saw his wife and the Harts slipping into the last row of seats. He put a book mark into his volume and laid it to one side. Mrs. Gruber was dismissed and Brush was called upon.

"What's your business, young man, and what are you doing in Ozarksville?"

"I travel for Caulkins and Company, publishers of textbooks for school and college. I came to town to call on Superintendent MacPherson."

"I see. Have you ever had an impediment in your speech?"

"No, Your Honor."

"Did you have laryngitis yesterday?"

"No, Your Honor."

"Can you explain why you pretended to be incapable of speech yesterday?"

"Yes, Your Honor, easily."

"I should like to hear it."

"Your Honor," began Brush, "I am very interested in Gandhi."

The judge laid down his pencil sharply and said, in a loud voice: "Young man, you will please give me the answers to my questions and nothing else."

Brush squared his shoulders. "I am, Your Honor. It's the only way I can answer them. I . . . I've been studying Gandhi's ideas lately and—"

Judge Carberry threw an ecstatic glance at his wife, then drawing his hand down his face he roared: "Stop that! Stop it right now! I will not be made a fool of in my own courtroom. Young man, this is no time for desultory conversation. Do you realize that you're standing here under two very serious charges? Do you?"

"Yes," said Brush, his jaws set.

The judge lowered his eyes and said, more quietly: "Now continue and let's have no nonsense."

Brush remained silent. There was a long pause.

The judge looked up. "Do you wish to add contempt of court to your other charges? Do you—Very well. Young man, perhaps you do not understand your position here. You have been charged with two offenses, either of which might send you to state prison for a very long time. You have been in Ozarksville for a little less than two days and already you have drawn across it a trail—a trail, I say—of suspicion and confusion such as it has not seen in fifteen years. And yet you conduct yourself before me *frivolously,* yes, *frivolously* in open court."

Brush turned even paler, but remained firm. "I'm not afraid of anything or anybody, Your Honor," he said. "All I want to do is to tell the truth, and you keep misunderstanding me."

"Well, begin again, then. And if you bring up the name of Gandhi again I shall put you in jail for a few days, where you can cool off."

Brush wiped his forehead. "The reason I didn't talk to anybody yesterday until four o'clock was that I had taken a vow of silence," he said.

The judge suddenly grasped the connection. When he reappeared, still panting, from behind his barrier of books, he glanced at his wife. Mrs. Carberry shook her fist at him.

"I see. Go on," he said.

"That vow of silence," continued Brush, "was in imitation of a certain leader in India. Soon after two o'clock I went out for a walk. I saw that girl sitting on the steps of her house. She had a sign around her neck that said 'I am a liar.'"

"What?" asked the judge.

"'I am a liar.'"

When this confusion was cleared up, everyone took a deep

breath and the judge took a drink of water. He asked, "What was your purpose in approaching the child?"

"I didn't think that was any way to punish a child. I think lying's a bad thing, but I don't think that's the way to punish a child that does lying."

"I see. Are you a father, may I ask?"

Brush was silent a moment. "No," he said, in a low voice. "I don't think I am."

"I *beg your pardon?*" asked the judge, learning forward.

"Not that I know of," said Brush.

Judge Carberry shuffled the papers on his desk. "Well, we won't go into that now," he said. He then asked, loudly, "Is this little girl in court?"

Rhoda May was led to the witness stand. She was given laborious instructions about the oath and the Bible, but she entered into the proceedings with perfect assurance and unbounded enjoyment.

"Will you tell us what happened, Rhoda?" asked the judge.

Rhoda May turned and faced the audience. She kept her eyes proudly fixed on her mother's face. For a moment she turned back to the judge. "My name's Rhoda May," she said. "I was sitting at my house and that man came up the walk to my house and I knew he was a bad man right away."

"Why were you sitting on the steps, Rhoda May?"

"Because I'd been bad."

"Yes, and what did this man do?"

"He said for me to go away to a bad place, and I said no, because I love papa and mamma best."

"He asked you to go away with him?"

"Yes, but I didn't go, because I love papa and mamma best."

"Rhoda May, be careful. You must tell the truth. Did he *say* this with his mouth, or did he write it down?"

"He wrote it down, Judge Car-Berry. But I knew he was a bad man kidnapper right off. He looked at me like *this* and then I gave him a good kick. I gave him a good kick. And he began to run away and I ran after him and gave him another good kick in the face, and—"

"Mr. Gruber!" roared the judge.

"Yes, Judge Carberry."

"Take your daughter home. We will now proceed to the second charge."

A shocked silence ensued while the Grubers with lowered heads passed down the aisle.

The judge then said in a courteous tone: "Mrs. Efrim, will you be so good as to give us an account of the events that took place in your store yesterday afternoon?"

Mrs. Efrim, rustling in a voluminous black silk dress, edged her way past her children's knees and took her place on the stand. The judge paid her a deference that touched on gallantry. Her hand was scarcely lowered from the oath when she broke out:

"Judge Carberry, I can't tell you how terrible I feel to be in court this way. I've lived in this town forty years—my husband and I, may his soul be at rest!—without ever coming in this building, beyond paying our taxes in the basement, Judge Carberry."

"But, Mrs. Efrim, there's no reflection on yourself. I assure you—"

"You can say what you like, Judge Carberry," she said, hugging her elbows woefully, "and it's very kind of you, but it don't change the facts."

"Now, now, Mrs. Efrim," said the judge, leaning forward, "The Court considers it an honor that you should be kind enough to appear here today. Yourself and my friend Nathan Efrim have been among the most respected citizens in this town for many years and the Court holds it a privilege to have you among us today."

Mrs. Efrim cast a mighty glance at her six openmouthed children and started to tell her story.

"Really, Judge Carberry . . . Your Honor . . . I have no charges to make against that young man. I guess he's just different from the rest of us, that's all. Even to this minute I don't know what happened. At first I thought he was a nice young man." Here she looked at him a moment. "I don't know what to think, Your Honor."

"Thank you, Mrs. Efrim, will you simply tell us what took place."

"Well, he came in. I was sitting by the window, knitting, when he came in . . . and he hadn't been there two minutes when it seemed like he began—I don't know how else to say it, Your Honor—he began *winding* himself into my confidence."

"You don't say?"

"I don't know what else I can say. Your Honor, Judge Carberry. There's nothing he didn't do. He tried to give me an apple; he threaded me needles—"

"I beg your pardon?"

"He threaded me three-four needles. He asked me my children's names. He . . . he bought a doll. Yes, sir. He asked me to eat an apple and he said himself he hadn't eaten a thing for twenty-four hours. And then he . . . and then he got me to show him where my money was hid."

"Why, Mrs. Efrim, I never heard such a story in my life."

"Well, it was funny, Your Honor. There's nothing he didn't do, but I must say I liked him until he began acting queer when the hold-up man came in."

"Will you tell us about that, please?"

Mrs. Efrim, however, was unable to tell it. From her confused narrative Judge Carberry received the impression that there were three or more hold-ups, a storm, broken window panes, and some very curious exchanges of money. He thanked her elaborately, however, and she resumed her place among her children, who scarcely so much as dared to look at her sideways, after her excursion into the important world. Mrs. Robinson was called. Her testimony was to the effect that there was no hold-up man with a handkerchief about his face—no one beyond the accused standing in the middle of the store with a revolver in his hand terrorizing Mrs. Efrim. This testimony was confirmed by Mr. Warren.

Finally Brush was called.

"Young man, did you obtain from Mrs. Efrim the secret of the hiding-places of her money?"

"Yes. She . . ."

"Did you tell the hold-up man where her money was hid?"

"Yes, Your Honor, but I meant to pay her back."

"Did you take the gun yourself and hold up Mrs. Efrim?"

"Yes, but I never meant—"

"Don't tell me what you meant or what you didn't mean. All I want is the facts, and the facts speak for themselves, don't they? Did you allow the hold-up man to escape when you knew the deputy sheriff was coming?"

Brush was silent.

"Are you going to answer that question?"

Brush continued looking stonily before him. The judge waited. Finally he began speaking in a low, penetrating voice:

"You've gone into another vow of silence, I suppose? And no wonder! There *is* nothing to say. The facts speak for themselves. You were going to tell me this is all a misunderstanding. You were sure we were going to be out of this courtroom in a quarter of an hour. . . . Put your hand down! . . . You wound your way into Mrs. Efrim's confidence, did you? You threaded needles for her! You even went so far as to buy a doll, did you? No wonder you found out where she had hidden her money."

Here the judge was so overcome with pleasure at his own wit that he descended behind the barrier of books and had a fit of coughing. When he emerged he discovered that Brush was descending the steps into the auditorium and apparently intended to leave the building.

"Where are you going *now?*" shouted the judge.

"I won't be talked to like that, Judge Carberry," said Brush.

"You're under arrest; Officer, restrain that man."

Brush said, "You won't let me speak!"

"Come back here. You're under arrest. So you've changed your mind? Now you want to talk, do you?—*Where are you going?*"

"Oh, I'm going to the jail, all right. I'd rather sit in jail and make rope than be treated like you're treating me, Judge Carberry. You haven't heard my explanations yet."

At this moment, to the great excitement of the already dazzled audience, Mrs. Carberry, very red in the face, advanced down the aisle of the auditorium.

"Darwin, you behave yourself," she said. Then turning to Brush, she added: "Young man, don't you mind what he says. You tell your story. That's just his way. He doesn't mean it. You go back and tell your story."

"Order! Order!" cried the judge. "Go back to your seat, ma'am, and leave the running of this court to me. . . . Now, Mr. Brush, I'll give you another chance." But the judge could not resist the addition of one further embellishment to his afternoon, and called after his retreating wife: "Ma'am, if you attend properly to the running of your home, I shall try to attend to the running of my court." Whereupon he disappeared behind the bulwark of his Blackstones, from which he presently appeared, much shaken, wiping his eyes. "Mr. Brush," he said, grandly, "have you an explanation for your astonishing conduct yesterday afternoon?"

"Yes, sir, I have."

"We are ready to hear it. And kindly remember you are under oath. . . . One minute!" He took a deep drink of water, mopped his face, and bade the stenographer look sharp.

Brush gave a clear and detailed account of the events in Mrs. Efrim's store. When he had finished, the judge sat in silence a moment, looking at his wife. He took off his glasses, breathed on them, and slowly polished them. The audience followed his movements in silence. He then turned to Mrs. Efrim:

"Mrs. Efrim, have you anything to add or correct in that story?"

"No, Judge Carberry. Everything he said really happened."

"Well, now at least we have an idea of what this is all about. Now, Mr. Brush, can you explain to the court your reasons for giving Mrs. Efrim's money to the hold-up man?"

"Yes . . . it's all based on a theory of mine. I mean on two theories of mine."

"What!"

"Yes, and a lot of it I owe to Gandhi."

"There's Gandhi again!" said the judge, resignedly.

"It's all based on *ahimsa,* Your Honor, but before I get to *ahimsa* I have to tell you what I think about money."

So Brush told the court about voluntary poverty.

"And do you live by voluntary poverty?" asked the judge.

"Yes, Your Honor. And the point of that is this: a *poor* person—even if he's a millionaire—is a person whose head's always full of anxious thoughts about money; and a rich person is a person whose head's not full of anxious thoughts about money."

"Thank you, Mr. Brush," said the judge, dryly, "I'm sure we're all the better today for that thought."

"And the poorest persons in the world, therefore are beggars and robbers. Now you'll see what I mean when I say that a robber is a beggar that doesn't know he's a beggar."

"And now, Mr. Brush, I'm going to ask you what good it does to give your money away to these robber-beggars of yours?"

"It's easy to see that. When you give money to a robber you do two things: you show him that he's really a beggar at heart, and you make a certain strong impression on his mind that—"

"Yes, you do. You give him the impression that you're a coward or fool."

Brush smiled and shook his head. "I think I can explain this idea in another way. It's my favorite idea in the world and I've spent a lot of time on it. Your Honor, I'm a pacifist. If they put me in a battle I wouldn't shoot anybody. Now suppose that I was in a shell-hole and I met an enemy who was about to shoot me, and suppose I tore the gun out of his hands. Naturally he'd expect me to shoot him, but of course I wouldn't. That would make an impression on his mind, wouldn't it?"

"Yes, it would."

"Well, and if I pointed out some hidden money to a burglar that was trying to steal some money from me, that would make an impression on his mind, too."

"Yes, it would: I say again they'd think you were a fool."

"Judge, that might be what they'd call it, but at the back of their minds they would be taught something."

"Have you finished?"

"Yes, Your Honor."

"So you gave forty or fifty dollars to a burglar in order to make an impression on his mind?"

"Yes."

"Suppose that the man in the shell-hole shot you. What becomes of your lesson to him then?"

"Well, Judge, *ahimsa* would have been in my mind. That's Gandhi's word for it, Your Honor. And if somebody has *ahimsa* in his mind, I believe it has a chance of jumping from mind to mind."

"What becomes of *ahimsa,* Mr. Brush, if you suddenly come upon a man who's attacking your sister?"

"Yes, I've heard that before. Everybody brings up that argument about your sister being attacked, and I get angry about it. What if a thousand sisters were attacked. Let them be attacked. If the attackers are met with *ahimsa* the attackers will learn about it.

That's the way the idea will spread. Somebody's sisters—millions of them—are being attacked all the time, and things aren't getting any better; so it's time to try a new way to cure it. Let some of your sisters be attacked. Before the new idea can jump around the world from one person's mind to another's there will have to be a lot of people attacked."

"I see. I see. And you want us to go about releasing murderers and thieves, on the chance that this impression is made on their minds. Do you advise the Department of Justice to collect as many thieves as possible and give them each a hundred-dollar bill? Is that it?"

"Well, look how things are now in your system. People go on committing crimes, and the government goes on committing crimes to punish them."

"Oh, it does!"

"Yes, sir. It's a crime to kill, and the government does that, and it's a crime to lock somebody up in a room for years on end, and the government does that by the thousands. The government commits thousands of crimes in a year. And every crime makes more crimes. The only way out of this mess of crimes is to try this other way."

The judge was silent, stroking his face. The silence was filled by the anxious scribbling of the stenographer and the sounds of automobile horns from the street. He glanced at the audience which sat watching him with fallen jaw.

"And where did you get that idea?" he asked.

"It's mine and Tolstoi's."

While the judge spelled out the name for the stenographer, Brush drew from his pocket a little blue pamphlet, *Sayings of Leo Tolstoi,* and passed it up.

"Have you any other sources upon your person, Mr. Brush?"

Whereupon Brush began to draw similar little pamphlets from all his pockets. They were gravely passed up to the bench— Epictetus, *Thoughts from Edmund Burke, Sayings of Great States-*

men, Sayings of Great Philosophers, Stories from Famous After-Dinner Speakers. The judge passed the books to the stenographer. He then collected himself and said, dryly:

"Well, it's all sort of poetical and sentimental, Mr. Brush; but it's all very unlike the facts of life. And it seems to be based upon a profound misunderstanding of the criminal's mind."

"I don't know what you mean by the criminal's mind, Your Honor. All I mean is, a criminal is a human being who thinks that the whole universe hates him. I think that awful things must go on in your mind when you think that the whole universe hates you. And the certain impression that we try to make on their minds is the impression that they are not hated."

Again the judge paused. Then he said, "And you expect the United States to—"

Brush interrupted him: "Judge Carberry, people like me, who believe in *ahimsa*—it's not our business to worry as to whether other people do or not. It's our business to do it ourselves and to take every chance, like this, to talk about it to other people. It's the truth and so it'll spread about the world of its own accord."

"Mrs. Efrim, do you feel that this explains what this young man did with your money?"

Mrs. Efrim rose hesitantly. "Judge Carberry . . . I guess he means what he says."

"Court is dismissed," said the judge.

The clerk said, quickly: "There's this other man, Your Honor—Burkin, charged with—"

"Court is dismissed," repeated the judge.

The clerk was required to repeat the announcement a number of times in addition, for the audience remained motionless in its seats, unwilling to quit so bewildering a display, but finally the Carberrys and the Harts took Brush in the mayor's car to the jail to call on Burkin.

"Let me explain about Burkin," said Brush. "He's a—"

"No. Wait 'til we get there," said the judge.

Burkin sat in his cell, rereading *King Lear*. He was brought into the office.

"What's it all about?" asked the judge.

Burkin was pale and contemptuous. "You wouldn't understand," he said. "You wouldn't understand. Go and give me your twenty days. I've got some letters to write."

The judge was silent, listening to him gravely.

Burkin continued: "Only leave me Little Rollo here. Big kidnapper and hold-up man. Big public enemy.—The law's a farce and you know it."

"Come on," said the judge. "What is it? Looking in windows?"

Burkin began to tremble and snap his fingers with excitement. "I tell you you wouldn't understand. Go tell the goddam mayor there never was anybody in Ozarksville who ever understood anything and there never will be."

Brush was suffering acutely. "Let me explain?" he asked, in a whisper.

"All right, Brush. What's the matter with your friend?"

Brush explained.

The judge turned to Burkin. "Even I can understand that, Burkin," be said. "Gentlemen, would you rather have your supper here in the jail or would you rather find it somewhere else? Have either of you got a car?"

"Yes."

"Well, I don't want to hurry you, gentlemen, but it would be less embarrassing for us if you decided to eat in some other town."

The prisoners gathered their things together and went down the hall.

Judge Carberry put his hand on Brush's shoulder and stopped him. Brush stood still and looked at the ground. The judge spoke with effort:

"Well, boy . . . I'm an old fool, you know . . . in the routine, in the routine. . . . Go slow; go slow. See what I mean? I don't like to think of you getting into any unnecessary trouble. . . . The human race is pretty stupid, . . . Doesn't do any good to insult 'm. Go gradual. See what I mean?"

"No," said Brush, looking up quickly, puzzled.

"Most people don't like ideas. Well," he added, clearing his throat, "if you do get into any trouble, send me a telegram, see? Let me see what I can do."

Brush didn't understand any of this. "I don't know what you mean by trouble," he said. "But thanks a lot, Judge."

They shook hands and Brush climbed into the car beside Burkin. Burkin bent over the wheel with a black expression on his face, but Brush waved back at the judge, the mayor and the warden and disappeared down the street.

11

A road in Missouri. Chiefly conversation, including the account of a religious conversion. George Brush again sins against ahimsa.

When they had reached the edge of the town, Burkin asked, "Where do you want to go?"

"Kansas City, if it's all right with you," said Brush. "You see . . . I expect to get married Monday or Tuesday and I want to get there Sunday so as to talk it over."

"You don't say!"

"Yes, it's a long story and I'd rather not tell it just yet."

"That's all right with me, but there are some other things I'd like to know. How did it happen the judge and the mayor had to come to the jail to see us off? What was all that diddling about? Are they all crazy in that town or did you infect'm?"

Brush gave him a detailed account of the trial.

"Well, well," said Burkin, shaking his head, "such goings-on! You'd better look out, Brush. You can't go about long with upsetting ideas like that and get away with it. One of these days you'll be teasing the bourgeoisie one too many and they'll crack down on you."

Brush looked at him inquiringly, but said nothing. They decided to postpone their supper indefinitely and drove on for a time in silence over the plain. In the distance an occasional silo rose among some farm buildings. The first stars began to appear above a spiritless sunset.

"Stop!" cried Brush as they passed a man beside the road, his thumb extended for a hitch. "Stop for him!"

"Not on your life!"

"Stop, I say!" cried Brush, putting his hand on the wheel.

"You can't do that in this country," said Burkin. "It's not safe."

Brush pulled back the brake. "What are you afraid of everything for?" he said.

"He might be another hold-up man, y'fool! He'd take our car off us."

"I'll buy you another car," said Brush. "Always stop for hitchhikers. Always do it, if you've got room."

Burkin gave in and began backing the car. He said: "Oh, you're rich enough for anything, aren't you? All right. He's your responsibility."

The man came running up.

"Get in, Pete," said Burkin. "The car's yours."

Not until the newcomer had been bestowed in the back seat among the suitcases, and the car had gathered speed, did Brush recognize who it was. "It's Mrs. Efrim's hold-up man," he said.

The man leaped for the door, but dared not jump out. "I gotta get outa here," he cried in a throaty voice. "Lemme out."

"Shut up and settle down," said Burkin. "We won't hand you

over. Brush here saved you from the law once already, didn't he? So pipe down and take a snooze. And as for you, Brush, don't you lecture him. The poor geezer's suffered enough from you already."

"I don't wanna stick around with you guys. Go on, lemme out," the man repeated but receiving no answer, he relapsed into a brooding silence.

Brush said into Burkin's ear: "I wish I knew what he was thinking. It would be very important to know. I think it's one of the most important things in the world to know what goes on in a person's mind when he's been treated with *ahimsa.*"

"Nothing goes on in his mind," said Burkin. "All he's got is a few visceral reactions. He lives like a fox at the edge of a chicken farm."

"You're wrong," said Brush. "He's got a soul, a complicated soul like anybody else."

"Lemme out, you guys. All I wanna do is get out and walk."

"What's your name?" asked Burkin.

"Hawkins."

"Where do you want to go, Hawkins?" The man remained silent. Burkin continued: "What do you do? What's your trade? Come on, tell us your story. We've got two or three hours ahead of us. Come on, out with it. How did it all happen?"

Hawkins refused to answer.

Brush said, in a low voice: "You see, he's pretty uncomfortable, and that's what I expected. It's this way: The Bible says that if a man does something bad to you, you ought to give him the chance to do more bad to you, like giving him your other cheek to slap. That's in the Sermon on the Mount. But I always thought that ought to be changed a little. If you do pure good to a man that's harmed you that shames him too much. No man is so bad that you ought to shame him that way. Do you see? You ought to do just a little bit of bad in return, so he can keep his self-respect. Do you see what I mean?"

"Pretty subtle for me," said Burkin.

Hawkins became violent. "If you don't lemme outa here I'll break every window in this car," he cried, and smashed one of the side windows.

Brush leaned over the back of the seat and gave Hawkins a cuff on the side of the head. "Sit down there quiet, Hawkins," he said.

"Brush, I don't like that," said Burkin. "Looks like you're reneging on *ahimsa* for us."

"I didn't really hurt him," whispered Brush. "I'm experimenting."

There was silence for a time, when Brush felt a sudden blow on the back of his head.

"Hawkins, you mustn't do that," he said. To Burkin he said, confidentially: "Isn't this interesting? You see what it means? It means that bad people can't bear to be benefited by anyone. Now I'll punish him a little so as to restore his self-respect."

Brush turned and, keeling on the cushions of the front seat, grasped Hawkins' shoulders and shook him violently.

The car was entering a village. Burkin said over his shoulder, "Have some eats with us, Hawkins?"

"No."

"Aw, keep your chin up, Hawkins! What the hell's the matter with you? Have some eats. We'll pay for it."

They stopped the car before a lunchroom. Hawkins leaped out and darted up an alley.

Brush smiled after him. "I think that proves everything," he said.

Burkin did not answer. They sat down on the high stools and had a series of hamburger sandwiches, pouring scalding coffee down on top of them. At last Burkin said:

"How did they take that about voluntary poverty?"

"All right, I guess. They listened."

"Did you ever gain any converts with it, Brush?"

"You never know. I think it works in people's minds and perhaps they begin to practice long after."

They ordered some pie, and Brush resumed:

"For instance, I once talked to some millionaires about it."

"My God!"

"They were the only millionaires I ever met and naturally I was very interested in them. When I'm on a train I talk to everybody, and once on a train I fell into conversation with a young couple and somehow the conversation got around to voluntary poverty."

Here Burkin began laughing and choking so that he had to be beaten on the back.

"I was telling you about this couple," continued Brush. "It seems she'd been a schoolteacher in a small Oklahoma town and she'd married the baggage agent down to the depot. He still had a red neck and red wrists, as though he ought to have been in overalls still, but he was a good serious fellow; and she was a serious girl, too. She had on a brown dress and she was pretty and serious, and I liked them both. And I told them all about voluntary poverty. Well, after they had been out to lunch in the dining-car they came back to see me and by that time they were pretty excited. They had been talking it over, and so they told me their story. They both talked at once, almost, and while they were talking she kept her hand on his hand. It seems that oil had been found on their land and they were worth almost three million dollars and they didn't know what to do about it."

"I can't wait for the end of this story," said Burkin. "Tell me, how much did they give you?"

"Naturally, I wouldn't take it," said Brush.

"All right, go on."

"They didn't know what to do with it. They'd already given a hospital and a park to their home town and they began by giving baskets of groceries to all the poor people, but soon they saw that was foolish, just to give hundreds of baskets of groceries every week."

"Well, what did you tell them to do?"

"You know what I told them? I told them they'd never be happy as long as they had it. I told them to go back to the school-house and the baggage depot."

"That's great. Don't you know that the townspeople would hate them?"

"The townspeople hated them already when they stopped giving groceries. But this couple didn't want to live in any other town."

"Tell them to go abroad for a while."

"They did go abroad. They expected it would cost them a good deal of money, but when they got back it had only cost them two thousand dollars. They said they hadn't missed a thing, either, but that they didn't like doing foolish things that cost money."

"What did they say when you tried to drive them back to poverty?"

"The girl cried."

"So they tried to palm the money off on you?"

"You see, the reason they came back from the dining-car was because they wanted me to give away some of the money for them. They were Methodists and they had read the Bible and they believed you should give away one-tenth of your earnings every year. Only they couldn't think of any real good ways of doing it. It was a kind of funny situation, because they were getting off at the next station and had to talk fast. There he sat with his fountain pen out, trying to write me a check up to two thousand dollars."

"Didn't you take it?"

"No, I couldn't take it. Don't you see that giving is a thing you can never do for anybody else? That's a theory of mine. If you give without feeling your gift with every inch of yourself—"

"That's all right. All I want's the facts. You can keep the theories to yourself. So you sent the little millionaires off like that?"

"Yes."

"Is the story over?"

"Yes."

"Let's get back to the car." When they reached the pavement, Burkin added, "God! you're a fool!"

They drove on in silence. Brush felt Burkin's soured resentment. Finally Burkin said, in an even, leaden voice:

"It's a good thing you haven't got more stuff. Yep, you might cause a lot of harm, fooling around with people's lives. You might start a new religion or something."

"What do you mean, stuff?"

"Brains. Brains. Personality. Stuff."

Brush was silent a moment. Then he said, "It's not very nice to say things like that."

"Take it or leave it."

They drove on farther in silence. When they approached the lights of the next town, Brush began leaning over the back seat where the luggage was. "I think I'll get out here," he said, pulling at his suitcase.

"What's the matter? Hell! What's the matter with you?"

"I don't want to ride with you if you think that way about me."

Burkin was all amazement. "What did I say?"

"What you said back there—that I hadn't any . . . brains or personality. I don't like what you said back in the jail-yard about the New Testament, either. And I don't like the jokes you keep making about . . . well, about women. So I think I'd better get out here, if you'll stop the car, please."

"God damn it! get out and stay out!" cried Burkin, violently. "I'm not going to twa-twa like a sewing-circle for anybody. Get out before I kick you out. You're the damnedest prig I ever saw. You're a bag of wind. Get out of here."

Brush was still leaning over the back of the seat, extracting his suitcase from Burkin's extraordinary collection of goods. His confusion was increased by his need to fumble for a handkerchief.

Burkin stared at him sharply, then exclaimed: "Oh, you cry, too, do you?" Suddenly he burst out laughing. "You weep and blush and everything, don't you? Brush, you're wonderful! Say, put the suitcase back, put it back. I apologize. I won't do it any more. I apologize for everything." And again he went off into a violent fit of laughter.

Brush hesitated. "I can't stay here . . . if you don't take me seriously," he said.

"Of course I do! What are you saying! You're all right. Stick around. I wouldn't dump you out in a forsaken hole like this for anything. I apologize, and of course I take you seriously. I don't agree with you always . . . but, oh! I take you seriously, all right!"

"Well," said Brush, relenting, "I'd have been sorry to have left you in the middle of a quarrel like that. It's happened too often lately, just when I had begun to be friends with somebody. That's why I did what you called 'cry.'"

So Brush dried his eyes and the journey was resumed. From time to time Burkin was shaken by after-reflections of his fit of laughter. This made Brush uncomfortable, but finally he smiled a little sheepishly himself. At last he said in a low voice:

"I think I know what you meant by saying I was a prig—and you aren't the first person that's said it, either—but I don't mean to be one. That's the only way I can be and still hold on to my main ideas about life. Do you see what I mean?"

"All right. Let's not talk about it," said Burkin.

It was now a cold starlit night. The road ran smoothly over the prairie. Brush was commanded to talk in order to prevent the driver from falling asleep at the wheel, so he explained the business of selling textbooks. From there he went on to relate some of the adventures of the road—of how he had called on the great singer,

Madame de Conti, at the Iowa City Musical Festival and of how she had taken a great fancy to him, even inscribing her picture "To my good friend, the true American George Busch, child of Walt Witmann's hopes"; of how he had been offered thirty-five thousand dollars to marry Mississippi Corey; of how he had gone for four days without food in order to experience what Russian students had suffered, and to share some of the trial of the Mahatma; of how he had taken a bus from Abilene, Texas, to Los Angeles in order to look at an ocean.

Burkin listened with an even level of attention that finally had something ominous in it. After a pause he asked:

"How did all this start, anyway? Where'd you catch the religious bug in the first place? At home?"

"Oh no! My people don't believe anything. They just live on from day to day. I didn't use to think about such things, either. Through the first years in college I just lived on that way, too. I was only interested in athletic scores and collecting stamps. Then suddenly I was converted in the middle of my sophomore year at college."

"What college was that?"

"Shiloh Baptist College, at Wallingkee, South Dakota, a very good college. I was president of the class, and I was very interested in politics, too—school politics, I mean. One day I saw a poster that a girl evangelist had come to town. She had set up a tent down by the railroad tracks and was holding meetings twice a day. Her name was Marian Truby. Her photograph was on the poster and it seemed like maybe her face was beautiful, so I went the first night just to look at her. Well, it turned out that she was not only a very beautiful girl, but a very wonderful speaker, too. I was converted that first night and I went forward to testify to it, and my life has been changed ever since. I went to every one of her meetings and after that I took every religion course there was in the college.

Then the next most important thing in my life was when I began to read about Gandhi. I got hold of the life that he wrote of himself, and that gave me a lot more ideas—"

"Hold on here! Did you ever talk to the girl evangelist?"

"Only a minute or two," said Brush, reluctantly.

"What happened?"

"I didn't want to tell you about it . . . but since you've asked me . . . The last night of the meetings I went around to the back of the tent to tell her what a lot she'd done for me. She must have been pretty tired after preaching two sermons a day for a week and leading the hymns . . . and besides that she used to walk up and down the aisles and talk to people who were hesitating. . . . I don't like to tell you this because you might not understand it like I do. . . . I waited until the rest of the people had gone so that I could make it a little more personal. There was no door to knock on so I went right in. She was sitting in a sort of dressing-room and she was sort of moaning—"

"Did you say moaning?"

"Yes, moaning and groaning. And an older woman was standing over her, sticking a hypodermic syringe into her arm."

"You don't say!"

"Now that I know more about life I know what that was. But even that doesn't change my idea about all the good she did to me and hundreds of other people."

"Did you speak to her?"

"Yes, but she didn't look up. The older woman was mad and drove me right away."

"Have you ever seen her since?"

"No. I wrote her a letter, but she never answered it. If you put on the flashlight I'll show you her picture." Brush took from his purse a discolored newspaper clipping with a picture of Marian Truby. "I ask about her everywhere," he continued, "but I think she must have retired. Maybe she's sick somewhere. If I find that's so, I mean to support her for the rest of her life. You see, it says she was born in 1911 in Waco, Texas. I wrote the postmaster there, but he said there were no more Trubys there now."

"So your big ideas about life were fed you by a sixteen-year-old girl while she was hopped up with drugs?"

Brush made no answer.

Burkin continued in a low tone, edged with contempt: "Think it over. It all goes together—voluntary poverty and Christmas baskets for burglars. It all goes together. You've got the gaseous ideas of a sick girl. It has nothing to do with life. You live in a foggy, unreal, narcotic dream. Think it over. Listen, benny, can't you see that what you call religion is just the shiverings of the cowardly? It's just what people tell themselves because they haven't got the guts to look the facts of life and death in the face. If you'd gone to a respectable college you'd have had the chance to get wise to these things. You've lived all your life among the half-baked. You've probably never been exposed once in your whole life to anybody who really had any practice in thinking."

"You'd better stop the car," said Brush. "I'm going to get out." Then he added, shouting: "I suppose you think nobody with brains ever felt any religion."

"I could talk to you. I could show you things. But in two minutes you'd be squealing holy-murder and starting to jump out of the car. You don't want to grow up, that's the trouble with you. You haven't read anything. You haven't seen anything, except through the eyes of a girl in hysteria and some old dodo in Shiloh Baptist College. All right. Let's talk about something else."

Brush remained silent. At last he said, in a low voice, "Nothing that you could say would change my mind."

"It's now half-past eleven," said Burkin, decisively. "Will you let me talk to you for one half-hour, without your interrupting me?"

Brush was staring darkly before him. "Where did you go to college?" he asked.

Burkin named an Eastern university, adding: "But that wouldn't mean anything, except that I added a whole batch more education to it. I've worked on these things. I hung around the University of Berlin for a year. I lived half a year in Paris. I didn't stick in the smoking-cars of Texas and read cheap paper pamphlets from a mail-order house. Give me half an hour."

"I have a hard enough time with my own doubts without adding somebody else's to them," said Brush, in a low voice.

"What are you so afraid of doubts for? There's one thing worse than doubts, and that's evasions. You're full of evasions. You don't even want to look around. You don't give a goddam for the truth."

"I have the truth."

"All right, if you have the truth, why not listen to my error for half an hour?"

Brush was very unhappy. He glanced sideways at Burkin's face, then brought his wrist watch close to the dashboard light. "Go ahead," he said.

Burkin plunged into primitive man and the jungle; he came down through the nature myths; he hung the earth in astronomical time. He then exposed the pretensions of subjective religious experience; the absurdity of conflicting prayers, man's egotistic terror before extinction. At last he said: "If you'd read more I could show you the absurdity of the scholastic proofs of the existence of God and I could show you how the dependency complex begins. Is the half-hour up?"

Brush said, slowly: "When you began I thought you were going to say things that would stick in my mind and trouble me. You've talked three-quarters of an hour and you've only said one thing that had any point to it." His voice rose and presently he was shouting: "I guess we'd better change the subject, because you haven't thought enough about these things to make it worth my while. Why, can't you see that you don't know anything about religion until you start to live it?"

"Stop yelling, anyway."

"All you've done is *think* about it as though it were . . . as though it were a *fish* a long ways off. Even your doubts aren't the right doubts to have."

"I'm not deaf, I tell you. Shut up and sit down."

"You—"

"Oh, shut up!"

They drove in silence awhile. Finally they entered a village. All lights were out, save in a lunchwagon by the railroad tracks.

"I'm getting out here," said Brush.

Burkin stopped the car. The nervous twitch on the left side of his face had returned. Brush put his suitcase on the curb.

"I owe you about three dollars for that broken window," he said, "and another dollar for gas."

"Yes, you do."

"Here it is."

"Good-by," said Brush, extending his hand.

Burkin drove off without answering.

✽

12

Kansas City. Serious conversation in a park. A wedding. Practically an American home.

Brush returned to Kansas City by train. It was the first time in his life he had traveled by train on a Sunday. Even so, he was almost late for his appointment in front of the Public Library. He barely had time to rush back to his room at Mrs. Kubinsky's, change into his best suit, and run next door to take a look at Elizabeth. Elizabeth had entered Queenie's house a big-eyed pale child that smelled bad; already, however, she had taken on color, and Queenie gave a good account of her disposition.

The girls were already at the Library steps when Brush came running up the hill. They pretended to be deep in conversation.

"I'm only one minute late," he said. "I just got in from out of town an hour ago."

"This is my sister Lottie," said Roberta.

"Yes," said Brush, smiling. "I remember you from that night I was at your farm."

Lottie threw a quick glance at him and did not answer. She was not so tall as her sister; she had brown eyes and hair and gave the impression of being matter-of-fact.

"Would you like an ice-cream soda?" asked Brush. "Let's go to the drug store and have one first."

Making conversation was not easy. The girls sat on the high stools, earnestly engaged with the straws in their mouths.

"Is it too cold to go out to the park on the bluffs?" asked Brush.

"No, I guess not," said Lottie; so they all climbed on to a street car. The car was almost full and Roberta took a seat some distance from them.

"What are you interested in?" asked Brush.

"I?" asked Lottie. "Oh, nothing. Anything. Pigs and chickens, I guess, mostly. You see, Mr. Brush," she added, dryly, looking into his eyes, yet giving the impression that she did not see him, "I'm just a farmer's daughter—I don't go in for big ideas."

"I see," said Brush, uncomfortably.

Lottie turned her head and looked out of the window, as though she were sitting beside a stranger.

Brush cleared his throat several times, then said: "When we get to the park I want to show you some marks left by the ice-cap."

"I beg your pardon?"

"You see, the North Pole ice used to come all the way down to here. It stopped at Kansas City; that's what made the rivers. The ice was two thousand feet thick right where we are now. It was so heavy that it crushed the earth out of shape as far as . . . as far as Pennsylvania and Oklahoma."

"Well!"

"Naturally it carried some big rocks along with it, and those rocks ground down the big rocks under them and it's the marks of that grinding that I'm going to show you in the park."

"That'll be fine," said Lottie, without expression. She turned about and glanced at Roberta, who was sitting five seats behind her. She asked Brush, "When did all this happen?"

"About eight hundred thousand years ago."

Lottie gazed at him with cold irony, then turned her head away. Another silence ensued. Brush broke it by saying, urgently:

"Lottie, I want you to help me in persuading Roberta. I think it's tremendously important."

"Well, it was all an awful mess," said Lottie, just as quickly, "and I think the less we see of you the better."

"When I've done wrong," said Brush, in a low voice, "I can't wait until I've done everything I can to make it all right."

"You both did wrong. But at least it's all over now and there's nothing more that *can* be done about it," replied Lottie, decisively; then added, "Anyway, let's get to the park before we talk about it."

Brush glanced at her sideways. "Can I say one more thing before we change the subject?" he asked.

"I suppose so. What is it?"

"Try not to have a prejudice against me before you know me. I'm not the usual kind of traveling salesman."

Lottie looked at him with a faint smile. "I think I understand that," she said, and thereafter things went a little better. Descending from the street car, Lottie gave Roberta a sharp pinch on the elbow.

When they reached the park they sat down on a bench overlooking the river. Lottie sat in the middle tracing designs on the ground with the tip of her umbrella. Brush waited a moment and then plunged into the heart of the matter:

"Don't you see, Lottie, that all serious-minded people would agree that I'm really her husband already?"

"No."

"Don't you see that we can never marry anyone else, unless one of us two is dead? There's . . . there's one of the Ten Commandments about that."

Lottie bit her upper lip and looked at the ground. Brush tried another approach:

"Lottie, what does Roberta want? Does she want to stay in that restaurant? I think it's an awful place. I can't let her do that. I owe her a living for the rest of her life and I can afford it easily. I've got more money than I know what to do with. Can't you tell me what she wants?"

"Well, to tell the truth, Mr. Brush, she . . ."

"You must call me George, Lottie. Don't you realize you're practically my sister?"

"All right. All right. George—to tell the truth, there's only one thing in the world that Roberta wants, and that is . . ." She glanced sideways at Roberta. Roberta was sobbing. Lottie paused, then stood up and whispered into her sister's ear: "Roberta, do go off for a few minutes' walk while I talk to him. Will you, honey?"

Roberta nodded, rose, and sat down on the next bench.

Lottie continued: "She wants papa to like her again." Brush stared at her. "She wants papa to have a good opinion of her; that's all. She was papa's favorite girl of the three of us. It's been terrible for him, really it has."

Brush whispered: "But you see I don't know anything about it. I don't know anything about what happened."

"Well . . ." began Lottie, then rejected her impulse to recount the past, and resumed her former thought: "What I think is, if perhaps—when she knows you better and all that—if perhaps you married Roberta, then some day you could call on papa and show him you're not an ordinary traveling salesman . . . and you could talk to him about the Bible and things like that . . . and then he'd forgive Roberta."

"Then that's fine, Lottie. That's all I ask to do."

"But, George, don't you *see*? What good is it you two being married, if you don't love each other? What I thought was—"

Brush leaned over her earnestly and said: "I'll love her pretty well. I'll love her almost perfectly, you'll see. She'll never notice the difference. I'll tell you, confidentially, that there's only one other girl in the world I love more."

Lottie looked at him long and a little sadly. Then she smiled and put a hand on his arm. "George, you're kind of crazy," she said.

"Yes," he answered, hastily, "I know what you mean, if you notice carefully, you'll see that I'm very logical."

There was a pause. Then Brush leaned forward and, looking at his shoes, asked, "Lottie . . . why did your father send Roberta away."

"Why . . . because . . . because . . ."

Brush raised his chin and looked at her.

"She was very sick and. . . . I thought you knew."

"No, I didn't know."

"Of course. You couldn't have known."

"No, I never knew," breathed Brush.

"Well, on the farm . . . we all went through quite a time . . . papa and . . . mamma . . . and Roberta . . . and I."

They gazed into one another's eyes for a moment.

"Lottie, I think you're fine," said Brush. "I hope I know you all my life."

Lottie became confused and looked away. "I guess you will," she said, almost inaudibly. But she had something else to say. It was such a difficult thing to say that she fell into a false casualness and for a moment her gestures became affected and contradictory: "I was thinking that . . . you might marry Roberta just to please papa . . . then separate right away . . . and after a while get a divorce."

Brush also turned red. "No," he said. "You see, there are two things against that. One thing is that I never believe in divorce, and if anybody stops to think about it they can see why. And the other thing is that I never believe in doing anything just for show. I . . . I don't believe in that. . . . Oh, Lottie, don't you see that everything's all right? That we're going to have a fine American home?"

"Well, I've said all I'm going to say. You two'll have to decide it for yourselves from now on."

"Are you going to advise her to get married to me, though?"

"George, unless people love each other I don't think—"

"Lottie, when you have a hard decision to make, you know what you should do? You should go back to the first principles of the matter. You shouldn't ask what you want to do. You should look at it as though it were somebody else and not yourself. And, that's all very clear in this case. Lottie, I'll take the responsibility. I know I'm right. I know I'll love and protect Roberta until I die."

"All right," said Lottie.

"Will you go and ask her to come here? And, Lottie, listen: we'll have a nice home somewhere and you can come in all the time for Sunday dinner, and the whole family can come in from the farm, too. We'll have some fine times, you'll see. For instance, I have a very good tenor voice and the people are always asking me to sing for them. . . . Oh, Lottie, all this that began so badly will end up all right; it'll end up all the better. Now do you see how important it is?"

Lottie, a little dizzy in the conflict of ideas, went over to where Roberta was sitting. They had a long whispered conversation.

"But he's crazy," said Roberta.

"Yes," said Lottie, "I know. But he's crazy in a sort of nice way." She began laughing. "I'd marry him in a minute, myself."

"You would, Lottie?"

"Yes, I think I would; only, he hasn't asked me."

Whereupon they both began laughing into their damp handkerchiefs. "One more ice-cream soda and I'd do it," said Lottie.

"But, Lottie, he's *terrible!*"

"I know. But I've decided I prefer him that way. Compare him, I mean, with Gus Brubacker, back home, or Oscy Deschauer. Besides, he told me to tell you he had a fine tenor voice."

"What'll we talk about?"

"What?"

"What'll we talk about? What'll we talk about when we're married?"

"Oh, he's full of conversation. Didn't you hear him telling me all about the ice that used to be over Kansas City? Besides, he's so rich that you can have a radio."

"Is he *rich*?"

"He talks that way. Hurry, Berta, and make up your mind. He's waiting and he'll think we're laughing at him."

"Lottie, help me! Shall I?"

"Don't ask me! Don't you like him?"

Roberta shook her head, her face suddenly somber. "You know why I could never like him."

"Listen, Berta, he'll never drag that up, never. I know. There's nothing mean about him. He's kind of stupid, but he's good as gold. If you ask me, I say you ought to marry him. Then take him to see papa."

"All right, I will," said Roberta, rising.

"Wait 'til I blow my nose," said Lottie.

While this was going on Brush sat on the bench, thinking. He had taken Lottie's umbrella and was abstractedly tracing initials on the gravel: a large R for Roberta, then an A for Adele, the widow to whom he had proposed marriage on his twenty-first birthday; and F for Frances, Miss Smith, his chemistry teacher in the Ludington High School; at a distance from these initials an M.T. for Marian Truby; whereupon, in a flood of reminiscence, he wrote a J for Jessie Mayhew, a V and S, a C; then erased them all and traced a large R and sat looking at it, Roberta and Lottie were laughing?—laughing or crying?

Finally they came toward him hand in hand. He rose and said: "Before I ask you to marry me again, there's something else I ought to tell you. I forgot to tell you before that I . . . I own a little girl. A friend of mine died and left me his little girl. She's the brightest little girl that you could find anywhere, and I know you'll like her."

This seemed to make no change in the situation and Roberta accepted his proposal.

He took her hand and said: "It's going to be fine, Roberta. You'll see. What you'll want to do will always be the first thing in my mind. At first, though, I'll have to be away a good deal on the road, but I'll write you a letter every day. Later I think I can get the firm to give me the Illinois and Ohio territory. We're going to have a wonderful life together . . . you'll see. There'll be lots of times when we'll be laughing a lot . . . while we're washing the dishes, and so on . . . and soon we'll have a little house of our own. I'm very good at fixing things, like electric lights and furnaces. And I'm good at carpentering, too. I'll build you an arbor in the back yard where you can sit and sew. And Lottie can come and stay with us long as she wants to. We could never find a better friend than Lottie. . . . Don't you think it sounds . . . like it'll be fine?"

Roberta, standing with lowered eyes, said, "Yes."

"I know I'm kind of funny in some ways," he added, smiling, "but that's only these earlier years when I'm trying to think things out. By the time I'm thirty all that kind of thing will be clearer to me, and . . . and it'll all be settled."

They were married on Wednesday and had their photograph taken—Queenie, Elizabeth, Lottie, Roberta, and Brush. Brush received a three-weeks vacation from his firm and they moved into a four-room apartment over a drug store. The first installment was paid on a second-hand edition of the Encyclopædia Britannica. On the first Sunday after the wedding the Weyerhauser family came into town from the farm to go to church with them and to stay to Sunday dinner. Brush sat at the end of the pew, his arm lightly but proudly lying along the back of it. During the sermon Elizabeth put her head on his lap and went to sleep, and his eyes made a guarded journey about the congregation to ascertain how other fathers met this situation. After church the three younger women busied themselves in the kitchen. Mrs. Weyerhauser had the shock of hearing herself called Grandma—for, Herb having died, Brush and Roberta were now Papa and Ma. The manners of the host and his father-in-law towards one another were still somewhat stately, but they gave promise of becoming more easy with time.

Apparently all was well with the new household, but only apparently, for some flaws began very gradually to reveal themselves. Roberta had been correct in her doubt as to what they would talk about when they were married. For some reason Brush, who had never in his life been at a loss for things to talk about, now found himself hard put to it to fill the long evenings with interesting matter. He took to taking notes during the day on subjects that would serve, and when Roberta called him to dinner he would take out his purse and run his eyes over the topics he had collected. He tried putting forth some of the theories that never ceased fermenting in his mind, and though Roberta listened with lowered eyes (their eyes never met at any time) he found that his eagerness to propound them had somehow left him in this company. He discovered that there was one subject that never failed to arouse Roberta's interest—the lives and appearance of motion-picture actors—and he took to culling from the papers such items on these subjects as were suitable for retelling in a Christian home.

Another flaw appeared when Brush became aware that he and Roberta were engaged in a furtive, unceasing, game of strategy to obtain the first place in Elizabeth's affection. The worst of it for Brush lay in the fact that Elizabeth all too often showed a marked preference for himself. This filled him with a satisfaction of which he was soon ashamed. He tried time after time to give the advantage to Roberta, only to be filled with ignoble pleasure when the effort did not succeed.

On the last night before he set out on his long three-months trip (the firm of Caulkins assured him that his approach suited the southern territory more than the northern and refused to consider his application for a change) Lottie came into Kansas City for the farewell dinner. She had a long, earnest conversation with Roberta in the afternoon, and during dinner Brush noted that they had both been crying. He looked at them in surprise, but made no comment. That was left to Elizabeth.

"Mamma cried," said Elizabeth.

"Eat prettily now!" said Roberta, hastily.

Brush was about to inquire further, when he caught sight of Lottie's raised eyebrows sending him a signal.

Brush had a theory that children should be permitted to see the stars. The custom that put them to bed at dusk seemed to him to overlook the fact that a frequent view of the stars was an important element in the spiritual education of mankind. For this evening he had obtained permission to delay Elizabeth's retirement until after dark. Roberta dressed her for the open air and Brush carried her up the ladder to the trap door that opened upon the roof. He moved a soap-box across the floor of tar paper and gravel to the chimney and, seating himself on it, held Elizabeth in his arms and waited for the benefits to show themselves. The child lay humming contentedly to herself, and looking down at her, Brush seemed to observe a strange indifference to the sky. She smiled up at him, a smile that seemed to allude to their wickedness in evading her mother's rules on an early departure to bed.

They were silent for a time. Then Brush put her to her nightly test.

"What's your name?"

"Elizabeth Martin Brush."

"What do you do if you're lost?"

"Policeman."

"Where do you live?"

"Twelve twelve Brinkley Street."

"What do you do?"

"Tell the trufe . . ."

"Yes."

". . . love God . . ."

"Yes."

". . . and brush my teef."

"That's right."

She was able to tell what country she belonged to; she counted to twenty, and repeated a portion of the alphabet. She was then allowed to relax. After a long silence he looked down to see that her wide eyes were gazing tranquilly at the stars.

The trap door was raised. "She ought to go to bed now, dear," said Roberta.

"All right. We're coming."

Roberta waited, holding the trap door open. As he took it he said in a low voice: "Roberta, is something the matter?"

She made no answer. While Elizabeth was being put to bed, Brush sat by Lottie, having another cup of coffee. Lottie's face was thoughtful. She played with the spoon in her saucer.

"George," she said, "there's no need to keep up this apartment while you're gone so long. Why can't Roberta come back to the farm? There's plenty for her to do there and it would be much better for the baby, especially when the hot weather comes."

"But, Lottie, this is our *home*. I think it's very important that a married couple has a separate home of their own, even if the husband has to be away some of the time."

"George, are you very happy with Roberta?"

"Why, yes, of course! I'm the happiest man in town. It's not like you, Lottie, to ask things like that."

"Roberta wants to go back to the farm."

There was silence for a minute, then Brush said: "I'll give up the business. I'll get a job in town here somewhere . . . because my home's more important to me than my business is."

"No, that wouldn't help. George, I don't want to hurt you or anything. . . . We're both tremendously fond of you, George, you know that. But . . ."

"What *is* it? What are you trying to say?"

"George, don't you see? Roberta wants to live alone."

Brush turned white, but did not raise his eyes. Then he rose and said: "I think I'd better take a walk."

Lottie went to him and put her arm around his shoulder and said: "George, don't be mad at me. I'm only trying to help you see what's best."

Brush muttered: "But that's terrible. I don't see how you can say a thing like that."

"George, you're both awfully nice people, but you know as well as I do that you don't really suit each other. Everything's fine now; you've been married and that awful thing in the past is all settled and forgotten. Don't you think—?"

But by now Brush was standing by the door with blazing eyes. He said: "Are you going to be one of those city people, too, with ideas like that? I'm ashamed of you, Lottie. Don't you know about God's laws? Roberta and I have been married and we'll be married until we die. The only reason you can say a thing like that is because you've never been married and don't know what an important thing it is. Roberta and I are one person, don't you understand that? I'm going for a walk. I've got to get some air."

Roberta had come into the room. "All I want is to live by myself, George," she said. "I like you very much, George, but . . .

we're different, you know we are." Whereupon she rushed into the kitchen, shutting the door behind her.

Brush said: "Isn't this just what all married people go through? ... and then they come out of it?"

"George!" said Lottie, sadly.

Brush put on his hat and coat. Then he said: "Why don't you say it right out? You want me to get a divorce like all those people in the newspapers, and so go on smoking and ... giggling and drinking to the cemetery. That's what you want. You want us to lead lives like ... like senseless, silly people that have no ideas and no religion and no thoughts about the human race. It's not important if Roberta and I are different, as she calls it. It's not important if we don't get on like some couples do. We're married, and it's for the good of society and morals that we stay together until we die."

"George," said Lottie, in a level voice, "go into the kitchen and tell Roberta you love her more than anyone in the world. More than anybody ever loved anybody else. Go on. Go on, do it. That's what a marriage promise is."

They looked at one another darkly.

"Let her have Elizabeth," continued Lottie. "She'll be perfectly happy with her; but don't make her stay in this apartment for three months, pretending that she's waiting for the—"

Brush's train left at midnight. His suitcases stood ready beside the door. He picked them up, then suddenly in wild emotion hurled them against the wall.

"I don't want to go on!" he cried. "What good does it do to go to work if I haven't got a home to work for?" He put his hands over his face. "I don't want to live," he said. "Everything goes wrong."

Lottie went over to him. She tried to pull one of his hands down from his face, but he would not let it go.

"George, don't act so," she said, quietly. "You're the finest person I ever knew ... but this is an entirely different kind of thing.

Be frank, look at things simply. See? Be kind to Roberta; this is the way to be kind to Roberta."

He put his hands down and looked at her. "Isn't the principle of a thing more important than the people that live under the principle?" he asked.

"Nobody's strong enough to live up to the rules," said Lottie, with the beginning of a smile in her gravity. "I guess we're all allowed an exception once in a while. . . . Say a nice good-by to Roberta."

Roberta had silently come into the room. He kissed them both good-by and, although it was only nine o'clock, went to the station. He walked around the station feverishly, then went up to one of the shops.

"Do you sell pipes?" he asked.

"Yes."

"I'll take one . . . that one. What's the best kind of pipe tobacco that you've got?"

With his new possessions he went into the smoking-room and tried to look matters over in a new light.

13

George Brush loses something. Last news of Father Pasziewski. Thoughts on arriving at the age of twenty-four.

Again George Brush set out on the long swing of the pendulum to Abilene, Texas, resuming the life in trains, buses, street cars and blank hotel bedrooms, his evenings spent in public libraries, and the long walks at night encircling the towns he was visiting. He refused to recognize the profound dejection that filled him; he pretended that he was enjoying his work, his Sundays, and his reading. There were two things that now somewhat mitigated his depression; one was his pipe, the other was his study of the German language. Caulkins and Company had decided to put out a First and Second German Reader, and as usual Brush felt himself called upon to make a personal experience of their superiority. He memorized the paradigms and wrote out all the exercises. He found three misprints. He learned by heart "Du bist wie eine Blume" and "The Lorelei." He began talking to himself and thinking in hog-German. He no longer lived by voluntary poverty, and with the addition of Herb's money he grew incredibly wealthy; he had over eight hundred dollars. Out of this superfluity he bought himself a portable gramophone, and while he was dressing he played himself the German instruction records. He became very enthusiastic about the German classics and prolonged all his conversations with the German teachers he called upon; Caulkins' Readers sold in great numbers.

But these consolations were more apparent than real. They could not conceal the stab of physical pain that went through him when, on the evening walks, he glimpsed through half-drawn blinds the felicities of an American home, or when in church he discovered that the old-fashioned hymns no longer had the power to render him inexplicably happy. From time to time whole nights passed without his being able to sleep; occasionally he sat down to a meal, only to discover that he had no appetite whatever.

One day he arose to discover, quite simply, that he had lost his faith. It was as though in some painless way he had lost his arms and legs. At first his only emotion was astonishment. He looked about him; he had mislaid something that would turn up presently. But it did not turn up and the astonishment was followed by a mood of cynical exhilaration. When he went to bed he would find himself falling on his knees as usual, but he would spring up at once, a little guiltily, and, getting into bed, would lie there, smiling grimly at the ceiling. "Es ist nichts da," he would mutter aloud to the sky, "gar nichts."

For a while this gave his life and his business interviews a new energy. Now he laughed and talked more in the chance encounters on trains and in hotels. He spent his evenings at the movies, laughing long and loudly at the least pretext. He began to take advantage of his expense account recklessly; he chose the dollar dinner, with steak, rather than the sixty-cent dinner, vegetable plate, or sausage and potatoes.

By the time he reached Texas something was happening to his health, and finally at Trowbridge, in western Texas, he went to the hospital. The doctor was puzzled and then alarmed. Apparently Brush had a little of everything. There was a touch of amœbic dysentery and a suggestion of sinus; there was something of rheumatism and more than a hint of jaundice. His respiratory organs weren't right, a kind of asthma, and his heart had a murmur. The whole machine had run down and he grew worse daily. He lay in the hospital for weeks, his face turned to the wall. His few remarks were quotations from *King Lear* translated into bad German. He knew what was the matter with him and on one occasion tried to explain to the doctor his theory of sickness, but he soon gave it up with the words: "Ich sterbe, du stirbst, er stirbt, sie und es stirbt; wir sterben, ihr sterbet, sie sterben, sie sterben." When he first arrived at the hospital he had filled out a card, giving his name, age, and business address, and the hospital office had written to Caulkins and Company about his condition. A number of letters from the firm and forwarded by the firm had come to him, but Brush left them unopened on the table by his bed.

Brush had had very little to do with hospitals, but he had a theory that trained nurses were the true priestesses of our time. Whenever he saw or met one he gazed upon her with profound admiration and reverence. Miss Colloquer, who was assigned to him, was faultless in the performance of her duties, but she seemed to have no inkling of the higher qualities that Brush expected of her.

One day she put her head around the edge of the screen that protected him. "Asleepums?" she asked, softly.

"No."

"Here's a nice, *nice* caller to see you," she said, straightening the sheets into a long line across his chest. "It's Dr. Bowie. He's my minister at the First Methodist. You want to see him, don't you?"

Brush shook his head.

"Oh yes, you do. He's a werry, werry nice man. Now let me make you booful a minute," she said, straightening the part in his hair, "There! Oo's a perfect lamb, yes, you are. As good as gold. Come in Dr. Bowie."

Dr. Bowie was an elderly, bearded man, wearing a frayed frock coat; a black string tie was tied about the collar of his blue flannel shirt. He came from a long talk with the director of the hospital.

Brush with both hands held his pillow over his eyes. He lowered it for a moment, glanced at his visitor, and replaced it on his forehead.

"What's this? What's this, my dear boy?" asked Dr. Bowie, drawing up his chair by Brush's bed. Brush did not answer. Dr. Bowie lowered his voice: "Now, isn't there anything you want to tell me?" Brush still did not answer. Dr. Bowie was slightly antagonized, but he controlled himself. "The doctor tells me that you're a sick man, a pretty sick man, my boy. We must think of that, yes, sir." He brought out a questionnaire blank and laid it surreptitiously on his knees, and drew out a pencil. "Are your dear parents living, Mr. Brush?"

The pillow moved up and down.

"Now don't you think we'd better telegraph them that you're sick? Don't you think that you'd get well right off if your father or your dear mother were here?"

"No," said Brush.

"What are their names and addresses?"

Brush gave the answer and Dr. Bowie licked his pencil and wrote it down. It turned out that Brush was a married man also, and Roberta's address was recorded, with the date of the marriage.

Dr. Bowie consulted the next question and murmured "Mm—no children—?"

"Two," said Brush. "One that's alive and one that's dead. The live one is Elizabeth Martin Brush. She's four. And the dead one's name is . . . is . . ." He consulted the ceiling, then added with decision . . . "is named David."

Dr. Bowie's eyebrows rose, but he recorded the facts. "Now isn't there some message you'd like to give me for your family, Mr. Brush?"

"No."

Dr. Bowie laid aside his paper a moment. "I want you to think seriously for a moment, my dear boy. I certainly hope that God will restore you soon to a life of Christian usefulness; but God's will is not always our will. He calls us when he wants us. Have you any church affiliation, may I ask?"

Brush took the pillow away from his forehead. "No," he said, clearly. "None."

Dr. Bowie drew in his chin and cleared his throat. "Now a great many people, a *great* many, have found it a comfort—what a comfort!—to ask forgiveness of God in the presence of his minister—oh, my boy!—for the things they've done wrong in this life. It lightens the load, my brother."

Brush's mouth straightened out. "I've broken all the Ten Commandments, except two," he answered. "I never killed anybody and I never made any graven images. Many's the time I almost killed myself, though, and I'm not joking. I never was tempted by idols, but I guess that would have come along any day. I don't say these things to you because I'm sorry, but because I don't like your tone of voice. I'm glad I did these things and I wish I'd done them more. I made the mistake all my life of thinking that you could get better and better until you were perfect."

There was a long pause. Dr. Bowie swallowed his soft palate several times; then said, in a feeble voice: "In spite of that, Mr.

Brush, it has always been my custom at the bedside of patients . . . in a critical condition . . . to say a few . . . words of prayer."

Brush raised his head a moment and looked at him fiercely. "Don't!" he said.

"My boy, my boy!" replied the other, his hands fluttering in midair.

"If there were a God he wouldn't like it," cried Brush, with unexpected force. "Don't you know that you're not supposed to ask for . . . for *facts*?"

"Mr. Brush!"

"You're only supposed to ask for things like being good or having faith or something like that."

"Very well . . . ah . . . !"

"But it doesn't get you anywhere. Look at me. The more I asked the worse I got. Everything I did was wrong. Everybody I knew got to hate me. So that proves it. When you were young I guess you asked to be all those things; and yet look at you; you're pretty stupid, if I must say so, and dry and . . . I'll bet you even believe in war."

Dr. Bowie had risen in horror and was nervously gathering together his questionnaire, hat, raincoat, cane, and Bible. Brush continued: "The second thing that shows that there is no God is that he allows such foolish people to be ministers. I've secretly thought that for a long time, and now I'm glad to be able to say it. All ministers are stupid—do you hear me—*all*. . . . I mean all except one."

Dr. Bowie's anger had so risen that his horror was gone. He leaned over Brush. "Young man," he said, distinctly, "are those the words and thoughts you're going to die with?"

They stared at one another. Brush greatly weakened by his outburst, closed his eyes. "No," he said. ". . . I'm sorry."

"I realize you're a sick man. I hope you'll think over the foolish proud things you've said. I'll come and see you again." He stood looking at Brush's closed eyes a moment. Then he said: "There seems to be a good deal of mail for you here. Would you like me to read it to you?"

"No. There's not a letter in the world that would interest me at all."

Miss Colloquer had come in, smiling. "Dr. Bowie, do open that little package that's come. Perhaps it's a present for Mr. Brush. You'll let *him* open it, won't you, Mr. Brush? It's from Kansas City."

Brush nodded wearily.

Dr. Bowie opened it. In the tissue paper lay an ordinary silver-plated spoon.

Miss Colloquer loved a mystery and would not let the matter rest until they had found the letter that accompanied the present. It was from a Marcella L. Craven. It said that she hoped Mr. Brush was well and enjoying his work. The boys on the top floor were all well and still had jobs. Roberta and Lottie and Elizabeth had paid a call on her one day and they were in fine health. The writer hoped Mr. Brush would come back soon because Elizabeth wanted more lessons. "She couldn't be fonder of you if you were her own father, Mr. Brush, that's the truth. I forget if I told you that Father Pasziewski died. I will tell you the details about it when you come. Mrs. Kandinsky and I called on him a few days before he died. And it seemed he knew he was going to die and he wanted to give us something to remember him by. So he sent Anna into the dining-room and he gave us each a spoon. And he asked me to give you a spoon from him, too. He said it was a sort of foolish thing to give, but that perhaps you could use a spoon some way. I told him you liked to hear about him, Mr. Brush, and he seemed to have a special feeling about you. It's a terrible pity you never met."

"Don't read any more," said Brush. "Thank you," and holding

the spoon in his hand he turned his face to the wall. Then looking back a minute he asked: "What day is today, Miss Colloquer— what day of the week?"

"Why, today's Friday."

"Thank you."

From that day he began to get well. At first he was silent and thoughtful, but gradually the talkativeness began to reappear, and finally he was able to resume his itinerary. He so arranged his appointments that he was able to revisit Wellington, Oklahoma, on his twenty-fourth birthday. He returned to the path through the deep weeds and came to the pond near the deserted brick factory. Again there were turtles on the log; again the bird-calls foretold a hot day. He lay flat on his face and finally fell asleep, but not before he had passed an earnest hour. A few days later in Killam, a man heard him sing at a community-chest bazaar and offered him a good deal of money to sing on the radio in Chicago. Brush said he'd like to do it, but that his route didn't pass through Chicago. The man doubled his offer; Brush replied that he'd do it free of charge, but that his route didn't pass through Chicago. The next day in Lockburn, Missouri, Brush came upon a very pretty waitress reading Darwin's *The Cruise of the "Beagle"* in her spare time. He arranged to put her through college. The next week, the manager and guests of Bishop's Hotel at Tohoki, in the same state, were astonished to discover that one of their number, a tall solidly built young man, had suddenly lost the use of his voice and was communicating with the outside world by means of pencil and paper. Several days later, in Dakins, Kansas, the same traveler was arrested and confined for a few hours in the jail. The charge was later found to have been based on a misunderstanding. He was released and continued on his journey.

A Nephew's Note to a
New Edition

"[American culture] is obsessed with moralities, both
for good and for evil. . . . The nation is bound for the
Kingdom of Heaven, beginning at the general store and
the barbershop. It is the guarantee of our greatness but
the impulses turn often to vagary and heresy."
—Amos N. Wilder, "Don Quixote in the American
Scene," 1943

HarperCollins published its first Twenty-first Century edition of
Heaven's My Destination in 2003, sixty-eight years after publishing it in 1935, under the corporate name Harper & Brothers. The

2003 version featured two "firsts": a foreword by a notable writer, and an afterword with related readings fashioned by the author of these words. In the afterword, I tried, using as many of Thornton Wilder's own words as possible, to offer a helpful glimpse of how *Heaven's My Destination* was conceived, the nature of its initial critical reception, and selected highlights of the novel's history down to the present. The 2003 edition of *Heaven's My Destination* passed the test, and readers found the additional information helpful in better understanding the novel. Seventeen years later, it is a pleasure to collaborate with HarperCollins once again to place *Heaven's My Destination* into the new Thornton Wilder Library. This latest edition features a revised afterword and updated readings, bibliographical references for readers interested in pursuing more of the story behind the story, and an arresting new cover befitting a tale about a salesman who loves his job but gets into troubles.

While the afterword of the book has undergone significant revision, the foreword by J. D. "Sandy" McClatchy continues to stand the test of time. Sandy, who, sadly, died in 2018, was a distinguished poet, librettist, editor, teacher, and spokesperson for the arts. Serving as president of the American Academy of Arts and Letters and chancellor of the Academy of American Poets are only two of his countless deeds on behalf of the arts and humanities over a distinguished career as a genuine Man of Letters. His notable Thornton Wilder credentials, spanning more than a quarter of a century, included his editorship of the three-volume Library of America edition of Wilder's fiction and drama, his libretto for the *Our Town* opera, his presidency of the Thornton Wilder Society, and his service as a one-man kitchen cabinet for Thornton Wilder's Literary Executor (and nephew). When I asked Sandy whether he would be willing to write the foreword for *Heaven's My Destination*, he responded in typical fashion: "My pen is in my hand."

❦

"In the tissue paper lay an ordinary silver-plated
spoon . . ."
—*Heaven's My Destination* p. *185*

In 2003, I did not reveal what I now put on the record: *Heaven's My Destination* is my favorite Wilder novel, and I keep a silver-plated spoon resting on the shelf next to my desk as a constant reminder of this choice. I am also the founder of The George Brush Irregulars Association, whose members live in a file in my study. Who are these members? What is the purpose of the organization? Here is a bit of background about this special group.

Thornton Wilder wrote seven novels, each set across an enormous range of space and time from 1920s Newport, Rhode Island, to 44 B.C. Rome at the time of Caesar's assassination to the 1902 fictional town of Coal Town, Illinois. While all of his novels are in print, none is as well-known as his Pulitzer Prize–winning novel, *The Bridge of San Luis Rey*, set in Peru in 1741 and published in 1927. Because of its great fame *The Bridge* inevitably casts a long shadow over the other six novels, leaving them to fight for light. On top of this first shadow, the fame of *Our Town,* which won Wilder his second Pulitzer Prize in 1938, looms even larger.

Competition can bring out the best in us—and this is where the George Brush Irregulars come in. Its members believe in *Heaven* and, be it in a dedicated essay or an aside, enjoy throwing laudatory light on the travels and travails of George Marvin Brush, the highly successful salesman for the Caulkins Educational Press who never cheats on his expense account. Its membership includes such figures as: playwright A. R. Gurney who, in his introduction to Wilder's *The Collected Short Plays* (vol. 2) published by Theatre

Communication Group, calls *Heaven* "Wilder's underestimated novel"; John Knowles, author of *A Separate Peace*, who concludes an essay exploring *Paradise Lost* with the following: "*Paradise Lost* is a mighty theme, one that can lead to the grisly ordeals of Candide or the sparkling confrontations of *Sense Sensibility*. It can lead downward to despair, or it can turn back and aspire to Paradise regained. *Heaven's My Destination*, Mr. Wilder called one of his novels. Yes"; John Barkam, who, while reviewing Wilder's 1973 novel, *Theophilus North,* in the *Philadelphia Inquirer,* observed in an aside that *Heaven's My Destination* was "one of the finest comic novels in our literature"; English professor John Henry Raleigh, who wrote in his introduction in a 1960 edition of *Heaven's My Destination,* "[George's] problems, his defeats, his quixotic destiny are timeless"; and a new Irregular, Michael Schmidt, Cambridge University, and author of *The Novel: A Biography* (2014). Prof. Schmidt's testimony in his introduction to the 2016 British edition of *Heaven's My Destination* begins with a bold declaration:

> Of all Thornton Wilder's novels, his fourth, *Heaven's My Destination* (1935), has kept its freshness best. "It's news that stays news," as Ezra Pound said poetry ought to be. Even though it was written in a specific period—the Great Depression—and about places and people who are generally spared the attention of novelists, it feels close in time and incident. It is not realistic; actions and character are larger than life; but it does seem— paradoxically—very real.

As the leader of the Irregulars camp, I applaud *Heaven*, a timeless tribute, clothed in humor and pathos, for ideals and idealism that make the world go 'round and can drive you crazy. That it has been translated in more than ten languages since 1935—and is present and accounted for today in Germany, Italy, Spain, the Russian Federation, and Turkey as well as Great Britain—pleases me to no end. George Brush's story has always struck me as real and immediate and universal. That Wilder saw this precious double-edged quality in himself and in his family can also make the novel an emotional experience for me to read. Thornton and his brother Amos saw in George Brush a significant—if not always attractive—piece of the American mind. In fact, Wilder responded to one reader's query expressing hope that his "remote cousin of Don Quixote" was a "demonstration of the idealistic and ethically preoccupied element in all human nature." Aren't we all familiar with a George Brush?

I find that two features of the novel's design help me deal with its emotional impact. The first is its humor. If you can't laugh, don't touch *Heaven's My Destination*. Of course, humans being human, laughter can quickly end up as quite a different emotion. "Life under the dictates of the *Sermon on the Mount* can be either tragic or comic—depending on one's point of view," writes the editor introducing an excerpt of *Heaven* in *And the Laugh Shall Come First: A Treasury of Religious Humor* (1986).

The second feature is the novel's theatricality. *Heaven* was written during a critical juncture in Wilder's creative life when he was turning away from fiction to follow his deepest artistic calling: drama. *Heaven* is a novel, but full of scene breaks, dialogue, and stage directions:

> The man lay down again. "My name is Zoroaster Eels. I live on benches for a living."
> Brush looked at him in surprise, but Eels turned his back on him. (p. 131)

Thornton Wilder wrote to former Lawrenceville teaching colleague Lesley Glenn that he hoped *Heaven's My Destination* would be a "big socio-historical document," a major take on the Great Depression. His novel, with the word "depression" quietly mentioned twelve times throughout its pages, is soaked in the 1930s with its depiction of job loss, despair, suicide, vagabondage, and even an iconic collapse of a bank. Today the Great Depression is commonly remembered in the Farm Security Administration's photographs, and in fading memory. The result, as J. D. McClatchy puts it, is that "We read *Heaven's My Destination* less for its anatomy of an era than for its brilliant storytelling." McClatchy also observes that "If John Steinbeck's mighty *Grapes of Wrath* is the tragic novel of the Great Depression, then *Heaven's My Destination* is its comic masterpiece."

I write these words in another era marked by a depression-causing event that has compromised the lives of millions throughout the world. But amid sadness and despair and death, what brave acts are visible all about. Returning to our journey, as we must and will, it is best to remind ourselves, as George Brush was beginning to learn, to take it one step, one spoonful, at a time.

—Tappan Wilder
June 2020

AFTERWORD

"I'm very fond of the book."
—THORNTON WILDER, 1934

OVERVIEW

Thanks to Wilder's notes and letters, we know that he began writing *Heaven's My Destination* on June 15, 1932, at the MacDowell Colony, the artists' retreat center in Peterborough, New Hampshire, which he visited frequently starting in the mid-20s. He finished the novel on September 28, 1934, during a two-week stay at another artists' retreat of sorts, Mabel Dodge Luhan's ranch in

Taos, New Mexico. Earlier, in November 1932, when he felt he was a third done, he described the book in this ambitious manner to his close friend and confidant, the celebrated English hostess, Lady Sibyl Colefax in London:

> The novel is very funny and very heartrending—a picaresque novel about a young traveling salesman in textbooks, very "fundamentalist," pious, pure and his adventures among the shabby hotels, gas stations and hot dog stands of Eastern Texas, Arkansas, Oklahoma etc. His education, or development from a Dakota "bible-belt" mind to a modern *grossstadt* tolerance in three years; i.e., the very journey the American mind has made in fifty years.

Wilder's own journey to *Heaven* is a tangle composed of his artistic roots in the Classics, his experiences as a wage earner and a citizen during the Great Depression, his temperament, and, perhaps most significant of all, values inculcated throughout his upbringing in a home presided over by his father, Amos Parker Wilder.

The principle literary influence driving *Heaven's My Destination* is the picaresque form, characterized by an episodic style that recounts the adventures of a somewhat objectionable, yet always appealing hero. Cervantes's *Don Quixote*, widely believed the first modern novel and a sire of the picaresque style, was of passionate interest to Wilder. (It is believed by Thornton's family that over his lifetime he had read *Don Quixote* in several languages—Spanish, German, English, and French.) *Heaven*'s literary roots were no secret; for good and sufficient marketing reasons, the reference was highlighted in the *Book-of-the-Month Club News* and mentioned on the back of the novel's dust jacket as Wilder's "Modern American *Don Quixote*."

By 1930, when Wilder's "Picaresque: Baptist 'Don Quixote'" appeared in a list of projects he envisioned, he was routinely teaching *Don Quixote* in lecture courses at the University of Chicago.

In the spring of 1933, the popularity of his college lectures led Wilder to offer a five-lecture version for the general public titled "Cervantes and *Don Quixote*," as part of the University's downtown program at the Art Institute of Chicago ("Five Lectures $1.50—Singles 50 cents"). The series sold out.

Wilder's time spent on the road giving lectures no doubt informed the dialogue, atmosphere, and settings of *Heaven's My Destination*. Between 1929 and the spring of 1937, Wilder traveled the country for several months on formal lecture tours managed by the well-known Lee Keedick Agency. By the time *Heaven's My Destination* was published in 1935, he had delivered nearly 100 lectures in twenty-three states, the District of Columbia, two Hawaiian Islands, and two Canadian provinces. He traveled from city to city on trains, and the occasional plane, autographing endless copies of his novels, and taking his signature walks to soak in the sights and smells of a given locale with nights spent in the notable downtown hotels of the era. It is not difficult to imagine a book salesman taking shape in Thornton Wilder's imagination.

On his way to speak on December 15, 1933, in Saint Louis on the subject of "The Relation Between Literature and Life," he made a special stop in Kansas City. Here, as he wrote a friend, "I shall stay . . . one day, taking long walks and peering about for specific details to put into *Heaven's My Destination*'s scenes of which are laid there." Of all the parts of the United States he encountered in this period, he chose to anchor George Brush and *Heaven* in Kansas City with forays into the Midwest, Texas, and the Southwest. Here is where Wilder found the representative voice for a story with mythic ambitions. As he wrote to the German translator of *Heaven's My Destination*, the novel "is written in the most limited local dialect of Middle West and is saturated with the atmosphere of a certain type of the American mind."

Below its fundamentalist exterior, George Brush's story is also an exploration and synthesis of the moralistic and idealistic elements Wilder inherited from his father and recognized in his older brother, Amos, and himself. While he never hid it privately, Wilder did not publicly reveal this identification with George Brush until some years after the book was published: "George Brush, that's me!" he told a reporter in 1953. Writing to his publisher's editor-in-chief shortly before *Heaven* appeared in print, he depicted the novel's roots this way:

> Naturally I'm very fond of the book; it's all about my father and my brother and myself, and my years among the missionaries in China, and my two years at Oberlin College, and the Texas and Oklahoma of my lecture tours. It appears to be an objective novel reporting merely the seen and heard; but it is really flagrantly subjective, and it will be many years before I will be able to stand off and appraise it, if at all.

The book's two epigraphs hint at the potentially rich quixotic elements in the life of one George Brush. The first, a doggerel which Wilder suggested that "children of the Middle West were accustomed to write in their schoolbooks," was, in fact, an homage to the great coming-of-age novel that influenced Wilder and his generation: James Joyce's *Portrait of the Artist as a Young Man*:

> *George Brush is my name;*
> *America's my nation.*
> *Ludington's my dwelling-place*
> *And Heaven's my destination.*

The verse appears this way in Joyce's book, first published in serial form in 1914:

Stephen Dedalus is my name.
Ireland is my nation.
Clongowes is my dwelling place
And Heaven my expectation.

Worth noting is that Wilder's "destination" is an appropriately firmer evangelically freighted noun than Joyce's "expectation."

The second epigraph, "Of all forms of genius, goodness has the longest awkward age," comes from Wilder's previous novel, *The Woman of Andros* (1930). The words appear in a scene in which a young man self-righteously and publicly condemns the book's heroine, Chrysis, for being a prostitute. Her rejoinder, said magnanimously and with "grave affection," was to take his hand and say, "It is true that of all forms of genius, goodness has the longest awkward age." A still earlier version appears in a group of aphorisms Wilder drafted in his journal in 1928, at the time he was writing *Andros*: "The so-called Christers at Yale: of all forms of genius, goodness has the longest awkward age." The word "Christers" was a code word, used humorously, if derisively, to describe those Yale undergraduates who carried out good works in New Haven's slums, schools, and churches through Dwight Hall, the campus YMCA. Dwight Hall was an institution that Wilder's father championed and in which his brother Amos was active, and a place where George Brush would surely have felt at home.

"ASPIRATION" AND "VAINGLORY"

Wilder had intended to complete *Heaven's My Destination* by April 1933, so that his publishers would have plenty of time to prepare for the all-important Christmas trade. He, however, had honorable reasons for not completing the on this timetable. During this period, he was the sole support for what he called "the House of Wilder"—his parents, his two younger sisters (including for one, college tuition); the upkeep of the house in Hamden, Connecticut, that *The Bridge of San Luis Rey* royalties had paid for in 1930; and his own considerable professional and personal expenses and Depression-era-related gifts. (His donations to so-called "radical" groups in the '30s earned him FBI monitoring starting in 1933.) The extraordinary financial success of *The Bridge* brought Wilder royalties amounting to well over one million in current dollars in 1928–1929, and cash flow was not a problem. But with the onset of the Great Depression, his net royalty income from books fell dramatically, from over $40,000 in 1930; to $13,300 in 1931; to $9,200 in 1932; and $6,700 in 1933.

To meet needs and avoid dipping into savings, he sought odd jobs to supplement money received from teaching and lecturing. In 1932, he also began to receive welcomed royalties from productions of his new one-act plays, among them *The Happy Journey to Trenton and Camden* and *The Long Christmas Dinner,* being performed widely in schools and "little theaters" throughout the country and in Great Britain. That same year, he also began translating, though the one play to reach Broadway, *Lucrèce,* failed. Two years later, he ventured into scriptwriting, which provided good money, great experience, and much fun, but meant that he lost precious weeks of freedom to work on *Heaven.*

To make up for lost time and complete the novel, for which both his American and British publishers had been setting type since August, he fled from Hollywood to Luhan's ranch in September 1934, turning down a major writing job on a Garbo film. He had another picture in mind, however, a film version of *Heaven's My Destination*. From the ranch he confided to his attorney that "Frank Capra (Columbia) and Gary Cooper" were the "one director and one star who could suit it," a deal that his Hollywood agent,

Rosalie Stewart worked on but never pulled off. Since then, many others have attempted or dreamed of putting George Brush on the silver screen, but none have come to fruition.

To Lady Colefax he confided these words about the completed book, written with the imprint of Hollywood's compressed, scenic style and a writer desperate to write plays: "The novel is very good. Less of course than the wonderful germ-subject promised when first it dangled before my imagination, but still one of the best things ever said about the American mind, and the poor struggling 126 millions forever alternating between the ethical puritan aspiration and the busy realist vainglory."

"ADJUSTING THEMSELVES"

As pointed out in "A Nephew's Note," of all Wilder's novels none is as famous as *The Bridge of San Luis Rey*, the success of which led the 1927 Pulitzer committee to depart from normal practice and bestow its prize on a story laid outside the United States. This was especially true in 1935. By then, thousands of readers around the world had discovered Wilder's first three novels, *The Cabala*, *The Bridge of San Luis Rey*, and *The Woman of Andros*, all of which dealt with esoteric characters and universal themes, set in exotic times and places. With *Heaven's My Destination*, Wilder achieved a distinct departure from his earlier works. Instead of a Cardinal of the Church, the Marquesa de Montemayor, or Greek islanders named Pamphius, Chremes, and Simo, *Heaven's My Destination* introduced Wilder's public to George Brush, traveling salesman, whom Wilder described as an "earnest, humorless, moralizing, preachifying, interfering product of Bible-Belt evangelism."

Would his public remain loyal for a book that was completely different in tone and subject from the three earlier novels? As he was finishing the novel, Wilder's sister Isabel expressed concern about *Heaven*'s prospects in a letter to the family's attorney and adviser, Dwight Dana: "It is excellent and we can't help but trust that others will recognize its merits, although a large part of his 'public' will have to adjust themselves to the idea of the tremendous versatility in the author of 'The Bridge' which this reveals."

Wilder raised his own red flag to Dwight Dana, predicting that his North American publishers would probably be "bewildered" by it. This was certainly the case with the firm of Albert and Charles Boni who had published Wilder's earlier novels and had held the option on *Heaven's My Destination*. As Wilder recalled later, Albert Boni "made it clear that I had no feeling for the American scene and that humor was not for me and he liked it so little that he gave up the rights." On August 29, 1934, Harper & Brothers bought the publishing rights to *Heaven* from the Boni interests for an advance of $4,000 and various considerations.

Harper & Brothers's internal opinions about their new author and his new book are unknown. What is known is that the publisher devoted more than half of the back page of the dust jacket in twelve-point type to this "Truth in Advertising" statement:

> THE FACT of first importance for the many thousands of readers of Thornton Wilder's books is that each novel has been an unexpected and original treatment of themes deeply embedded in human emotions and experiences of all of us. This new novel is no exception. The element of surprise will take the reader's breath away for its sheer novelty, but will not diminish the shock of the electric charge. . . .

Wilder's readers did not desert him. The good news began with an unexpected double salute when both major book clubs in the United States and Great Britain chose *Heaven's My Destination* as their main selection. Over the months that followed domestic sales held up well enough to earn it seventh place on the 1935 list of ten best-selling novels. So fast did books fly out of the door when it appeared in January that the author heard on the grapevine that Harper had to borrow ten thousand copies from the Book-of-the-Month Club to meet demand. Altogether, in 1935, for telling the story of George Brush, Wilder earned $27,000 or some $500,000 in today's money. After *Heaven*'s success with the English Book Society, Wilder's British publisher, Longmans, Green & Co. moved the novel quickly into its humor series.

Royalties from *Heaven's My Destination* not only restored Thornton Wilder's finances, but also made it possible for him to begin to break free from teaching and lecturing to devote himself entirely to what he was now desperate to do: write plays. Wilder's path to fame on the stage during this period has its twists and turns, but there is much truth in the statement that the most famous George in all his works, George Gibbs in *Our Town*, owes a significant debt of gratitude for his birth to his older cousin, George Brush.

It is no surprise that the outstanding sales of *Heaven's My Destination* in 1935, a Great Depression year, were bolstered by strong and favorable critical reception on both sides of the Atlantic, especially in England where its humor and its portrait of an American type were enthusiastically received. William Plomer, in *The Spectator*, spoke for many when he hailed it "an uncommonly skillful and good-natured entertainment." The *London Mercury*'s V.M.L. Scott saw humor in the novel but also posed a big question: "Are we not to believe that Mr. Brush's goodness will one day be directed by intelligence; that it is America in the end who will save the civilization of the West?" Predictably, positive comment was often joined with collective surprise at how different *Heaven* was from Wilder's earlier fiction, leading reviewers to be "puzzled" by what Wilder was getting at. Had he written a satire, a comedy, a farce, a religious tract—what? Ted Robinson, in the *Cleveland Plain Dealer* thought he knew, calling the novel an "uproarious farce" and predicting, "In a week or so everyone in the country will be reading it." More typical was John Chamberlain's view in the *New York Herald Tribune*. He found the book "unusual and entertaining" but asked, "What is [Wilder's] intention?" Donald Adams in the all-important *New York Times* review summed up the issue beautifully. He said *Heaven* "will be read for its forthright entertainment; it will be discussed for its ambiguity." Also predictably, a number of reviewers would compare the book—fortunately not unfavorably—with his blockbuster, *The Bridge of San Luis Rey*, noting that philosophical and moral themes appear in both works, despite the striking differences in setting, character, and style. No reviewer knotted the two books together tighter than one of Wilder's former Yale College professors, Henry Seidel Canby, who sagely observed in the widely read Book-of-the-Month Club, "The truth of the matter is that *Heaven's My Destination* is just *The Bridge of San Luis Rey* written over and again in homely humorous Americanese. It is the same unworldliness marveling at the world and its inexplicable complications when it is so simple to the good."

If in the minority, *Heaven's My Destination* also had its critics. As a general comment, they found George Brush's story lacking in import and realism, charges soon to be leveled against *Our Town*. Herschel Brickell wrote in the *North American Review* that *Heaven* lacked "blood and bones" and was "not of any particular importance." The distinguished critic R. P. Blackmur, writing in *The Nation*, found that Wilder's treatment of the theme of goodness lacked "authority." And we know (see p. ix) that Sigmund Freud threw it across the room.

No overview of the novel's sources and initial critical positioning would be complete without mention of Marxist-Communist critic Michael Gold's 2,300-word assault on Wilder's previously published works (three novels and one book of short plays). In the October 22, 1930, issue of the *New Republic*, two years before Wilder began work on *Heaven's My Destination*, in brutal language, Gold painted Wilder as a poster boy for a "genteel bourgeoisie" literary tradition devoted to hiding from real "problems and subjects. Where are the modern streets of New York, Chicago and New Orleans?" Gold asked of Wilder whose work he summarized as a "synthesis of all the chambermaid literature, Sunday-school tracts and boulevard piety there ever was." He concluded his diatribe with a challenge: "Let Mr. Wilder write a book about modern America. We predict it will reveal all his fundamental silliness and superficiality, now hidden under a Greek chlamys." The challenge was met by an outpouring of letters, of which twenty-seven were published—the majority defending Wilder—in six of the next seven issues of the the *New Republic,* until December 17, 1930, when the editors ended the Gold-Wilder controversy and called it "an account of darkness."

In his Foreword to this book, the late J. D. McClatchy mentioned this attack, to which Wilder never responded publicly, and its possible influence on the author's next novel. What is known is that Wilder privately demised it as "wretched affair," and appears to have let it go. By the time *Heaven* was published, five years after Gold challenged Wilder to write a book about "modern America," his assault was referenced by only a handful of reviewers. A notable exception was the influential voice of Edmund Wilson, editor of the *New Republic,* who had been involved in the earlier controversy. Wilson not only praised *Heaven*, calling it "much Mr. Wilder's best novel," but also believed it was written specifically to answer Michael Gold's challenge. Revisiting the matter twenty years later in his influential *Writers on the Left: Episodes in American Literary Com-*

munism (1961), Daniel Aaron saw it differently: "Wilder, the genial lay-preacher and *histrio*, is closer in spirit to Cervantes (the real inspirer of his novel, not as Edmund Wilson believed, the attack of Michael Gold), and his teasing satire on human aberration implies no despair or alienation."

What was Wilder's view of the critics' questions about what he was up to? He explained himself forthrightly to his friend, the actress Rosemary Ames, soon after *Heaven's My Destination* appeared in print on January 2, 1935:

> My book's selling like pancakes but almost everybody misunderstands it. I should worry.
> It's no satire. The hero's not a boob or a sap.
> George Brush at his best is everybody.

—Tappan Wilder
2020

READINGS
A NEW WILDER NOVEL AVAILABLE

This 1935 postcard announcing *Heaven's My Destination* highlights two selling points of compelling interest to readers: a novel by the acclaimed author of *The Bridge of San Luis Rey* inspired by the iconic novel *Don Quixote*.

The small print reads: *The author of one of the most popular books of this generation offers the story of a modern Don Quixote—a novel as moving and as finely written as anything he has ever done.*

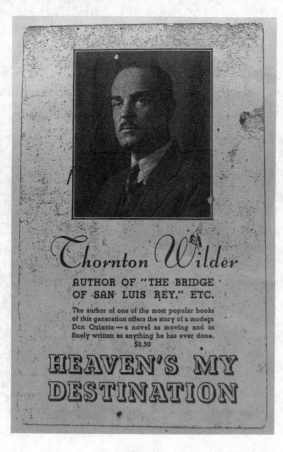

A BAPTIST DON QUIXOTE

On June 27, 1930, with *The Woman of Andros* published and selling well—third on the 1930 best-seller list, and a free summer ahead, Wilder drew up his typically eclectic list of eight "projects to choose among." The third under fiction, and the second of two "picaresque" ideas, is the first sighting of *Heaven's My Destination* in Wilder's records and only one of three ideas from this list to be developed into actual stories or plays. The other two are the Far Inglun idea developed into the short story "The Battleship," published in 1936; and "The House in Concord, N.H," found in his 1931 short play "Such Things Only Happen in Books."

(Deepwood Drive, New Haven, June 27, 1930) Now
after six months work I have free time to work again and
I have the following projects to choose among:

NOVELS OR NOUVELLES

1. Captain Faring: (the group: the nun: the children: alcohol).
2. Picaresque: "Lafcadio" Spanglian Europe: diary: "I have been reading Casanova": "Who was my mother?" "I mean to be a writer."
3. Picaresque: Baptist "Don Quixote." Selling educational textbooks through Texas. Oklahoma etc.
5. Far Inglun: The castaway civilization.
4. The Empress of Trebizond: homage à Händel

PLAYS

1. Capt. Faring. See Entry 71 in this book.
2. The Pilgrims (long talk with Jed Harris two days ago about this.) N.B.: Jed Harris was the producer-director of *Our Town* (1938).
3. The house in Concord, N.H. Criminals return to the scene of the crime. The cult of love & hate. The sentiment of all old houses—those who have died in them. The Indian mound; the 1790 builder who fell from the roof. "What will it matter in a 100 years?"
4. The pension on the Riviera. "See that little plump feminine widow: across the barriers of language, social background and poverty: she will addle a man." "Nature only eager to fill as many go carts as possible."

IN HANDWRITTEN FORM

The "4th copying of the opening" draft of the novel's first lines, the text of which appears below, shows the epigraph taken from

The Woman of Andros. Later drafts tighten the language and deepen characterization. Note that Wilder changed Brush's middle name to Marvin, possibly because Marvin was a family name. Misspellings in the draft remain as Wilder wrote them.

4th copying of the opening

"Of all forms of genius, goodness has the longest awkward age."

Chapter One: George Brush attempts to save some souls in Texas Arkansas and Oklahoma. His theory of poverty. His Criminal Record: Incarceration Number Two.

~ in western Texas

One morning in the late summer of 1930 the proprietor and several guests of the Union Hotel at Crestenego, Texas, were annoyed to discover Biblical texts freshly written across the blotter on the public writing desk. The next morning the guests at McCarthy's Inn, Usquepaw, in the same state were similarly irritated and the manager of the Gem Theatre next door was terrified by the spectacle of a young man who tore down and trampled upon a poster advertising a motion picture being exhibited there. The same evening a young man passing the First Baptist Church and seeing the announcement that the annual Bible Question Bee was to take place, paid his fifteen cents, took his place against the wall and won the first prize, his final triumph being his recitation of the Kings of Judah backwards. The next night several passengers on the Pullman car Quarritch bound for ___ were startled to discover a man in pyjamas kneeling and saying his prayers in the aisle before his berth. His concentration was not shaken when copies of two Western Magazines and Screen Features hit him sharply in the back. The next morning a lady who had retired to the platform to enjoy a meditative cigarette after breakfast returned to her seat to discover that someone had written across her window with a piece of soap the words: "Women who smoke are unfit to be mothers." A business card had been inserted at the corner of the pane. It read: "George Mercer Brush. Representing the Clay Educational Press, New York, Boston, Chicago. Publishers of Caulkins' Arithmetics and Algebras, and other superior textbooks for schools and colleges."

George M. Brush   This novelist and census descended from the train at Wellington Arkansas and settled himself at the Wellington House where some exigency in his business required his remaining for three days. He passed the time in taking long walks, in memorizing a speech of Abraham Lincoln's, in reading the Encyclopedia Brittanica at the public library and in troubling the librarian to find everything she could for him that had to do with Mahatma Gandhi. He fell into conversation with eleven people, of eleven of them he eventually asked whether they were saved. He made notations of them

"Of all forms of genius, goodness has the longest
awkward age."

Chapter One: George Brush attempts to save souls
in Texas, Arkansas and Oklahoma. His Theory of
Poverty. His Criminal Record: Incarceration Number
Two.

One morning in the late summer of 1930 the
proprietor and several guests of the Union Hotel at
Crestcrego [in Western Texas], Texas were annoyed
to discover Biblical texts freshly written across the
blotter on the public writing desk. The next morning
the guests at McCarty's Inn, Usquepaw, in the same
state were similarly irritated, and the manager of the
Gem Theatre next door was terrified by the spectacle
of a young man who tore down and trampled upon
a poster advertising a motion picture being exhibited
there. The same evening a young man passing the First
Baptist Church and seeing the announcement that the
Annual Bible Question Bee was to take place, paid his
fifteen cents, took his place against the wall and won
the first prize, his final triumph being his recitation of
the Kings of Judah backwards. The next night several
passengers on the Pullman car *Quarritch* bound for
~~Saint Louis~~ Dallas were startled to discover a man in
pyjamas kneeling and saying his prayers in the aisle before his berth. His concentration was not shaken when
copies of the Western Magazine and Screen Features
hit him sharply in the back. The next morning a lady
who had retired to the platform to enjoy a meditative
cigarette after breakfast returned to her seat to discover
that someone had written across her window with a

piece of soap the words: "Women who smoke are unfit to be mothers." A business card had been inserted at the corner of the pane. It read: "George Mercer Brush. Representing the Clay Educational Press, New York, Boston, Chicago. Publishers of Caulkins' Arithmatics and Algebras, and other superior textbooks for schools and colleges."

George M. Brush ~~This moralist and sensor~~ descended from the train at Wellington, Arkansas, and settled himself at the Wellington House where some exigency in his business required his remaining for three days. He passed the time in taking long walks, in memorizing a speech of Abraham Lincoln's, in reading the Encyclopedia Brittanica at the Public Library and in troubling the librarian to find everything she could for him that had to do with Mahatma Ghandi. He fell into conversation with eleven people; of eleven of them he eventually asked whether they were saved. He made notations of these. . . .

TWO LETTERS

As pointed out in the Afterword, critics and readers were puzzled by what Wilder was getting at in *Heaven*. Was George Brush an idiot, a fool, a boob, a saint, etc.? Indeed, the whole controversial business, as it played out in the papers, became a significant selling point for the novel. The following excerpts from two of Wilder's letters at time of publication express the author's feelings about the character of George Marvin Brush.

"Dear Doc"

This letter was written January 3, 1935, a month after publication, to Dr. Creighton Barker, the Wilder family's physician in New Haven. In his first three novels, of which *The Woman of Andros* was the third, Wilder consciously explored love, religion, memory, imagination, and other resources at an individual's command to oppose life's inevitable tragedies. He wonders here whether a more explicit statement about what interests him in George and his personal growth and education, might have helped readers better understand his viewpoint. Wilder never revisited the novel to "examine the point" raised in this letter.

> *There's no satire in it. It's about all of us when young. You're not supposed to notice the humor—you're supposed to look through it at the fellow who not only has the impulse to think out an ethic and plan a life—but actually does it.*
>
> *George Brush is the continuation and externalization of all the little private illuminations that in other people wilt and die under fear and reticule or under the acquirement of our singularly inadequate world wisdom . . .*
>
> *Five years from now when the testimonies pro and con have begun to subside, I'm going to examine the point as to whether I made a big lapse of artistic judgement in present[ing] the matter so objectively.*
>
> *Perhaps the note [epigraph] should have been from phrases from Andros: "How do you live? What do you do first."*

"Dear Mr. Saxton"

The letter is to Eugene Saxton, editor-in-chief at Harper & Brothers. It was written on November 20, a month before publication. Wilder admits hurrying *Heaven* at the close, with the possible cost, he suggests gently, of a lack of clarity about George Brush's development and growing wisdom at the end.

> *I would like to think that the present last chapter ties up the suspended knots however brusquely:*
>
> *The family-life with Roberta is understood to have been impossible. My sister [Isabel] scolds me when I tell her that for me the important words about that lies in the parenthesis ("Their eyes never met at any time.")*
>
> *We have seen in the pipe, for example, the breaking up of all that was most rigid and dialectic in his ethical background.*
>
> *His loss of faith and sickness were just what was needed to instruct him that his faith was hitherto too glib an optimism and too dogmatic a bundle of planks. His insults to the visiting Dr. Bowie show that a lot of fresh air is blowing through his fundamentalism. . . .*
>
> *His disappearance in the last paragraph shows that he is still the same fellow, trying to think, always turning his experimental thoughts into acts—but after one year's growth, doing it better, less bound, etc.*
>
> *Except for considerable improvement he is still the same person as in the opening paragraph,—fundamentalist, but more flexible, earnest, but less obstinate; humorless, but wiser.*

GEORGE BRUSH IN THE FAMILY

Wilder saw George Brush's idealism as a factor in all youth and in all families, and certainly in his father, Amos Parker Wilder (1864–1936); his older brother, Amos (left) (1895–1993); and himself, all shown here in a photograph taken in 1915. Their father was determined that his boys not only survive in a world of constant danger and temptation, but also "enter into the larger world and bring knowledge from the stars."

In order to achieve success, the elder Wilder prescribed faithful religious practice, the best possible liberal arts education, foreign travel and study, and, for good health and for understanding America and its people, manual labor on farms. His father's dream for his boys is reflected in one of Wilder's favorite lines from *Heaven*: "I didn't put myself through college for four years and go through a difficult religious conversion in order to have the same ideas as other people have." This photograph was taken shortly after the senior Wilder's resignation from the consular service in China for health reasons, and the subsequent establishment of the Wilder family home outside New Haven, Connecticut. Thornton was an Oberlin College freshman and Amos a Yale College junior in 1915.

THE OLDER BROTHER AS INTERPRETER

The younger, Amos, was variously amused and troubled by the simplistic use of the term "strict Puritan" to describe his father's religious stance and, by implication, its impact on his brother's life and work. In this extract from *Thornton Wilder and His Public* (1980), he seeks to set the record straight about the character of the intellectual world in which he and his brother grew up, with an emphasis on their father and his values. Amos Niven Wilder (1895–1993) was a clergyman, biblical scholar, poet, and literary critic.

> The term "Puritan" applied to our parents and to the culture in our home is . . . imprecise and misleading. It is also an exaggeration to say, as does one biographer, that my brother came of "a long line of New England divines." On the Wilder side they are hard to find in any direct line. The kind of New England tradition represented on our mother's side is suggested by her grandfather, Arthur Tappan, friend of William Lloyd Garrison and himself the first president of the American Anti-Slavery Society (1837). A philanthropist like his brother Lewis Tappan who financed the defense of the Spanish slaves in the Amistad slave ship case all the way up to the Supreme Court and helped fund the establishment of Oberlin College because it was the first to welcome Black as well as women students. He and his New York store were repeatedly in danger from proslavery mobs. This kind of Puritan tradition is no reproach.

The kind of piety represented by the Congregationalism on my father's side was similar, as is suggested by the fact that he chose schools like Oberlin, Mt. Holyoke, and Northfield for his children's education. The books of our father in our possession, which are the most marked up and annotated by him, are Boswell's life of Johnson, the four-volume life of Garrison by his sons and Whittier's poems. Favorites in our family Sunday reading along with the Bible were the works of Bunyan, John Woolman, George Fox, and Thoreau. This kind of Nonconformist tradition is very different from some kinds of Bible-belt piety and life-style as well as from familiar strains of Calvinist orthodoxy. . . .

The early Wisconsin years of our family (1894–1906) suggest a number of observations. Although through our parents we had Maine and Hudson River antecedents these were now overlaid with Middle Western experience in depth. It was not just a question original but of the social variety. A newspaperman like my father was involved in the full gamut of town and country life. Madison, though the state capital and seat of a university, in those days before the motor car was still only a large town. The *Wisconsin State Journal* served the county and the region. My father's editorials for which he is still remembered show his immersion in the folkways and plebeian sympathies. Well prepared by his doctorate in political science and his years in journalism in New York and elsewhere, he identified himself vigorously with the "Wisconsin progressivism" of the time which was drawing national attention. But it was especially his inimitable "human-interest" editorials

which were cherished and copied far and wide. Here
sentiment, fancy, eloquence, and humor combined.
Those same antennae for the common life and those
fine filaments of the poetic and the histrionic which
later evoked Grover's Corners in the son had their
antecedents in the father . . . From his college days
at Yale as "fence orator" and Glee Club antic he was
remembered as word painter, mimic, and clown. In
Wisconsin as scribe and as favored speaker at county
fair and at Chautauqua he was a poet and wit of the
Midland. . . .

The tone of the following editorial, occasioned by an event
witnessed on the streets of Madison, Wisconsin, sounds not unlike
George Brush's habit of seeking a quiet spot each year far from the
tread of the elephants, to reflect on his life.

A "HUMAN INTEREST" EDITORIAL PUBLISHED BY AMOS PARKER WILDER IN THE *WISCONSIN STATE JOURNAL*

"Somewhere on the lake shore in Dane County tonight
is the boy to whom a hayfield will never seem quite the
same. A lady from the marvelous world smiled on him
and took his modest gift, and her gentle voice thanked
him.

And somewhere in the confusion of wagon wheels
and ghostly mountains of canvas and gilt and gold that
look best at a distance—somewhere in that scene of Jeru-
salem and the Crusades is a woman whose heart quick-
ened today because a barefoot boy was proud to pass
her a waterlily, and because its fragrance wafted into

her dusty, tired life memories of some quiet spot where she dreamed and perhaps loved, and where there was no tread of elephants nor noisy blare of bands, but only green trees and a brook . . . and the sweet memory of the wind through the trees."

ENVOI
"ENTHUSIASM FOR EVERYTHING"

Whatever their differences, Thornton Wilder and George Brush shared an enthusiasm for *everything*. Perhaps no reporter in the '30s caught this side of the novelist better, both the joy and passion of living, than Hollywood syndicated columnist Mollie Herrick in her September 14, 1934 column, "Hollywood Sidelights." Her piece was written just as Wilder was leaving Hollywood to complete *Heaven's My Destination* at Mable Dodge Luhan's ranch in Taos, New Mexico. (Herrick has him incorrectly returning to Chicago.)

Thornton Wilder—none other—leads, most success-fully, two utterly antipathetic existences and yet man-ages to weld them in his spirit in such a way as to be a most satisfied and satisfactory person. *A Lion at Par-ties* A couple of days ago, Thornton Wilder finished the script of "Dark Angel," on which he had been work-ing for some time for Sam Goldwyn and . . . took the train for Chicago . . . in order that he might resume his chair as professor of comparative literature in that seat of learning. But before he took the train, and outside of the busy hours given to polishing up the script, he went from party to party—no actor has ever been more popular—and at each party was the lion of the moment. This is something few writers have experienced. An unbelievable blond is most often the high-spot of a truly Hollywood fathering and mere brains are often relegated to obscurity.

This colony has many circles that touch at cinematic crossroads and then diverge widely . . . Thornton Wilder seems to have penetrated many of these groups and to have been a tremendous success with all of them. ***Enthusiasm for Everything*** His grey-blue eyes are filled with an endless enthusiasm for everything. All mutations in thought, action intrigue him. He analyzes eternally but with such a friendly eye that nobody minds it. He has genius for laughter and play but his plummet-like drop from nonsense to profundity is something unprecedented in my experience.

ACKNOWLEDGEMENTS AND BIBLIOGRAPHICAL NOTE

The back matter for this volume in the original and revised form is constructed in large part from Thornton Wilder's words found in unpublished material or publications hard to come by. My hope is that readers will find this approach brings *Heaven's My Destination* (*HMD*) and its author into view in a special, even personal way.

A definitive biography and formal treatment of Wilder's letters remained unpublished when HarperCollins first reprinted the novel in 2003. However, both works exist today. It is thus a pleasure to refer readers interested in Thornton Wilder's life, work, and family to these foundational works: Robin G. Wilder and Jackson R. Bryer, eds. *Selected Letters of Thornton Wilder* (HarperCollins, 2008) and Penelope Niven's *Thornton Wilder: A Biography* (Harper-

Collins, 2012). Intrigued by the religious elements in *HMD*, readers are directed to Christopher Wheatley's *Thornton Wilder & Amos Wilder: Writing Religion in Twentieth Century America* (University of Notre Dame Press, 2011) and Amos N. Wilder's *Thornton Wilder and His Public* (1980/Wipf & Stock reprint 2017). Those similarly interested in his use of classical material, a subject of growing interest among Wilder scholars, can consult the information and titles found through the *HMD* page on www.thorntonwilder.com. Additional material can be found on the Thornton Wilder Society website, www.ThorntonWilderSociety.org.

Sources and Permissions

A NEPHEW'S NOTE

Amos N. Wilder's epigraph is taken from "Don Quixote in the American Scene," *Anglican Theological Review*, Vol. XXV. No.1, (July 1943), p. 212. George Brush Irregular quotations are found as follows: A.R. Gurney, "Introduction," *The Collected Short Plays of Thornton Wilder* (TCG Press, New York, 1998) p. xviii; John Henry Raleigh, "Introduction" to *HMD*, Anchor Books (Garden City, 1960), p. 2; John Knowles, "A Protest from Paradise," *Art and the Craftsman: The Best of the Yale Literary Magazine* 1836–1961 (Southern Illinois University, Carbondale), p.203; John Bankham, "Thornton Wilder Visits the Past," Review of *Theophilus North*, *The Philadelphia Inquirer*, Nov. 18, 1973; Michael Schmidt, "Introduction" to *HMD* (Apollo/Head of Zeus, Ltd., London, 2016), p. ix. William H. Willimon edited *And the Laugh Shall Come First: A Treasury of Religious Humor* (Abington Press, Nashville. 1961) with the quotation cited found on p. 101. Wilder's observation of George Brush as "a remote cousin of Don Quixote" is taken from his letter to Norman W. Drey, held by the Manuscripts Department of the University of Virginia.

AFTERWORD

With the exception of Thornton Wilder's correspondence with Lady Sibyl Colefax, all excerpts quoted are found from unpublished correspondence, manuscripts, and related records and ephemera held by the Wilder family or drawn from the Wilder Family Archives, Yale Collection of American literature (YCAL) housed in the Beinecke Rare Book and Manuscript Library in New Haven, Connecticut. This material is published with the permission of the Wilder Family LLC. Spelling errors have been silently corrected unless otherwise noted. The Colefax letters are found in the Thornton Wilder Collection, Fales Manuscripts, Fales Library, New York University, and Marvin J. Taylor's assistance is acknowledged. In addition to Daniel Aaron's views expressed in *Writers on the Left: Episodes in American Literary Communism*, the Overview cites his opinion found in "Morley Callaghan and the Great Depression," David Staines, ed., *The Callagham Symposium* (Ottawa: University of Ottawa Press, 1981), p. 15. Data covering Wilder's lectures for Lee Keedick is drawn from the literary executor's personal collection supplemented by research in the records of University of Chicago held in The Joseph Rogenstein Library. The research assistance there of Naomi Scharlin is gratefully recognized.

READINGS

Mollie Herrick's syndicated "Hollywood Highlights" column appeared originally on 13 September 1934 through the North American Newspaper Alliance. It is reproduced from "Joan of Arc: Treatment for Motion Picture," Introduction by A. Tappan Wilder

(*The Yale Review*, Vol. 81, No. 4, October 2003), p. 4. The cited letters, photographs, handwritten samples of mss, and list of projects are found in the Wilder Family Archives, YCAL, and published with permission of The Wilder Family LLC. The reading from Amos. N. Wilder's *Thornton Wilder and His Public* appears on pp. 49–51 and a reprint of his father's "Human Interest" editorial on pp. 51–52.

★   ★   ★

For their invaluable work on this publication I am deeply indebted to three gifted and committed professionals: Barbara Hogenson, Wilder's literary agent, Rosey Strub, manager of his intellectual property, and Jennifer Civiletto, his editor at HarperCollins. This team makes literary executorship a pleasure to practice—and I thank them many times over. We all regret that Sandy McClatchy could not be with us to celebrate this new chapter in the story of George Brush who said of himself, "I'm not the usual kind of traveling salesman."

THORNTON WILDER

In his quiet way, Thornton Niven Wilder was a revolutionary writer who experimented boldly with literary forms and themes, from the beginning to the end of his long career. "Every novel is different from the others," he wrote when he was seventy-five. "The theater (ditto). . . . The thing I'm writing now is again totally unlike anything that preceded it." Wilder's richly diverse settings, characters, and themes are at once specific and global. Deeply immersed in classical as well as contemporary literature, he often fused the traditional and the modern in his novels and plays, all the while exploring the cosmic in the commonplace. In a January 12, 1953, cover story, *Time* took note of Wilder's unique "planetary"

mind"—his ability to write from a vision that was at once American and universal.

A pivotal figure in the history of twentieth-century letters, Wilder was a novelist and playwright whose works continue to be widely read and produced in this new century. He is the only writer to have won the Pulitzer Prize for both Fiction and Drama. His second novel, *The Bridge of San Luis Rey,* received the Fiction award in 1928, and he won the prize twice in Drama, for *Our Town* in 1938 and *The Skin of Our Teeth* in 1943. His other novels are *The Cabala, The Woman of Andros, Heaven's My Destination, The Ides of March, The Eighth Day,* and *Theophilus North.* His other major dramas include *The Matchmaker,* which was adapted as the internationally acclaimed musical comedy *Hello, Dolly!,* and *The Alcestiad.* Among his innovative shorter plays are *The Happy Journey to Trenton and Camden* and *The Long Christmas Dinner,* and two uniquely conceived series, *The Seven Ages of Man* and *The Seven Deadly Sins,* frequently performed by amateurs.

Wilder and his work received many honors, highlighted by the three Pulitzer Prizes, the Gold Medal for Fiction from the American Academy of Arts and Letters, the Order of Merit (Peru), the Goethe-Plakette der Stadt (Germany, 1959), the Presidential Medal of Freedom (1963), the National Book Committee's first National Medal for Literature (1965), and the National Book Award for Fiction (1967).

He was born in Madison, Wisconsin, on April 17, 1897, to Amos Parker Wilder and Isabella Niven Wilder. The family later lived in China and in California, where Wilder was graduated from Berkeley High School. After two years at Oberlin College, he went on to Yale, where he received his undergraduate degree in 1920. A valuable part of his education took place during summers spent working hard on farms in California, Kentucky, Vermont, Connecticut, and Massachusetts. His father arranged these rigorous "shirtsleeve" jobs for Wilder and his older brother, Amos, as part of their initiation into the American experience.

Thornton Wilder studied archaeology and Italian as a special student at the American Academy in Rome (1920–1921), and earned a master of arts degree in French literature at Princeton in 1926.

In addition to his talents as playwright and novelist, Wilder was an accomplished teacher, essayist, translator, scholar, lecturer, librettist, and screenwriter. In 1942, he teamed with Alfred Hitchcock to write the first draft of the screenplay for the classic thriller *Shadow of a Doubt,* receiving credit as principal writer and a special screen credit for his "contribution to the preparation" of the production. All but fluent in four languages, Wilder translated and adapted plays by such varied authors as Henrik Ibsen, Jean-Paul Sartre, and André Obey. As a scholar, he conducted significant research on James Joyce's *Finnegans Wake* and the plays of Spanish dramatist Lope de Vega.

Wilder's friends included a broad spectrum of figures on both sides of the Atlantic—Hemingway, Fitzgerald, Alexander Woollcott, Gene Tunney, Sigmund Freud, producer Max Reinhardt, Katharine Cornell, Ruth Gordon, and Garson Kanin. Beginning in the mid-1930s, Wilder was especially close to Gertrude Stein and became one of her most effective interpreters and champions. Many of Wilder's friendships are documented in his prolific correspondence. Wilder believed that great letters constitute a "great branch of literature." In a lecture entitled "On Reading the Great Letter Writers," he wrote that a letter can function as a "literary exercise," the "profile of a personality," and "news of the soul," apt descriptions of thousands of letters he wrote to his own friends and family.

Wilder enjoyed acting and played major roles in several of his own plays in summer theater productions. He also possessed a life-long love of music; reading musical scores was a hobby, and he wrote the librettos for two operas based on his work: *The Long Christmas Dinner,* with composer Paul Hindemith, and *The Alcestiad,* with composer Louise Talma. Both works premiered in Germany.

Teaching was one of Wilder's deepest passions. He began his teaching career in 1921 as an instructor in French at Lawrenceville, a private secondary school in New Jersey. Financial independence after the publication of *The Bridge of San Luis Rey* permitted him to leave the classroom in 1928, but he returned to teaching in the 1930s at the University of Chicago. For six years, on a part-time basis, he taught courses there in classics in translation, comparative literature, and composition. In 1950–1951, he served as the Charles Eliot Norton Professor of Poetry at Harvard. Wilder's gifts for scholarship and teaching (he treated the classroom as all but a theater) made him a consummate, much-sought-after lecturer in his own country and abroad. After World War II, he held special standing, especially in Germany, as an interpreter of his own country's intellectual traditions and their influence on cultural expression.

During World War I, Wilder had served a three-month stint as an enlisted man in the Coast Artillery section of the army, stationed at Fort Adams, Rhode Island. He volunteered for service in World War II, advancing to the rank of lieutenant colonel in Army Air Force Intelligence. For his service in North Africa and Italy, he was awarded the Legion of Merit, the Bronze Star, the Chevalier Legion d'Honneur, and honorary officership in the Military Order of the British Empire (M.B.E.).

From royalties received from *The Bridge of San Luis Rey,* Wilder built a house for his family in 1930 in Hamden, Connecticut, just outside New Haven. But he typically spent as many as two hundred days a year away from Hamden, traveling to and settling in a variety of places that provided the stimulation and solitude he needed for his work. Sometimes his destination was the Arizona desert, the MacDowell Colony in New Hampshire, or Martha's Vineyard, Newport, Saratoga Springs, Vienna, or Baden-Baden. He wrote aboard ships, and often chose to stay in "spas in off-season." He needed a certain refuge when he was deeply immersed in writing a novel or play. Wilder explained his habit to a *New Yorker* journalist in 1959: "The walks, the quiet—all the elegance is present, everything is there but the people. That's it! A spa in off-season! I make a practice of it."

But Wilder always returned to "the house *The Bridge* built," as it is still known to this day. He died there of a heart attack on December 7, 1975.

WORKS BY THORNTON WILDER

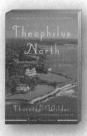

THEOPHILUS NORTH
A Novel
"An extremely entertaining array of American life in a bygone era."
—*New Yorker*

THE BRIDGE OF SAN LUIS REY
A Novel
"One merely has to consider the central question raised by the novel, which, according to Wilder himself, was simply: 'Is there a direction and meaning in the lives beyond the individual's own will?' It is perhaps the largest and most profoundly personal philosophical inquiry that we can undertake. It is the question that defines us as human beings."
—Russell Banks, foreword to *The Bridge of San Luis Rey*

THE CABALA and THE WOMAN OF ANDROS
Two Novels
"No matter where and when Wilder's novels take place, his characters grapple with universal questions about the nature of human existence."
—Penelope Niven, author of *Thornton Wilder*

THE EIGHTH DAY
A Novel
"We marvel at a novel of such spiritual ambition."
—John Updike, foreword to *The Eighth Day*

HEAVEN'S MY DESTINATION
A Novel
"If John Steinbeck's mighty *The Grapes of Wrath* is the tragic novel of the Great Depression, then *Heaven's My Destination* is its comic masterpiece."
—J. D. McClatchy, foreword to *Heaven's My Destination*

THE IDES OF MARCH
A Novel
"Full of the wisdom of the ages—as well as satirical observations on man's political instability, loves, joys and terrors."
—*Chicago Tribune*

OUR TOWN
A Play in Three Acts
"Our Town is probably the finest play ever written by an American."
—Edward Albee

THE SELECTED LETTERS OF
THORNTON WILDER
"A remarkable collection. . . . What emerges from these pages is a new and
sometimes surprising self-portrait of a great American artist."
—Marian Seldes

THE SKIN OF OUR TEETH
A Play
"For an American dramatist, all roads lead back to Thornton Wilder."
—Paula Vogel, foreword to *The Skin of Our Teeth*

THREE PLAYS
Our Town, The Skin of Our Teeth, **and** *The Matchmaker*
"These plays are a gift." —John Guare, foreword to *Three Plays*

THE MATCHMAKER
A Farce in Four Acts
"Loud, slap dash and uproarious . . . extraordinarily original and funny."
—*New York Times*

THORNTON WILDER: A LIFE
by Penelope Niven
"The best kind of literary biography, one likely to send the reader back (or
perhaps for the first time) to the author's works." —*Washington Post*

HARPER ● PERENNIAL